Higher Than Jesus

Robert Chazz Chute

Ex Parte Press

Higher Than Jesus
Robert Chazz Chute

Published by Ex Parte Press

Copyright 2012 Robert Chazz Chute
ISBN 978-0-9880082-6-7

First Edition: October 2012
Second Edition: September 2014
Cover design by Kit Foster of
KitFosterDesign.com.
Formatting by Lionheart Publishing House.

Dedication

She Who Must Be Obeyed makes it all possible.
She Who Must Be Driven makes it all worth it.
He Who Must Be Wrestled makes it all fun.

Special thanks to my graphic designer and friend, Kit
Foster of KitFosterDesign.com.
There's no one better to work with and certainly none
more patient and kind.

Welcome to Book 2 of the Hit Man Series
In the first book of The Hit Man Series, Cuban hit man
Jesus Diaz battled New York's Spanish mob to escape the thug
life with stolen mafia money and the lovely Lily Vasquez.
Read Bigger Than Jesus, the book that started the series.

"Bigger than Jesus is wickedly real and violently funny."
~ Claude Bouchard, bestselling author of Vigilante

From Amazon Reviews of *Bigger Than Jesus*

"This new thriller by the author of *Self-Help for Stoners* is a crime story worthy of Elmore Leonard with a backstory that is shades of Thomas Harris. An unusual mix of some stock characters and a gangland scenario which is made fresh by great, punchy dialogue and plot twists that keep you moving from one calamity to the next with no time to catch your breath..."

"This can't-wait-to-discover-how-he-gets-out-of-this-situation nail biter will keep you entertained to the last page!"

"With *Bigger Than Jesus*, Robert Chazz Chute proves that genre fiction can be inventive and unconventional in its use of language while delivering a suspenseful story."

"With comedy throughout and a wonderful cast of characters, *Bigger Than Jesus* pulled me right in and wouldn't let me go."

"At times it has the brutal violence that I expect from crime novels, but mostly it is funny. Jesus Dias has a sharp tongue and it seems that he modelled his life after Mike Hammer from Micky Spillane's books and after numerous characters he has seen in movies."

"For a murder book, the way it was written had me smiling through it, the scene on the roof had me laughing. It was a light and enjoyable
mob mystery."

"I enjoyed the twists and turns of this novel and was not able to put it down until I read the whole thing."

From Amazon Reviews of *Higher Than Jesus*

"Jesus is a bad guy you hate to love."

"In between all the funny cultural references is a solid, well-plotted crime thriller that is thoroughly enjoyable from start to finish. There is nothing slow or dull about this book. So do we need yet another series about a hit man? Only if it's about Jesus Diaz."

"A quick-moving plot with lots of surprises and a clear-eyed examination of addiction."

Books by Robert Chazz Chute

Fiction
Bigger Than Jesus
Higher Than Jesus
Hollywood Jesus, Rise of the Divine Assassin
The Divine Assassin's Playbook, Omnibus Edition
Self-help for Stoners
Murders Among Dead Trees
This Plague of Days, Season One
This Plague of Days, Season Two
This Plague of Days, Season, Season Three
This Plague of Days, Omnibus Edition

Poetry
The Little Book of Braingasms

Non-fiction
Crack the Indie Author Code (Book One)
Write Your Book: Aspire to Inspire (Book Two)
Six Seconds

Higher Than Jesus

UNFORGIVEN

Thirteen years ago, Tia Marta taught you how to please a woman who was hard to please. She took away your name and beat the Cuban accent out of you. She also taught you the word "sidle", which, she explained, was acting sneaky and casual at the same time. "It pays to improve your word power," she said, waving a *Reader's Digest*.

"Get on your knees, boy. You may look me in the eyes if I see love and devotion in them. If I do not see love and devotion, I'll take out one of your lovely brown eyes."

Tia Marta taught you English. She taught you how to lie well, when to hate and how to kill.

Early on in your confinement in a Miami basement, you once dared to complain to your other captor, the Bug Man, how terribly mean Tia Marta was.

"Actually," the Bug Man replied, "Marta's little bits of fun sound pretty close to my British boarding school experience." Then he slipped a plastic bag over your head until you almost passed out.

He did that several times until you lost consciousness, but somehow, lots of brain cells survived. For instance, you remember the word "sidle" and tonight you used that knowledge in the commission of a murder.

A few hours ago, as soon as *It's a Wonderful Life* ended, you sidled up beside the target at the bar and asked him if you could buy him a drink. You want to get out of the business of

1

sidling up to strangers and thinking of people only in terms of predators, prey and potential witnesses. However, this is a special case. You were doing this job for a damsel in distress. Whether she thinks she fits that quaint description, the guy who ordered the hit sure thinks so.

Suspicious, the target asked you why you wanted to buy him a drink.

You checked your watch. "It's officially Christmas."

"I'm more of a Hanukkah kind of guy."

"We're in a shitty bar."

The Bartender of Undetermined Asian Descent cutting limes into wedges looked up from his knife.

"Sorry," you told the bartender, "but it's no secret."

He shrugged and returned to his work. To the target, you offered, "All over Chicago, people are either asleep, having Christmas sex or swearing up a storm trying to put a toy together for their greedy, ungrateful kids. We should be much more hammered than we appear to be, don't you think?"

"Test: name your two favorite TV shows."

"*Dexter* is uneven but delivers great moments. *Breaking Bad* is best overall."

The target smiled. "I would have also accepted *The Walking Dead*." He turned to the bartender, "Gimme a Singapore sling. He's buying."

"Make it two," you said. "What is a Singapore sling?"

"It's a sweet drink that was popular when I was in college."

"Sad holiday nights are for nostalgia."

"Yeah, or, through the magic of association and sense memory, I'm getting back in touch with the slutty college girls I remember." He swept his hand in an arc. "When I was a journalism major, *this* place used to be quite the hot spot. A meat market! Sense memories like taste and smell are strong. For me, a Singapore sling is a time machine. Fires up the brain full of Jon Bon Jovi, feathered hair and girls falling out of their tank tops."

The bar looked dusty and the only sense you got was the feel of old beer on the sticky floor and, over toward the bathroom, a bottle of bleach did battle with the sharp stench of fresh Christmas Eve vomit. Somebody toasted Christmas with something red and green, so at least the puke was festive.

The Bartender of Undetermined Asian Descent had to check his iPhone to look up how to mix a Singapore sling. When the slings were finally mixed, they arrived sweet and went down easy. You'd already tipped the bartender not to add alcohol to anything he gave you. For the job ahead, the target had to get obliterated mentally before you could finish him physically. You had to be able to find the door and drive.

"Grenadine," the target said. "I don't know if that's just sugar, or flavored syrup or something else."

You nodded to the little TV mounted high on the wall behind the bar. *It's a Wonderful Life* was over, so whoever was in charge of irony at the TV station had switched to news reports that featured the year in review. The riots, both foreign and domestic, looked disturbingly similar. Plumes of smoke and fire rose behind grim-faced correspondents speaking into microphones in news stories that looked interchangeable with all news reports since 9/11.

"We're just consumers and destroyers now," you said. "We buy everything made from anywhere but here and we don't make anything besides guns and ammo. How would we know about anything nice, especially sweet stuff like grenadine?"

The target turned and looked you over, apparently considering you seriously for the first time. "Nice suit. I like the red tie. Christmasy."

"Thanks. Silk. The last gift my ex-girlfriend gave me."

"*Ex*, huh? So that's what brings you to this hole on Christmas? I'm guessing the 'ex' part is recent?"

You gave him a cagey shrug and, perhaps reassured you weren't coming on to him, he offered his hand. "I'm Thomas."

"Sully," you lie. "Sully Martinez."

He shook your hand. "You look like a Martinez, but I never met a Sully who looks like you."

3

"It was Sal, as in Salvador, but when you get called *Sally* in elementary school enough days in a row, you switch to Sully as soon as you can."

"Heh. *Sally*. Can't blame you there, son. Bad bounce."

"What brings you out in the snow tonight, besides memories of college girls?"

Thomas finished his drink and ordered another, switching to Scotch. "I read a novel a while back. It was called *Still Life with June*. Good stuff. I'm here a lot, sure, but I remembered something in the book about how people in a bar on Christmas have the best stories. How about it? Got a story?"

You could have told him you'd been following him off and on for a week and he'd gotten wasted in this bar five days out of the last seven. Instead, you told him, "I'm only here because my girl broke up with me. Not much interesting in that. Happens all the time. Sorry."

"Shit. I'm a bit worried, Sully. There's only you and me in here and Chinese Rick doesn't talk. Not much English, anyway. It's a bit concerning when I come here for the sad stories and I might be the saddest ass in the place."

"Rick's Chinese? I couldn't tell."

Thomas burst out laughing. "I don't know his *name, Sally*, but he's running the bar and the original title of *Casablanca* was — "

"*Everybody Comes to Rick's*. I get it. And it's Sully," you added, curiously defensive over your fake name.

He toasted you, tossed back his Scotch in one go and winced. "A cinemaphile, huh? Or is it cineaste? I used to know lots of shit like that. I should have gotten a job in journalism, but I got into it too late, born too late. Freelanced for a while here and there, but it wasn't paying the bills. Now so-called journalism is all about working for free and linking to some shit-for-brains blogs. No money in that and I'm *still* paying off my student loan."

The line of work he ended up in, he can easily pay off those loans.

"Why'd your girl dump you on Christmas, Sally — uh, Sully?"

"She wanted freedom and travel and I wanted to settle down."

"You're too young to settle down."

"I'm one of those guys who needs stability, I guess. This time next year, I'll either be sleeping in my own bed or having Christmas sex with my new wife or maybe even swearing up a storm, trying to put a crib together."

"Christ, you're young and in a hurry."

"I've always been in a hurry to get married. Feels...safer, and love — especially *new* love — is a drug, right? Besides, it's always later than you think." You made a show of trying to catch up and knocked back your Cuba Libre. Only you and Chinese Rick know that it's only Coke.

You bought the target all his drinks and watched him get steadily plastered. He did most of the talking and he did have some interesting stories. "Kennedy said we had to beat the Russians to the moon, but that was really about developing rocket technology. He had to justify those huge budgets so he told America it was about the Space Race instead of developing better ICBMs to nuke the Russians."

He switched to Seven and Sevens — two ounces of straight grain whiskey, five ounces of 7-up and a wedge of lemon. Chinese Rick just gave you the lemon and 7-up.

"Now NASA is all about *unmanned* space missions," the target said, gesturing with his glass. "We don't even have *shuttles* anymore. Unmanned missions, just when we need the best flying killer robot drones possible. You think that's a coincidence? It's the Space Race all over again, but this time, with the tech they're developing, they'll use it on us, on American soil. Just wait until those DEA and Homeland Security douchebags get hold of surveillance drones that are the size of houseflies!"

Thomas ordered again without even pretending he might reach for his wallet. You kind of liked him. You might have liked him more if he wasn't so cheap, but you'd had that problem, too, lately. You reminded yourself that your

5

annoyance was really a case of the reformed sinner getting more annoyed at an unrepentant offender.

"I'll tell you another thing. Nixon said, go after marijuana users and keep the whole *Reefer Madness* propaganda going. Our government is *still* doing that shit. We got a recession and they're spending billions on policing weed instead of making billions taxing it. Organized crime — this should tell you all we need to know — *wants* to keep weed illegal so their business model isn't interrupted."

You nodded, knowing from personal experience that this was true. You're not surprised that he sounds informed. He bloviates — thanks Tia Marta and *Reader's Digest* for more word power — but he's informed. Given the main reason you're killing him — besides the money — his views on drugs surprise you.

"You know why Nixon and all the other douche nozzles in authority wanted to go after marijuana? Because weed is the drug of all those protesters and the jobless and the kids with student loans they'll never pay back. Cocaine users aren't protesting shit, but you want to have another handle on Occupiers so you can lump more charges on them when you arrest them for getting the snot beaten out of them? That's how you do it, son, and the scared middle class just nod and say, 'Thank you, sir, may I have another? Hope you don't come after me with a cannon that shoots sound and melts my eyeballs.'"

"Somebody once said, 'Question Authority before Authority questions you.'"

"Hell, yeah!" He toasted you again.

His politics bored you, but the more toasts, the better.

"Have you noticed that there are no major drug busts anymore? The feds have all this new technology and weaponry that Homeland Security gave them so they're all militaried up, but you hardly ever hear of huge cash and drug seizures like in the old days. I think it's because the cops are doing the seizing *before* they get the drugs and cash back to headquarters. Safer to send SWAT through a door to squeeze a bunch of stoners.

Try that shit with a bunch of meth heads and they'll shoot your balls off and fry 'em for breakfast."

You gently pushed that subject, seeing where Thomas would take it. "I've done some weed, but I never thought about it like this. I mean, I know the underground economy is tied up in the regular economy. Gangsters mix with banksters."

"Heh. That's not the half of it! In the late '80s, the locals...big Chicago gangs like the Black Kings and the Latin Kings? Crack was the drug of choice then. It's a cheap, quick high. Now we got meth, which is some crazy shit. But it's the prescription drug companies that are the huge pushers. International conglomerates, and they're the ones killing off all our celebrities. Prescription drugs have their uses, but a bunch of these kids have no idea what the wrong dose of Vicodin will do to their livers. I've seen some crazy shit. You see that earlier this year? Sly Stallone's kid? Sage? Gone. Too many prescription pain meds. And Heath Ledger? Shit. He's gone, too."

"Heath Ledger played the Joker the best it has ever or will ever be played," you said. That was the first earnest statement you'd allowed yourself tonight.

Thomas slammed his glass down so hard, you thought it might shatter. His words had grown more slurred. "Right! To Heath Ledger! Best Joker ever! Hot damn! Made you totally forget Nicholson's Joker and the totally unrealistic anal sex in...in...!"

"I hope you're talking about Heath Ledger having 'totally unrealistic anal sex' in *Broke Back Mountain*."

"Right." After a few minutes he leaned closer. You resisted curling your lip and turning your head from his boozy breath. "You say you've done a little reefer, Sally?"

"Sully, and yup."

"Do you realize the resources that go into stopping people from sacrificing a harmless plant to the fire gods? The government is so stupid, they even outlaw hemp. Hemp can't even get you high. Makes the best clothes, paper, fuel and rope and, just because William Randolph Hearst wanted to keep his lumber companies profitable in the last century, we *still* can't have hemp in *this* century. This country is crazy. Henry Ford's first car was made out of hemp and you could hit the fenders with a hammer and not leave a dent!"

Thomas fell forward. You caught him before he could fall into your lap.

"It's about time," you said. "I thought you were going to bore me to death."

You slipped one of Thomas's arms across your shoulders and helped him to his car. You already knew which car was his just as you knew where he lived and that his garage door opener was clipped to the sun visor over his driver's seat.

You slipped your gloves on before touching his car door. As soon as he was inside, Thomas lay slumped in the passenger seat. You fished his keys out of his pants pocket, but he didn't stir. "No more political lectures," you ordered, sure now that the murder would be righteous, if only to shut him up. Thomas began to snore.

Twenty minutes ago, you parked the car in the target's garage, pushed the button to close the door and left the engine running.

Every assessment of a crime scene is based on the easiest theory of the case. It's Christmas day, so when detectives are eventually called, Occam's Razor will go in your favor. The easiest narrative is that Thomas drove home, drunk and depressed. The cops will think he decided to end his life as a Christmas gift to himself, though you happen to know his death will be a gift for a stunning blonde.

Christmas, you reasoned, is for suicides, domestic and child abuse and family fights. Even though holiday suicides are really a myth — you Googled— it's a persistent lie and who could say the victim himself didn't believe the myth so much he acted upon it? More people commit suicide than murder and someone offs themselves once every seventeen minutes — Google again — so why wouldn't the police jump to the easy conclusion?

Besides, hit men usually take Christmas Day off. Not you, but most.

When you were a Military Policeman, you saw far too many suicides. The target's crime scene would look open-and-shut clean and DIY. Checking out via carbon monoxide is one of the easier ways to leave this world and find out if hell has room. Bullets and blood get complicated and you've had all the complications you can stomach.

You left him in the car, engine chugging and tailpipe spewing. You planned to go out and check on him once you completed your search. If he had receipts or any clue he was in Chinese Rick's bar, the evidence leaves with you. The hardest part of this hit would be to muscle Thomas into the driver's seat.

Five minutes ago you checked the refrigerator and freezer. You looked in, under and behind the stove. The cupboards stood nearly empty except for bags of chips. The client promised the money and drugs would be hidden in the house. However, Paulie, your only remaining contact with The Machine back in New York, didn't know where the target stashed the drug money. Paulie owed you his life, but more important, you're pretty sure he's too afraid of you to screw you over. You continued the search.

The tough part of the job was not to make a mess. Tossing the small house wouldn't take so much time if you didn't have to worry about keeping the suicide narrative intact. You moved from room to room, confident you were alone, but losing faith in Paulie as you searched. The house seemed too bare for this to be the target's only flop. The cupboard held one dish and one water glass. Where were all the empties and the cleaning supplies or even a bottle of ketchup in the fridge? The living room held just one chair, a large square glass coffee table and a plasma TV with a PS3 game system beneath it. He only had one game: *Lego Batman 2*.

Only one small picture hung in the entire house and it was in the bedroom. You paused to note that it was a photo in a cheap frame: a stacked blonde in a red tankini whose face was turned away from the camera toward the setting sun. Since it was the only picture in the house, you were sure you'd found the treasure. You checked behind the frame for a hidden wall safe but again, came up zeroes and snake eyes. You looked under the mattress and found nothing but dust bunnies. There were no sheets, just a sleeping bag and a stained pillow. Despite your surveillance from the street, from where you stood, the target's house looked more like a front by the minute.

Finally, you discovered Thomas's stash of Vicodin — a bundle of pill bottles wrapped in plastic held tight with thick blue elastics. He'd hidden the stash behind the toilet tank in the upstairs bathroom.

A few seconds ago, you heard the crash and tinkle downstairs. You pulled your SIG from your waistband and raced downstairs, pausing at the landing to peer around the corner.

"H-help!"

Of course, it was Thomas.

And now, having stumbled in from the garage, Thomas smashed through the glass coffee table, ass first. He's trapped on his back, helpless as a turtle. He looks up at you through red, bleary eyes, coughing and bewildered. "Dude...Sally...my car's out of g-gas, man."

You thought you were cool, but you forgot to check the gas gauge.

A trickle of blood drips beneath him, but he doesn't seem to notice. It takes him a while to work through the equation that you're standing in his living room, a pistol in your fist, the business end pointed at him.

"Where's the money, Thomas?"

"Wh-what? What are you doing here, Sally?"

"Jesus. My name is Jesus Diaz."

"R-really? *Hay-soose?*"

"Where's the money, Thomas?"

"H-hey, man...are you...are you the bad guy?"

"No, man. I'm not the bad guy. I'm just *a* bad guy. You're *the* bad guy."

He tries to get up. You push him back down.

Thomas straightens his legs, which makes him sink deeper into the well of the broken table. It's like he's trying for a sit up with his ass in shattered glass.

"This is not Cirque de Soleil, Thomas."

Still, as he reaches up awkwardly, his pant leg slides back and — surprise! — he's packing a little .22 in an ankle holster. Ankle holsters suck to wear and are slow to use, so you have just enough time to shoot Thomas in the upper chest once. His body jolts, his arms fall back and he makes a sound that starts with a growl and ends on a high note of despair followed by a long wheeze.

He looks up at you, glassy-eyed, draining and fading fast. Breathing in tiny birdlike gulps, he manages to say, "I'm not...*Thomas*."

Tomorrow you will skim the news websites and find a reference to an unidentified man found dead in a nearly empty house on Chicago's east side. Police will say they found $20,000 behind the kick plate under the kitchen cupboards.

Paulie told you the target could have at least $80,000, maybe more, and Paulie expected a heavy finder's fee for being your agent in addition to your cut of whatever cash you found. The rest would go back to the guy who ordered the hit. Maybe the guy who called himself Thomas was right. Maybe the DEA doesn't have major drug and money busts anymore because cash and drug seizures are the only reliable retirement fund left. They've got kids with student loans to pay, too. You pop some pills because the only thing you know for sure is that you will never know.

It will bother you that you missed out on at least $20,000, but you'll be so high on Vicodin, it will lessen the pain. You will stay in your room, play *Lego Batman 2* on Thomas's PS3, and dream of finally meeting the woman in the red tankini face to face.

The Vic-induced euphoria will kick hard and sweet, but you will wish the Vicodin could do more, like make the woman in the photo speak to you. You will hold up her picture close to your face and whisper, "I'm not really the bad guy. I'm just a guy. I can dance and we'll play pool and have fun and I'll never leave you. It'll be good. I'll be good. I've been trained to make people happy who were very hard to please."

But who is the real you? Which is the higher self who will graduate from this life and deserve the girl in the red tankini? What happened to the innocent kid from Cuba, pushed into this life?

"Jesus," you coach, "you're losing the thread. You're losing yourself. You can't think in terms of what you've done. You have to cut the past off and burn it. You have to forgive and forget. Everybody says that so it must be true."

When you start to hyperventilate, you resolve to stop taking any more Vikes for a while.

You tell yourself aloud, your voice bouncing off the hotel room's walls, "It's always later than you think! You've got to live in the *now*, not think about what might have been."

The counsellors at Veterans Affairs call what you're doing "dissociation". You call it the only way to be you and live.

You will fall asleep holding the photo of the girl in the red tankini to your bare chest, so only she will see your scars. You hope she's as nice as she seems from a distance. You want her to be pure. You want to be pure for her.

TICKING CLOCK

Ordinarily, you would never sit with your back to the entrance but, halfway down the middle of the diner, you get the best continuous view of the girl from Thomas-not-Thomas's photo. You'd have chosen differently if you knew that ten minutes from now, two thugs are going to burst in the front door of this greasy spoon and point their Tech 9s in unsafe directions. You don't know that yet. You're just trying to enjoy the Blue Plate Special: tough steak and runny eggs. The food is bad, but the waitress who took your order and brought it out to you is the girl from the photo. That red tankini did not lie, but now that you can see her face — those cheekbones! Those eyes! If you could order a pot cookie with your decaf coffee, you'd stay here all night.

Still, you're never off the clock. People are after you. Before you could even look for the girl of your dreams, you scoped out the diner's clientele. An old couple left as you arrived and you held the door open for them. They looked at you with suspicion and hurried into the street.

The only other person in the diner when you arrived was the big, black bald guy in the rear booth by the bathroom. It was Ving Rhames, the actor. Then you decided it wasn't him, couldn't be, not here in a greasy spoon on the edge of Logan Square late at night. Then you wondered if Ving Rhames has a twin brother. You felt the same startling jolt everybody gets when they spot a celebrity. You'd felt it before. You saw Kevin

13

Smith, the director, in Times Square once and you'd even said hello to Christopher Walken twice in the street in New York.

The guy in the rear booth looks up and scans you, too. Celebrity or not, you try to do a threat assessment in a glance. You should have given the guy more serious consideration when you first spotted him. His size is intimidating, but he passes the can-I-take-him test for two reasons: he seems more interested in reading his Kindle than looking at you and the vest under his suit jacket is bright purple. The vest was a bold choice for the otherwise conservative, dark pinstripe suit. The dude has style. On a lot of big guys, a suit either fits them like a paper bag or they look like they're stuffed into a sausage casing. His suit is tailored and fits well. With that purple vest, there's no way he's a cop, so he seems safe. You take him for a musician having a bite after a gig at a local jazz club, but when you get up to go to the bathroom, you spot the big Bible on the table in front of him and decide he has to be an evangelical preacher. He has the look of a former football player who has found Jesus — not you, the other one.

Settling into the booth and watchful for the goddess from the photo, you try to live in the now because that's what the counsellors at the VA say to do. They tell you to look for details and notice things, like where the exits are and how many windows are in a room. They call it "mindfulness." You call it being on high alert every day of your life, as if memorizing wallpaper patterns is the answer to your problems.

Your life coach says you should live for today, too. Sgt. Billy doesn't work at the VA. He lives on the street but he still has lots of advice, telling everybody who comes within a few feet of him how to live their lives. Mostly you just politely nod to him as he babbles at you and pretend you don't speak English.

But Sgt. Billy said something Christmas Eve Day that caught your attention as you passed him. "The three most powerful words are 'I love you.' Say it more and you live better! Now gimme a dollar!"

With the money from the Christmas Day hit lost to the cops, you're off to a slow start on beginning again. Either way, you will try to start fresh. You may as well since you're starting at zero. You ran from New York. Yes, "ran" is the right word. There wasn't a lot of dignity in the way you left. That wasn't a retreat. That was a run-away-before-the-FBI-arrests-you situation. That was a disappear-before-the-Machine-shoots-you-for-treason sort of deal. You may as well have run away holding your hands over your head and screaming like a little kid. Even the Romanian mob wants you dead and they barely know you.

Ah, but when you're in the greatest city on earth, where do you run? East was the ocean. North was boring. They'd know where to come looking for you if you'd bolted south to Miami. That left running west, so you ran away to Chicago to lose yourself in another big city. The cops and the mob probably won't find you as long as you start being the smart ninja you only thought you were when you got in that mess in New York.

The key to staying alive and living in the now is to keep your profile low, avoid playing with guns and, above all, don't fall for the first pretty girl you see. Not again. Of course, you're already screwing that up as soon as you look up and see your waitress walking toward you smiling. Even though the photo didn't show her face, you know who she is. You've seen her before at a distance. You memorized her rack then, but it's her blue eyes that hold you now. You've never gone out with a blue-eyed girl.

She's already plenty tall so she sure doesn't need the two-inch heels in a place like this. Most diner waitresses wear white orthopedic shoes with lots of cushion for all the miles back and forth from the kitchen. Occasionally a hand reaches up and dings the bell on the counter, but the short order cook must be awfully short because you haven't spotted him yet. Maybe the waitress is trying to give the diner some class. She's fighting a losing battle with the neon sign out front that says "Good Eats". The second *o* has flickered so it looks like "God Eats". Still, the high heels do wonders for her calf muscles and it's impossible not to imagine how her long legs would feel wrapped around you, urging you on.

"More coffee?" she asks.

The name tag on her left breast says Willow. The old joke is "What do you call the other one?" You resist the urge. Instead you give her the nod. As tough as the steak is, there's nothing wrong with the view and you want to make the good times last. You dip your head slightly and give her your slow smile. Tia Marta instructed you in how to throw down your most seductive look and this is it.

"Undress me with your eyes," Tia Marta said. "Look hungry. Make me feel desired, like you want to tear my clothes off with your teeth. Even women who prefer shy men don't want men who are shy about their desire. Make me believe you are the answer to all my questions and all my needs, boy."

Of course, the context of Tia Marta's instruction was kidnapping, statutory rape and murder, but your seductive look still has juice. Willow doesn't call the 14th District cops. Instead, she smiles back as she refills your cup. A flame leaps up where your heart has been cold.

As she turns away, you savour the way she moves. There's something different about the way Willow carries herself, like she spends a lot of time at the gym when she's not slinging hash on the edge of Logan's Square. If you can get your shit together, Willow is the perfect girl for getting over the last girl, She Who Must Not be Named.

You pour in the sugar and cream. You need the calories. Your suit is stylish, but it's hanging off you lately.

You applied for a job at a gym just before Christmas, but it wasn't the sort of place for a woman like Willow. Stale sweat and anger hung in the air and every few minutes some juice monkey would grunt and yell with effort and drop his weights to the floor with a clang. All the guys at the gym looked the same: big biceps and spindly legs. They're making bar bodies so they can pose with their beer and wait for somebody to ogle. Men who can't dance do weights until their muscles fail. The place had looked promising from the outside, but the moment you climbed the stairs you knew this wasn't the sort of place that would need a Salsa instructor.

"You box?" the bored-looking guy behind the counter asked. His name tag read: Dravon MNGR. You didn't ask him what he'd named the other tit, either, though his chest was a muscled shelf that a flat-chested girl in junior high would envy.

"Yeah, I box."

"Any good?"

"Golden Gloves."

"I knew right away. Your face says you've been in the ring a lot."

Your face had been pounded harder outside the ring than inside it, but you didn't correct Dravon's assumptions.

"We could use a boxing instructor on Friday nights in the New Year. Just Friday nights. The regular guy always wants to start his weekend early. Start at five, teach a few members one on one. Maybe a class with a few more people if I can get them to sign up. People keep asking for it. You know, the weight loss people, not the regulars, so it's an easy gig. I pay you by the hour at the end of the night. We good?"

"Part-time's better than no time. Sure, I'll be your boxing instructor."

"Got a name?"

"Jesus Diaz."

"You Cuban, *Hay-soose*?"

"Yeah."

"I knew that, too. All Cubans make great boxers."

"Yeah. My Mom was Cuban. She had a surprise hook. My grandmother's uppercut was mean."

Dravon looked at you a moment too long, trying to decide if you were messing with him and how much smartassery was okay for a guy he'd just met. "You got the look is what I'm saying."

"If I were prettier, like Ali, you'd know I was great. You know that scene in *The Magnificent Seven*? Yul Brynner is in a bar looking for hired guns to protect a Mexican village from marauders. One of the farmers he's working for says, 'What

17

about him? Did you see his face? Lots of scars. He must be tough.' And one of the other farmers says, 'No, we're looking for the man who gave him that face.'"

Dravon looked at you like he was going to change his mind about giving you the job. "Don't know that movie. Is that just out? I haven't heard of that one yet. I don't see many movies stuck behind this counter."

That's what passed for the first regular conversation you'd had in a while. You couldn't remember the last long conversation you had that didn't end with you having to kill somebody. Dravon seemed nice enough, but sadly, Thomas-not-Thomas was a better conversationalist.

You do talk to the people at the VA, but they're too hippie earnest and never want to just talk about movies and things that don't mean something else. They make a big deal about staring you in the eyes to make sure you're listening or to let you know they're sincere when they tell you they care. If they really cared, they wouldn't have to try so hard.

Even Sgt. Billy, your life coach from the street, stares in your eyes as you pass. He street preaches about how he was a stand up citizen before he got behind on his credit cards, started drinking and got in trouble kiting checks. Your first day in Chicago, he sat on a stoop a few doors down from your fleabag boarding house and offered you a drink from his bottle. You shook your head wary of what might crawl from his mouth to your lips if you drank from it.

"Good, man!" he said. "Stay off the wrong drugs! The wrong drugs release the bad mojo of our true natures. I can tell by looking at you, that's a valve you want to stay stuck. Stay out of trouble! Now gimme a dollar!"

You watch Willow wipe tabletops and straighten chairs. She wanders to the last booth by the bathroom to offer the huge, well-dressed bald, black man ensconced there more coffee. Maybe the salad is as bad as the steak because the Ving Rhames lookalike ignores the salad bowl at his elbow. Instead, he focuses on reading a book. Maybe he's just camping here to stay out of Chicago's winter chill. He waves the waitress away with a smile.

Willow lingers and straightens menus and salt and pepper shakers. She's doing busy work, going slow and enjoying your unwavering attention. You would love to have a conversation with Willow. She's the sort of woman who makes you think you should plan things out and think about what you're going to say so you sound as smart and funny as you imagine you are. You want to dance slow and close with no music at all and she could talk into your neck about movies or TV shows or nothing much, her hot breath measuring out each soft syllable. You could have a conversation and not be anyone's burden or case. With a woman like Willow, you could feel so good, you could skip over all the stuff you have to fix about yourself and just be who you only imagine you are. You could claim your best self and not be a bad guy.

The people at Group, the people who say they've heard it all before, are do-gooders who can't understand people like you. They think they've heard it all, but they don't know the horrors you've seen. And the worst things? That's when you're standing outside yourself, seeing yourself do bad things and seeing bad things done to you as if you were another person while light and shadow battle for who gets to drive your brain around in this body. There are a few people at the VA, the do-badders. They might understand, but they might understand far too well and turn you in for the reward.

Your coffee cup isn't half-empty when Willow's back at your table, smiling sweetly. She doesn't show her teeth when she smiles, but her lips are full and her eyes light up when you give her your I-am-the-answer-to-all-your-prayers look. "You okay?" she asks.

"Um." What had you planned to say that sounded so smart and funny in your head?

"For coffee, I mean? You okay?"

"Um." Beat. "Yes."

"You took too long between the 'um' and the 'yes' and maybe I'm reading too much into it, but there was a hint of a question mark in there. Like you said 'yes' but I heard 'yes?' "

"Uh." Two beats. "Okay."

Willow's giggle makes you want to laugh, too. It's a Betty Rubble giggle, lips closed and her head nodding ever so slightly. It's the most charming thing you've seen a woman do since She Who Must Not Be Named woke up in the morning wrapped only in bedsheets with her hair mussed (but sexier for not even trying to be sexy). You shouldn't be flirting, using your head dip and slow smile on her. You should keep this to business, but you've also heard the best cure for an ex is sex with the next.

"Sure you don't want me to brew a fresh pot?" Willow says, but she's already pouring and leaning closer.

What is that perfume? It's subtle. You didn't catch it over the smell of fried food before, but at this range, you can't miss.

"You know you've been talking to yourself, right?" she asks, not unkindly.

You stare at your spoon like it contains all the secrets to the universe. "It's an old habit. Sometimes I do that. Sorry."

"Don't be sorry."

"Did I say anything..." — *incriminating* — "interesting?"

"No, no. It was all an under your breath sort of thing. Don't worry. I didn't hear anything. You know, they say if you talk to yourself, you must have money in the bank." Before you can bark out a laugh, she rushes to tell you she has another theory. "But whoever 'they' is, they're idiots. It's pretty obvious. I think the people who come in here and talk to themselves are lonely."

"Ah."

Willow surprises you in a way that delights: "Like Tom Hanks and his volleyball on that island in *Cast Away*."

Then Willow surprises you even more by setting the coffee pot in front of you and sliding into the seat beside you. Her perfume, you decide, is made of roses. You imagine her in bed, wrapped in a thin sheet and the smell of roses in the air. You gaze at her, stunned and wordless.

After a moment, she says, "Dude, you do speak English, right?"

"Yes," you say. "I had a very mean teacher who made sure."

"Good, because I just gave you your opening. I can't make it much more plain without one of us getting embarrassed. I caught the way you looked at me, but don't stick with the shy thing. The cute and shy thing will only take you so far."

"It's so funny you say that. That's exactly what the mean teacher said."

"Well, mean teacher or not, it's true. A girl likes to be chased by a go-getter, you know? When a girl flirts with a guy, the polite thing to do is to flirt back harder and ask me out, for Christ's sake!"

"It's the twenty-first century," you say. "A guy likes to be chased sometimes. If you make me feel pretty and keep the free refills coming, this might be the start of a beautiful friendship."

There's the Betty Rubble giggle again. "Since you've already got the cool trench coat, you be Bogart and I'll be Louis."

"Willow, you picked up on my *Casablanca* reference."

"Netflix," she says.

"Still weird. My life seems to have more *Casablanca* references than usual lately."

"Sure, though who wouldn't catch that?" she says and you almost fall in love with her right then. "Happens all the time. You think of a word or a person you haven't thought of in ages and suddenly it seems like it's everywhere. It's called synchronicity. It's also why we have to watch what we're thinking so the bad things don't creep in too much."

"I agree completely," you say, though you have reservations about the whole synchronicity thing. "I try to watch my thoughts all the time. Where'd you pick that up?" already guessing the answer.

Willow shrugs, looks away and says she reads a lot of self-help books. You already know the problem she's struggling with. Maybe you're the answer to that, too. Some people would say she's way too tall for you. Fuck those people. You're her answer and she is yours, no matter what the question is.

"I'll be your Bogart," you say. "You know the coolest thing about Casablanca?"

"That it's the film that launched a hundred movie cliches? That it has the most romantic end in movies? The 'Maybe not today, maybe not tomorrow,' speech where you know Rick Blaine loves Ilsa but he sacrifices himself and tells her to get on the plane and he loses her forever for the greater good?"

"Um. I was going to say that the plane at the end was just a cardboard prop and they used little people for the ground crew to make the plane look big.... Your answer's better."

Willow's lips part to break out a killer smile. She shows her teeth. One tooth on the top is doubled up a little, like she has two canines that decided to live side by side rather than insist the adult kick out the baby. Willow is a beautiful woman made more beautiful by one precise flaw. A flaw like that can stop a gorgeous woman from knowing she's gorgeous. A flaw like that can perfect her so she never becomes a bitch. That's the moment the scales tip over hard and you go from almost falling for her to deep in love. You told yourself not to fall in love with the first pretty girl you see. However, when you look at Willow and smell roses, the pain of She Who Must Not Be Named recedes, the same way you can't remember an old tune when you hear a new song playing.

That's also the moment the two thugs burst through the front door of the diner, guns out and looking for trouble. They find it.

RAGE IN HEAVEN

Two black guys, a big handsome, tattooed thug and a thin, rat-faced banger, rush in. They carry Tech 9s, so scarily inaccurate that your weapons instructor referred to them, and all machine pistols, as spray and pray guns. You assume they're on a mission from Big Denny De Molina, once a brother in The Machine and now the guy who wants you dead — well, *one* of the guys who wants you dead, anyway. Though the diner is long, it's also narrow, so missing you is a long odds bet.

Your hand is on your SIG, but if you get into a firefight with Willow beside you, she's dead. You hold off, take a breath, and wait to die. You close your eyes and your last thought is, "Gee, I hope they're good shots and don't screw it up." Your heart ramps up to pound at the inside of your ribs as if it's trying to get out of its cage. You are definitely living in the now.

"Samuel Clemont!" the thin one at the door screams.

You open your eyes. Neither of them spares you more than a glance. New York's Machine is not going to kill you tonight, but there's a better than even chance one of these guys will. The big guy steams your way and grabs Willow by the hair, yanking her up from her seat in the booth. You wish they were here for you. Not only have they taken Willow hostage, but Samuel Clemont is the client who hired you for the Thomas-not-Thomas hit. Paulie was pissed when you told him the cops confiscated the dough, but you argued that services were rendered and the client still had to pay up.

"Jesus, you were supposed to find the money *and* the drugs."

"There weren't any drugs, either," you lied and swallowed a pill. "Guess the cops took them, too. I'm told, they do that sometimes, but I'm not interested in making the client's problems mine. I gotta get paid."

Paulie wasn't even going to tell you who the client was until you reminded the idiot that if you didn't get paid, neither did he. Only when he understood how the problem affected him did Paulie give up Clemont's name.

"Paulie, you're what's wrong with this country," you said and hung up.

Back to living in the now: "Samuel Clemont! We need a meeting!" The big thug turns to his partner and with a tilt of his head, indicates the rat-faced guy should come closer and cover you. The slim guy is light-skinned, which does nothing to conceal the red and purple birthmark plastered across his throat. Even though he's wearing a mock turtleneck — that's probably all he wears — the raw mess crawls up to his chin. Mr. Bad Birthmark should think about wearing scarves until he can grow a thick beard. The birthmark is such an obvious identifying feature, he is not meant for this type of work. When God gives you a birthmark like that, He's saying, "Get in a police line up and go to jail, sucker!" The dude really should have studied harder in school. He could have been something more useful, like a tax collector dying of a heart attack in an empty office after hours. You would have preferred that happening to him in the now. That would be most excellent compared to what he's doing, which is pointing the mouth of his Tech 9 your way.

"Anybody moves, shoot them in the face," the beefy one says. He has the air of entitlement most leaders have. He reminds you of a young army officer you once knew who got the rank for the wrong reasons. This guy is as jumpy as that guy. Busting in here without scoping the place out was a stupid move. After all, you're in here. Only an idiot assumes he's the only one with a gun.

The slim guy is the smarter one. He at least thinks to go back to the front and turn the sign on the door around to read: CLOSED, and lock it.

"Samuel Clemont!" the beefy guy yells again. "I've got your girl here. You come out and we'll have a chat. You make me come back there and it'll be bad. Don't make me come looking for you or I'll make it real bad. You got cleavers and a deep fryer and all sorts of things to play with back there so do *not* fuck with the Lone Wolf!"

The way he announces it would make you giggle under different circumstances. It's not just that he's not busting in alone. No one sane gives even a street name in the commission of a crime any more than a bank robber would give a bank teller his account number, though some idiots have actually done that. What it tells you about the Lone Wolf is that he's stupid and reckless. You might have to jump to taking a chance with Willow's safety and shoot him in the head. The Lone Wolf will have to be put down first, in any case. The guy who is the most aggressive is the one who wins most fights, true. However, this guy is too jittery. He's liable to shoot Willow. Considering you've just decided she is the love of your life, that would prove untimely.

"All right! All right!" a gravelly voice comes from the back.

You slide one hand off the table and reach under your trench coat again. Right about then is when you glance straight ahead and catch the eye of Ving Rhames's twin brother at the back of the diner. The shake of his head is so subtle, you almost miss it. Watching the big man watch the bad guys now, you see how you read him wrong earlier. He's not the kind of guy to save sinners. He looks back at you and, with the slightest narrowing of his eyes, a hint of a smile in one dimple and another subtle head shake, tells you: *I've got this. Do not to go for your weapon.*

You smile back and quirk an eyebrow. *Your move.* You're trying to look cool, but you feel like an idiot. Appropriate. Only a moment ago you were telling yourself that only an idiot assumes he's the only one packing.

You're still sure he's not a cop, not with all the expensive fashion and style he wears. Ving Rhames's twin is so cool he's not even staring at the Tech 9 in the Lone Wolf's hand. Under stress, most people focus on the wrong details and stare at the gun. Talk to any witnesses after a crime with a gun involved and they can probably describe the weapon, but descriptions of the assailant will range from a clubfooted Asian pygmy to an albino basketball player.

The lookalike slips a massive hand up to his mouth, takes out his two front teeth, and drops the plate into his water glass. He picks up his Bible, touches it to his forehead and slides out of the booth.

The beefy guy holding Willow by the hair swings his machine pistol around and screams for Ving's twin to sit. Your hand tightens on the grip on your SIG as you glance back at the slim guy with the unfortunate birthmark. He's looking out the front window nervously and trying to cover you, too. They should have brought three guys for this job.

The Lone Wolf gets even more jittery. "Get down you big, dumb sonofabitch! I will shoot you in your goddamn face if you don't get back in your seat!"

Instead, Ving's twin goes down on one knee, holds his big Bible up in front of his face and begins to pray with a lisp in a surprisingly high voice: "Oh, Lord, deliver us from evil!" The us comes out "*uth*." "Though we may walk through the Valley of the Thadow of Death, deliver uth from theeth two men who have lotht their way! Pleathe, Lord! Deliver uth by releathing the Devil'th hold on their thoulth!"

The word *thoulth* strikes you as particularly ridiculous. If you could watch this as a *Saturday Night Live* sketch, it would be *hilariouth*. You knew another big, scary guy with a high voice and a lisp. Everybody you've ever known who suffered a lisp either came out of the closet early or they became very motivated to lift weights and get huge. Nurture or nature? Bullies or genes?

The Lone Wolf shakes and screams louder for Samuel to come out of the kitchen. He doesn't know what to do with the man praying for his "thoul", whose entreaties to God wail louder. "Oh, Lord, spare us from death, despair and dismemberment. Spare these sinners, these thieves in the night, from Hell's tortures."

"Thpare theeth thinners"? This guy should have been an actor considering how thick he's laying it on. You're 100% sure it's a con and that man is a killer. Fortunately, the big jittery guy still has no idea there's a train coming down the tracks. The thug doesn't even know he's tied down yet.

Your job will be to take out the rat-faced banger with the birthmark. In your mind, it's already done. Some civvies think guys like you have faster reaction times than normal humans. Not true. It's just that people like you plan how to take people out, even if you're just at the store, shopping for almond milk and egg whites. Planning ahead and preparation only makes it *look* like you're faster than average. You measure the distance between you and Rat Face.

Meanwhile, the preacher who is not a preacher is speeding up his train: "Don't, please, don't Lord, make them gargle each other's genitals in a lake of fire! Don't send them to hell and make them give each other blowjobs with an unholy gnashing of teeth, each forever consuming the other, and the fire consuming them to ash and yet devouring them anew, never letting them expire, that they may be pierced by flaming swords wielded by their dead mothers in a gleeful dance of ecstasy at their bastard sons' infinite punishment!"

It's such a fine performance — you might have laughed if the asshole with the Tech 9 wasn't holding your future wife hostage by the hair. Maybe that really is Ving Rhames. It's not just the lisp. It's the tears in his eyes and the high sing-song pitch, like a Mike Tyson lullaby, that sells the con. It's like he's high on helium.

"Don't shoot!" another voice calls from the kitchen. "I'm coming out!"

Samuel Clemont, you judge by his greasy white smock, is apparently the short order cook who undercooked your eggs, overcooked your steak, and sent you to kill Thomas-not-

Thomas. Since you couldn't see him back there earlier, you'd assumed he was what people used to call a dwarf. Since Peter Dinklage rocked his role on *Game of Thrones*, pretty much everybody's got the memo by now that the label is not "dwarf" or "midget". They're now called *little people*.

However, though technically Samuel Clemont *is* short, he is not, in fact, a little person. Both his legs are missing below the knee. He rolls his wheelchair out, just into view. Judging by the high and tight haircut, the tatts snaking out from his three-quarter length sleeves and the M-4 Carbine across his lap, Samuel is a former Marine. No one, no matter how short they become, is ever an *ex*-Marine. It's an easy guess that he probably became a double amputee in a desert war started by a lying Texas oil man and wannabe cowboy. You were sent on that errand by the same Texas oil man and still have a locker somewhere that holds a neatly folded uniform with a few grains of sand in it.

Willow's crying. Just thinking about that really makes you want to shoot somebody. The angle's wrong to take out the big guy. You could shoot him, but there's an excellent chance you'd shoot your future wife in the head before the bullet drilled into the Lone Wolf. And what about the rat-faced baddie with the Tech 9 at the front door? The Lone Wolf's death depends on the man who is not Ving Rhames, or a preacher, either.

When you were an MP, you got called to a PMQ one night. Private Married Quarters are like regular homes, but everything is smaller. The doorways are narrower. There's less room to move around so, though a happily married young officer might enjoy the privacy and married bliss of a little house away from the pure animal raunchiness of the barracks, it didn't work out that way all the time.

The night you're thinking of in particular, at the base in Germany, you got a call over the radio to respond to a domestic disturbance. Some lieutenant was drunk and beating on his wife again. She wanted him to get out. He threatened to kill her. It wasn't the first time you'd been to this lieutenant's house. In the civilian world back home, the drunk asshole would have been dealt with differently. Instead of breaking his nose, you had to call him sir and pretend that his wife's beatings wouldn't end tragically some night.

When you arrived, another MP — a guy named Leland — was already on the stairs, backing up from the young lieutenant and screaming, "Stay back! Stay back, sir! Please!"

The drunk asshole kept coming down the stairs with a combat knife in his hand, held high and heading toward the MP. You drew your weapon and shouted warnings, too. Leland stumbled backward a couple of steps, grabbed for the banister and shot the lieutenant in the wrist.

Stunned, the asshole officer dropped the knife. The lieutenant slowly raised his arm to stare at the blood pumping in spurts into his face and blinding his unbelieving eyes.

Astonished, you congratulated Leland on his amazing marksmanship. "Good shot!" Even if it was an accident, it was an amazing accident. The rule is: pull your weapon, mean it and aim for the center of mass. In stumbling backward, for a few seconds there, you were sure Leland had managed to save the asshole lieutenant's life with a fortunate wound. Your relief didn't last long.

Dead, the asshole wife beater dropped and slid down the stairs to the landing face first. Leland's bullet hit the bones in the wrist and a fragment zipped up and ripped into the bad husband's heart.

Hostage situations can go so wrong even when you have the advantage, which, in this case, you certainly don't. If the preacher's train is going to obliterate the guy with the gun to Willow's head, it better pull into the station soon.

The scene in front of you slows: Ving's twin brother says, "Let us read from Galatians!" He pulls a blued .357 Magnum out of that big Bible and puts the muzzle to the Lone Wolf's forehead as Willow yanks herself away and drops to the floor. The beefy guy goes wide-eyed and freezes, one arm still in the air, a hank of Willow's long blonde hair still clutched in his fist.

In his soft, high, Mike Tyson voice, the preacher who is definitely not a preacher lisps, "I think ith time you guyth thtarted prayin'." A big smile cracks his egg head wide open to reveal the empty space where his top front teeth should be.

The Lone Wolf — the big beefy bad ass with whom no one was supposed to fuck — lets go of his Tech 9 and control of his bladder. The gun clatters to the yellow linoleum as he pisses his pants. Samuel Clemont raises his M-4 Carbine to lock on to the skinny guy at the front of the diner. By the way he stares into the mouth of death, his birthmark bobbling up and down as he swallows hard, the Lone Wolf's accomplice knows he's outgunned. Mr. Bad Birthmark lowers his weapon and turns his back to the short order cook's mercy, scrabbling at the front door's lock.

You could leave it at that, but that's your future wife crying on the floor and you don't want to be the guy who did nothing to defend your future wife. She'd always remember this night as the time you watched her be taken hostage. You've got too much pride to be the guy who sat back, helpless and humiliated by your helplessness. What kind of future could you have with Willow if she always wondered what you would have done, how far you would have let it go before even saying a word when Evil grabbed a Tech 9 and a hank of her beautiful hair?

You are caught up in the moment. You want to be a hero. You are not being a smart ninja. You'll understand all this in the future. You don't know it yet. You're living in the now.

You make your move.

THE UNDERCOVER MAN

There are stereotypes about Cubans. When people think about Cuba, they often think baseball players. There's often some truth in stereotypes. That's how stereotypes begin. However, you never played little league. Your parents were always too busy working at the hotel to take you. Instead, you stayed home, cared for your baby brother, Rodolpho, and kicked a soccer ball back and forth.

But you do have a good throwing arm. To take out Mr. Birthmark, you have several choices of weapons available to you: the SIG in your waistband and the steak knife are the obvious choices. Instead, you go for the weapon Willow left in front of you. You grab the handle of the coffee pot and stand in one smooth motion, twist and throw it at the bad guy as hard as you can.

The scene slows down as the coffee pot turns in the air. He has the door unlocked and yanks it open. Glimpsing some movement in his peripheral vision, he swivels slightly. His head turns to the right as the glass shatters and the coffee scalds his face and neck. His scream is high and loud. He stumbles into the street in misery.

"And stay out!" you roar.

The scene speeds up again as the big bald black man strikes the Lone Wolf with the butt of his pistol in the temple. The Lone Wolf's limbs go loose and he collapses the way a building implodes. When his head hits the floor, there is nothing left in him to resist the fall or to cushion the sickening smack of his shaved head against the linoleum.

Mr. Bad Birthmark is still screaming down the street as you look down and offer Willow your hand to pull her to her feet. She cries and rubs her scalp where the hank of hair was ripped out, but, honor defended, she smiles at you. She closes the gap and throws her arms around you in a desperate embrace. Willow is warm and soft and strong.

The last time you saw your mother, she clung to a tire in rough water off the coast of Florida as you were kidnapped. You have dim memories of being hugged by your mother. Willow is so tall, her embrace is kind of like getting a hug from your mom. Strangely, you feel like a very young boy again. You like it. A lot. It feels like...beginning again.

She pulls back, still holding you, and says, "I-I only saw you sitting down! I had no idea you were...uh."

"Short?" You manage a laugh. "How tall are you?"

"6'2"."

In her two-inch heels, she's seven inches taller than you. "I'm 5'9". No wonder your name is Willow. You're a tree."

"You think that's the first time I've heard that, don't you?" she says.

"Sadly, I thought it was original. And 5'9" isn't so short."

You look up at her and pull her close again, holding tight. "I'm so glad you're okay."

"Me, too."

"No, you don't get it," you whisper in her ear. "I'm glad you're okay because I don't know you, but I'm going to know you. I don't know if the height thing is an issue for you. If it is, that's too bad, because when we lie down, I'm going to make you forget about it completely."

Samuel Clemont rolls out and nudges you in the knee with the butt of his rifle. "Hey! Will, who the hell is this?"

When you and Willow part, she does so reluctantly. She turns to the man in the wheelchair and says, "Dad, say hello to my little friend!"

Ouch. And a nice *Scarface* reference! You love her even more so you are going to forgive her. Still, *ouch!* And *"Dad"?* Oh, sweet Christ.

You stick out a hand. "Nice to meet you, sir. I'm Jesus Diaz."

He looks at your hand as if you just pulled it out of your ass. "Christ."

"Common mistake, but it's pronounced *Hay-soose.*"

He gazes back at you sourly.

The Ving lookalike stands over the Lone Wolf, who was thinking about getting up until the big man pushed him back down with his foot. He does not need to use any martial arts finesse or leverage to trap the beefy man beneath him. He pushes the bad guy down like he's stepping on an ant. He scoops up Lone Wolf's Tech 9 from the floor. "Easy, son. You are messed up!" The Lone Wolf doesn't look near as scary as he did a moment ago.

The big black man looks at you, nods and kicks his prisoner hard in the ribs with the toe of one of his pointy shoes, which you suspect, despite their style, are steel-toed.

Samuel Clemont zips forward and rolls over the Lone Wolf's right hand.

The Wolf shudders. "Mother— !"

"Don't talk. Don't come back." Clemont sticks the muzzle of the carbine behind the Wolf's ear. "If I have business with you, I'll call you. Tell your boss, he's not the only one with muscle. If you understand, moan softly." He raises the butt of the rifle and brings it down on the Lone Wolf's collarbone with a thunk and a crack. It only takes twenty pounds of pressure to snap a collarbone, so that's done. The bad guy moans, but not softly, gets up and stumbles his way to the door holding his right arm with his left hand, his mashed fingers to his chest.

"Lock that door after him," Willow's father says. "We're done business for the night. At least, we're done with regular business."

You recognize the tone. Before he was in that chair, he was an officer. He's used to giving orders. Officers have that sure tone of entitlement. They don't say please and they have no doubt whatever they command will be acted upon immediately.

The big man locks the door, and turns to look at you.

"Oscar-worthy performance, Mr. Rhames."

"Thanks, but that's not original, either. I hear the Ving Rhames thing all the time. People used to say I looked like Michael Clarke Duncan, but they really meant Ving Rhames when they said it. Since Michael Clarke Duncan's death, they don't make that mistake anymore."

Michael Clarke Duncan would have been easier on him. There's no lisp when he says, "Michael Clarke Duncan." Now he has to deny he's "Ving Rhameth."

"The resemblance has probably got you laid plenty, though, huh?" you ask.

He finally breaks into a tight smile, but crosses his arms. Mixed signals. He's still trying to figure out your place in his universe.

"Good job taking that guy down," you say. "It was a smooth con. I didn't see the .357 coming out of that Bible. That's something out of a western. I saw you reading an ebook, but for pulling a cannon out of a book, you can't beat an old Bible."

"You a pro, Jesus? Or are you just a good Samaritan? You have the look of a pro. You talk and move like a pro."

Sharks recognize each other as sharks. Still, you shrug. "A pro? I dunno. Right now I'm not getting paid. It preserves my Olympic status as an amateur."

That makes the big man smile more, but Samuel Clemont eyes you up and down like you're a rusty car at the back of the used lot. "You from around here, smartass?"

"I've only been in Chicago a couple of months."

"You plan on staying?"

You look at Willow like she's a new and shiny Ferrari. "Oh, hells yeah."

"Then, for your own safety, I guess you're on my team. Maybe our safety, too, if you're useful."

"He's useful," the big man says, although with his speech impediment, it sounds like he's calling you youthful. Your hand disappears into his as he shakes it gently. It's like putting your hand into a warm loaf of bread. Most guys squeeze your hand hard to prove how strong they are. He doesn't have to prove a thing.

"I'm Chilli Gillie," he says. "My friends call me Chill. The way you nailed that guy with a coffee pot from half-way across the room? You call me Chill."

"Cool."

"How'd you do that, anyway, man? Just overhand a coffeepot like a baseball and nail him like that?"

"Dunno. It's only my second time scalding somebody with hot coffee. A few more times and I could reach expert level, but I'm afraid the act might get stale."

He looks at you like he's still trying to figure you, fails, shakes his head and smiles. Smiling seems to remind him he doesn't have all his teeth so he goes to the back booth and retrieves his top plate from the water glass. When he turns away and dips his head to pop his false teeth into his mouth, his back looks like a wall. He reminds you of Big Denny De Molina. It's nice to have a new friend who is well armed and just as big as the one who wants you dead.

You don't know how much to say in front of Willow, but you can't very well talk to Samuel Clemont about the money he owes you for killing Thomas-not-Thomas.

"Jesus, you escort Willow home," Samuel says.

When he catches your grin he tells you to come right back. "I'm guessing we got a lot to chat about. No dawdling."

He gestures to Willow and she bends to bring her ear close to his mouth. It's a long way down. He whispers and she shakes her head. Then she nods.

You were hoping Willow would take you home and pump you. Instead, she'll be pumping you for information.

NIGHT AND THE CITY

Willow has questions, but not the ones you expect.

"Do you drink?" she asks.

You take a deep breath. You already had your lies all lined up and here she is, getting the truth out of you. "There was this girl I really liked once. I was at a bar and she asked me if I wanted to buy her a drink. Of course, I did, and then she asked me what I was drinking and I made the mistake of telling her I was drinking a Coke with a lime in it. She called me a pussy and walked off with the drink I bought her."

"So you don't drink. Does that mean you drank too much before or — ?"

"Sometimes I'll drink alcohol, but not often." You could tell her that the last time you were in a bar you only faked drinking to set up a target so he looked like a carbon monoxide suicide. You hold back. "I just never liked the taste. Those uh, fruity drinks with umbrellas, are sweet. The kind that disguises the sharp taste of alcohol, like a Singapore sling. Is that the right answer?"

"Fruity drinks with umbrellas? Really?" She lets go with her Betty Rubble giggle. "That girl who called you a pussy might have been right, but not drinking is the right answer. "

"Great. Just what I was hoping to hear."

When Willow laughs next, she snorts a little and covers her nose. Embarrassed, she laughs and snorts again. You're charmed. This *must* be love.

As you both walk up the street toward the apartment she shares with her father, people bustle back and forth, heedless of the fact that you and Willow had guns pointed at your heads just a few minutes ago. "Nobody knows what we just went through," you say. "Weird, isn't it?"

"You think I'll get PTSD, like all those soldiers?"

You shrug. "When I was a little boy in Cuba, my father, my brother and I built a treehouse. It was just scraps of wood and it didn't hold together very well. We weren't exactly a handy bunch of guys."

"More evidence of being a pussy. It's not looking good for you."

"Anyway," you continue, "I was trying to drive a nail and I hit my thumb instead. I dropped the hammer and started dancing around in pain and my father looked at me and said, 'That hammer probably hurt a bit, but at least it wasn't on long.'"

"Helpful."

"Made me laugh. And you just laughed...*at* me, but you laughed. All things considered, I think you're getting over your life being threatened remarkably quickly."

"I'm sure it looks that way to the casual observer."

"I'm looking at you, but not casually, Willow." You look away when you realize your look veered off into a leer. "There are military folks who go through a lot and they don't fall into the stereotypes about Post Traumatic Stress Disorder. There's people who go through several tours, look fine, then kill themselves. I hear that even those guys in Nevada who pilot drones to kill people halfway around the world? They're eating dinner at home every night with their families and their work looks like they're playing a video game. Some of those guys get PTSD even though they're safe. Maybe I'm wrong, but you weren't held hostage very long before Chill and your Dad and me did our thing. Don't worry about PTSD."

That doesn't seem to comfort her. "Makes me think of Dad. Even when he was safe, he was pretty messed up," she says. "After he got hit with the IED and his wars were over — at least until now I thought they were over — there was a while there when I thought he was going to kill himself. Maybe it was the drugs he was on then, but once, when he looked up at me after one of his surgeries.... He was coming out of the anaesthesia and he told me, 'Will, we should never have gone over there. Not just because it was what the enemy wanted. By going after them, we bring ourselves down.' "

"Wow."

"It didn't last. As soon as the drugs wore off, he was back to wanting to kill them all. 'Nuke 'em and turn the desert into a glass parking lot,' is Dad's annual Christmas toast."

"Mental note: I do the Christmas toast from now on."

She laughs, squeezes your shoulders and leans down to lay her head on yours for a moment as you walk together.

The air is crisp and a light snow begins to fall. You and Willow pause to watch the flurry fall out of the darkness and into the city lights. *You and Willow.* What great words they are when put together. "Look," you whisper. "We're having a moment and God approves."

"Thanks. I guess I am feeling pretty safe with you. Seeing you get that guy..." She gives a full-throated laugh that exposes her fang. "If you'd asked me an hour ago if I thought that was a good thing, I would have said no, but as soon as that guy hauled me up by the hair, I didn't just want them dead. I wanted them to suffer. I wanted to watch them burn in hell and I wouldn't even piss on them to put out the fire." She does something with her jaw. She looks a little harder. You suppose you look that way all the time.

"Priorities rearrange themselves, Will. Somebody once said that a liberal is a conservative who hasn't been mugged yet."

"Oh, I've been mugged before, but this was more personal. That guy was calling Dad out by name."

"Yeah, you gonna tell me what tonight was all about and why I'm on the team for my safety and possibly yours?"

"What?"

"What Samuel said. Not exactly a ringing endorsement, thanking me for swelling the ranks."

She shrugs with one shoulder. "It's about protection money. Those guys have come around before. Dad says they want too much. It's not like the diner is doing that well."

That one-shoulder shrug bothers you. Is she telling the truth? Her face tells you she knows more than she's saying. You want to press her, but the snow is falling. "I can't imagine why the diner isn't doing better. *You're* there. Why doesn't everybody come there? At least all the hetero guys and a platoon of lesbians."

"It's a diner, not a strip bar, pal."

Pal. A girl has never called you that before. The way she says it reminds you of a moll from an old Jimmy Cagney movie. That makes you feel warm. You love those old movies, and like you, Jimmy could fight *and* dance. When done right, fighting is dancing.

"Besides," she adds, "they still have to eat the food. I told Dad we should class the place up with some fancy coffees. In fact, coffee is *all* we should sell. I don't think he's a very good cook."

"You say that like it's a matter of opinion. It's a fact. I don't usually do this, but since we're pals with an option for more, I agree with you. The steak and eggs were awful."

Willow punches you in the shoulder. "You don't usually agree with people?"

"I don't usually tell the truth. Not on a first date."

Willow pulls you around a corner to head south on North California Avenue. "Nobody tells the truth on the first date. The first couple of months of a relationship, at least, it's like a job interview that just goes on and on. No farting!" She laughs and snorts again.

"No farting, I promise. Not for a while. For you? Not for *years.*"

"Maybe we should try something different," she says. "I'll tell you the truth. I'm laughing and having a good time with you but I'm also on the edge of throwing up. Those guys... I don't know what Dad and Chill are going to do about them, but I'm glad I'm not them. And with what they did? Just grabbing me like that, like I was nothing? I don't really care what they do to them. I know I should care, but it's like looking for something on a shelf. You think it should be there, but it just isn't. Wishing doesn't make it so. If it makes me evil to want them dead, then I'll be evil. You know what I mean?"

"I know exactly what you mean. You're not evil. You're a brave woman."

"No. I'm all exposed nerves. Feels like I'm a toothache. It's worst over my heart. I'm like my mom. While my Dad was in Iraq for his first tour, she was diagnosed with breast cancer. She was all nerves, too, but the deeper she got into her treatment — the chemo, the radiation — the funnier she got. The sicker she was, the more jokes she made. You remind me of her, actually."

"Oh, no. I remind you of your Mom."

She pulls you by your lapels and kisses you hard.

"If you kissed your mother like that, it's not PTSD you gotta worry about."

"Shut up. We're still having a moment, smartass."

"Kiss me again."

She does.

"Okay, go on."

"At the beginning? When Mom went into surgery, this orderly wheeled her down to the OR and while they were waiting, she made him laugh and laugh until he was just about to pass out. Later, one of the nurses asked how my mother knew that guy. The nurse had never seen him laugh like that. Mom didn't know him, but getting scared, just opened something up in her."

"I've seen that. I've even done it and felt it. I used to be an MP in the army. Cops, medics, paramedics, funeral home directors...they all have a weird sense of humor. When you're that scared all the time, it's a reflex. When you see the world the way it really is, you can cry, but it's mostly so hopeless, you might as well laugh."

"Mom was funny right up until the end. I guess you're right. You can be hysterical or in hysteria. Better to make jokes on the way out."

"It's why I always liked the *Spider-Man* comics," you say. "Spider-Man is one of the few superheroes who makes jokes while he's beating up the bad guys."

"I've never gone out with a short guy before. I don't know if I can handle it if you turn out to be an ubergeek, too." She lessons the sting by leaning down and kissing your cheek.

"One more," you say. "Jesus said, turn the other cheek." You tap your other cheek and when she leans in, you turn your head at the last minute and your lips touch again. This turns into a softer, sweeter, lingering kiss. It's a *real* kiss. This is the one. This is the kiss you will count as your last first kiss. Her lips taste like cherries.

She looks you in the eyes for a full minute and you think, just for a moment, that she recognizes you. She's seen you before, maybe in a glimpse, but she's seen you. But she didn't *consider* you then. Not like this. The moment passes and you're relieved when she puts her arm over your shoulder and you walk on. You slip your arm around her waist. Her hip is against your side, but the mismatch doesn't bother you a bit. Sure, this is the sort of abrupt start to a relationship that addiction counsellors warn about, but since this must also be what lottery winners feel like, fuck that noise.

"I'm supposed to find out more about you."

"What does Samuel want to know?"

"The way I'm feeling, he can ask you himself. I have my own questions."

"Can I ask you one?"

She shakes her head. "It didn't actually occur to me that the whole question and answer thing would go two ways."

"Too bad. When your mom got breast cancer, did your dad come home from overseas?"

She takes a deep breath. Blinks. Her jaw is moving but no words come.

"Never mind," you say. "I know all I need to know about that. Ask me something."

"I asked about drinking," she says.

"And we established I'm a pussy."

"Yeah." The smile is back. "What about drugs?"

"Weed makes the inside of the top of my skull feel like it's packed with peppermint gum if I smoke it. I prefer edibles."

"Weed doesn't count."

"Not unless I'm a pussy and —"

"You can throw a full pot of steaming coffee with deadly accuracy and take out a guy who's threatening me and my father. I'm going to take a risk and declare, you aren't a pussy."

"I worked on my ninja skills since the hammer and thumb, treehouse debacle. It's a good skill, but it's difficult to monetize."

"Ah, have you got a job?"

"I teach boxing over on North Fairfield on Friday nights." You haven't actually done that yet, but Dravon gave you the job for the new year, so you're managing to stick remarkably, unusually and excruciatingly close to the truth so far. You hurry on, "I could teach Salsa, but I haven't found a place to teach it yet. I play guitar, too, but I'm not good enough to teach that and the pay's for shit, anyway. The economy — well, you know how it is. Everybody knows how it is."

"You said you were an MP. You ever think about being a cop? They need lots of guys. The mayor keeps talking about cracking down on gang violence. It's gotten crazy, like those assholes tonight. Last Memorial Day, there were a bunch of people killed not far from here, including a kid in the crossfire. They also need a lot of police for crowd control. I swear with the economy and the protests...it's all just getting bigger. Things are getting worse."

"I thought about being a cop. Lots of times, actually. But I don't have the temperament for it. I don't take orders well. I've been given a lot of orders from a young age. I decided I don't like it. I don't like wearing a leash."

"That must have been a tough way to go in the military."

"It was."

"Huh. Well, Jesus, so far you're enough like my father to like a lot and so different from him I might..." She doesn't finish.

"I'd like to hear the end of that sentence."

"This is my building." She gestures up at an old apartment building indistinct from all the others. "And you should get back to the diner. Dad will be waiting."

"Let him quiver in anticipation a few minutes longer. Suspense is good for the adrenals. You were about to say something interesting."

"We giants don't reveal everything to our dwarves." Willow wraps her arms around you and kisses hard. Heaven must be like this and chocolate croissants all day long. She's shaking when she finally pulls back.

"You are Queen of the Giants. Queens need knights. I'll be yours."

"So are you going to tell me about the gun in your waistband?"

"Yes. On our next date."

"My dad will want to know about the gun when you get back to the restaurant."

"Then let him ask me."

"You won't tell me?"

"Only if you agree to a date tomorrow night."

"What will we do?"

"I don't care as long as I make you laugh and snort."

"That's not something you tell a girl on the first date."

"I'm feeling unusually confident and truthful tonight."

"The way you say that, I'm not sure if you're messing with me or telling the truth."

"Truth. It's a new thing, but I'm trying it out. When you meet the Queen of the Giants, it's a rule: either tell the truth or leave out the tough stuff. It's the custom of my people, the noble dwarves."

She laughs and snorts again. "This is going to be strange, isn't it? It's the custom of my people to slouch a lot and deal

43

with a lifetime of back and neck pain. It's that or only date basketball players."

"Don't slouch for me, Willow. You don't have to be anything less than you are for me. And obviously, since a gorgeous queen like you is available, the basketball players aren't working out. It's time to try a dwarf. We all Salsa and, if your back hurts, I'll just stand on the front steps and you stay on the sidewalk. The goodnight kiss will work out fine."

"I'm not into basketball, anyway."

"Whatever you're into, I'll be that, though getting taller might require ropes, pain and some persistence."

"I've never met anyone quite like you. You're funny."

"The secret is the same one your mother figured out. I'm terrified all the time."

"Is that why you carry a gun?"

"That's second date talk and I like mystery and suspense, don't you?"

"Okay. Tomorrow night, meet me at the diner."

"As long as we don't have to eat there, fine."

"Huh. Okay. I'll play, as long as you can answer one question correctly. If you don't like that rule and don't want to wear my leash? I'll have to say goodnight and we'll just have to part ways and chalk all the smooching up to facing death without pissing ourselves."

"I did piss myself a little, but I wouldn't mind wearing a leash if you're on the other end of it."

She laughs and snorts again and struggles to give you her serious face. "For reals, though. One correct answer and we go on from here. Wrong answer and we do not proceed. Got it?"

Reluctantly, you give her the nod. "Respect."

"Do you do any drugs besides weed? I can't be around anybody who does hard drugs. For serious."

"I don't." It's your first real lie to Willow, but you were almost honest for at least eight blocks.

MEAN STREETS

There's great power in pointing a pistol at someone who deserves it. When you aim, you feel a connection to the point of impact, like a line of energy ties the path of the bullet to the spot between the target's eyes. When someone points a gun at you, you sense that same energetic connection. You've felt it several times: a spot between your shoulder blades; a crawling feeling on your forehead where the slug was to drill through; a laser's dot over your heart. New love is like that.

After you check Willow's apartment — no monsters under the bed or hiding in the closet — you kiss her goodnight. You take it slow, your hands in her hair. Her lips are soft. After, even though you're on the other side of her thick, reinforced steel door secured with three deadbolts, you still feel her presence.

As you walk down the street, you feel light. You want to keep this feeling. When you wake in the dark on sweaty sheets and the walls lean closer, crawling with shadows, this is the feeling to hold onto until the sunlight finally marches to Chicago's dawn and outlines the city's horizon like uneven, broken teeth against the sky. To sleep at all, you always need a room with a window, so when Tia Marta's basement nightmares return, you can wait and watch for the softness to disperse Miami's memories.

Big Denny De Molina used to laugh at you for falling in love too quickly. He never understood your need to share the night with someone. While he was out trying to get laid, you had few girlfriends, you were often too serious too quickly. You drove a lot of young women away and went into a funk for months at a time over each one. "Jesus, the answer to an old love is a new one, or at least a booty call," Denny said. "Why you gotta fall so hard?"

Big Denny never understood because, back when he was still Little Denny, you saved him from Tia Marta's chamber of horrors. But don't think of Tia Marta tonight. Tonight is for love and cherishing first kisses. Kissing Tia Marta doesn't count as a first kiss. That wasn't your choice.

But it's already slipping away. Happiness reminds you to be sad. Telling yourself not to think of the past ensures you will.

In Union City, you learned the power of choices. For the first time, you had them. Bankrolled from what you stole from the Bug Man's mansion, you and Little Denny ran away from the crime scene in Miami, got on a bus and wound up in Havana on the Hudson. Tia Marta's master, The Bug Man, took Denny from his parents like he took you away from your mother. Denny was sure he'd find his parents in Union City. They were on their way there when he was kidnapped.

Union City, New Jersey is small but dense. From its streets, New York beckoned. The twin towers still commanded the city's skyline and commuters streamed through Havana on the Hudson, always on their way somewhere else. If anyone asked, you told them Denny was your brother. Little Denny couldn't replace Rodolpho, your real brother, but he was fun and didn't hesitate to dumpster dive with you. Denny was small, but he wasn't a whiner.

Back then, when the homeless did it, everyone called it dumpster diving. Now, with the economy all messed up, a new movement of poor people and nouveau hippies call it living Freegan. Most people who live on discarded food aren't part of some anti-consumerist movement. They're hungry. Maybe some wackos think that's "progressive" or maybe they're trying to make people without choice think poverty is cool and noble. When soccer moms and Wall street banksters take up the freegan lifestyle — not just white stoner hippies in dreads — you'll reconsider.

The dumpsters behind grocery stores were best. Denny would sniff the thrown food and declare most everything "Vamos a comer!" *Let's eat!* You stopped him to look at the best before date. If the food was only a day or two past that date, it was dinner.

The Bug Man owned a mansion, fine clothes and slaves. All you had was what you could steal and stuff in a hockey bag. During the day, you and Denny scouted places to stay and each night you counted the Bug Man's money, trying to make it last. Your first job was washing windows up and down the Miracle Mile. While you worked the squeegee, Denny carried the water bucket and soap, pitched pennies and searched the crowds for his parents' faces.

As that first summer in Union City ended, you had to find a warm place for you and Denny. A lanky blonde hustler named Jinx often wandered the Miracle Mile. You weren't sure how old he was. He couldn't seem to grow a beard and his skin was cracked from too much time in the sun. His thin hair looked like mange on a lost dog. You often saw him getting shooed away by the local store owners. Jinx said one of his tricks owned a rug warehouse where you and Denny could squat.

"I'll tell you where it is, if you and the boy want to party."

"We're not into that," you said. "Leave us alone."

"Everybody's up for a party when it gets cold, boy."

He shouldn't have called you "boy."

"Jersey's so cold at night in the winter, you little brown boys have no clue. But hey, it's a free country. You let me know when you're ready not to freeze to death some night."

A couple of weeks later, bleary from a night spent shivering in a big metal Salvation Army donation bin, you could see the steam of your breath even at noon. That night, you told Jinx you were down for a party. Little Denny looked worried, but you soothed him. You would take care of everything.

The rug warehouse was a large old gray building that stood by railway tracks. Jinx surprised you by producing a key to the big padlock on a side door.

"How'd you get a key?"

"It's *my* key, dummy. I broke the old padlock and put on my own. I take all my tricks here when there's no place else to go. Lots of guys' wives wouldn't appreciate me in their living rooms, but their husbands don't mind me in their mouths."

The darkness beyond the doorframe freaked Denny out and he pulled on your arm. In a torrent of Spanish, he pleaded with you to run with him back to the Salvation Army clothing bin for another night of shivering. When you tore your arm away, he cried and tried to pull the hockey bag off your shoulders. You slapped him across the face and pulled him inside.

"Easy! Easy! This can all be easy, boys. All that carpet makes for a good flop. Just cover yourselves with the rugs and you can be cozy. We can all be cozy. Just be out at six. Nobody shows up to work here until nine. Leave the place as you found it and it's fine. There's a scuzzy bathroom past the freight elevator, but the water works."

There were no light switches, but Jinx showed you where to find the circuit breakers. When the lights snapped on, the rolls of carpet looked like hills, big and small.

"You boys can sleep here whenever you want. All you gotta do is pay the tax."

Without ceremony, Jinx pulled his pants down to his knees, his hard penis bouncing up. "I suggest you work together!"

You'd never pointed the Bug Man's SIG Sauer P220 at anyone. Your hand shook. The bullet was to go through his belly button. Where life had first come to him as a baby, death would enter and it would be deliciously agonizing. You could see Jinx's guts explode in your mind's eye. You relished the power because it was the first time you had ever felt any power.

You took a deep breath before pulling the trigger. That was just enough time for Jinx to slap the pistol from your hand. It spun off into the darkness and Jinx laughed so hard, it sounded like a howl. His next slap burned across your face and Jinx howled louder and longer in delight.

Plan B kicked in: Little Denny leapt from a rug roll to Jinx's back. Jinx kept to his feet but, with his pants at his knees, staggered. Denny used the Bug Man's switchblade, cutting him off mid-howl. Jinx burbled and fell, his neck spraying blood. He grabbed at his wound, trying to stop from bleeding out, but once the carotid is cut, it takes about four minutes to die.

Technically, Jinx would have been your third kill. Denny didn't seem so bright, but he had a head for this. You cut the rug on which Jinx bled to death and rolled up his body. Together, you carried and dragged him outside to the railroad tracks. It was Denny who suggested you take off Jinx's clothes, fold them neatly and put them beside his shoes. "People who commit suicide do that," he said.

You took his suggestion and, despite the cold, you and Little Denny De Molina huddled together and waited for the train to decapitate Jinx the hustler. You never knew his last name. All he had in his pockets were a few dollars, three condoms and the key to the padlock. That rug warehouse kept you and Denny alive that first winter in Union City. The killing itself was distasteful. You were afraid and sick as you carried Jinx to the tracks, but you clung to that rush of power, the feeling of holding the SIG and pointing it at a target who needed killing.

Now, as you look up into Chicago's city shine, you pick a snowflake and follow it to the ground. The sound of a distant train shuttling into the night reaches out. It's probably just the El, Chicago's elevated train system, but the sound of a train always gives you a familiar warm feeling. After Jinx, you were less afraid. You learned that to survive, you didn't have the luxury of indecision and hesitation. You learned you had to grab life by the balls and squeeze.

A wino, listless and palm up, sits on a stoop. He looks at you from under a black hood with white lettering that reads: Ezekiel 25:17. The Bible reference looks like it's scrawled on with white paint or seagull shit. You've seen him on the street before, another of Chicago's permanently disenfranchised. His eyes look scared. The street is a time machine that makes people age faster.

"Hey, guy," you say. "The shelters are closed to new guests this late at night. Better go crash somewhere safe or at least find a heating vent."

"Yup. Already colder than a witch's tit, praise God," he says. "You been saved? Do you know Jesus loves you? Do you know the truth? Do you know someone's watching over you, sir?"

"That's too many questions, buddy, and I only have one answer. The truth I know is that life is too long if it's bad and way too short if you live it right," you reply.

He nods. "Amen."

You give him five bucks. "Stay warm, brother."

Chilli Gillie and Samuel Clemont are waiting. You trudge off through the deepening snow toward the diner with hope that your new life is about to start. This is the happiest you've been in a long time, but you try not to think about how happy you are for fear you'll jinx it.

THE UNKNOWN MAN

When you get back to the diner, Chill is waiting outside the front door holding his hollowed-out Bible. "Before you go meet with Mr. Clemont, I wanted to talk a second, man."

"Shoot."

"Funny you say that, because I was wondering if Mr. Clemont hired you as a troubleshooter. I told him all I do is provide security. No black bag and wet work nonsense for me. The man wanted to turn downtown Chicago into downtown Baghdad. When I told him that's not my thing, Clemont was pissed. Now you show up. Are you a hired gun, Jesus?"

"I didn't come in on the noon stage."

"Huh?"

"Look, I didn't have to shoot tonight, so I didn't."

"Technically, you didn't have to burn that man, either. You appear to be afflicted with a temper."

You note that there was not a single s in that sentence and it's vaguely disappointing. You didn't realize how much stupid, juvenile enjoyment you were getting out of hearing Ving Rhames with a lisp.

"If Sam had hired me to shoot somebody," you say, "I didn't do that job tonight. And I wouldn't have gone through some kind of play just to convince you. I'm mostly here for the girl."

"It's pretty clear Mr. Clemont hates that idea."

"I'm charming. He'll come around."

"Jus' helluva coinkidink, you showing up, packing heat and ready to rock." The way one eyebrow shoots up, you know for

51

sure he's not buying your con at all. He's too good at cons himself to be fooled.

"Everybody's gotta be somewhere," you say. To change the subject, you ask how he knew you were packing heat.

"You had the look when you strutted in."

"Really? That makes me sound like a douchebag. Maybe I'm not quite as charming as I thought."

"Well, mostly it was that your belt buckle's pulled over a few inches and riding low on your concealed carry."

"I should have gone with the shoulder rig, but I wanted to be casual."

Chill looks your suit up and down. "You dress pretty fancy for a guy trying to look casual. Usually it's fat guys trying to conceal a gut who dress up this nice to go to a greasy spoon so they won't be too embarrassed to order a milkshake."

"Like I said, I'm here for the girl."

Chill checks the street. "No girl here now. Why you back? You could just date her. You don't have to get pulled into her father's business."

The way he says the word business — *bidnith* — reminds you of Eddie Murphy in *Beverley Hills Cop II*. You have to suppress a smile. That's one hell of a speech impediment he's rocking. If you laughed, you'd feel bad though. Chill is one of those guys you want to like, and not just because he's so big you pray he's always on your side.

"Jesus. Be real with me. I'm a good listener. I don't believe in coincidences. You try to sell me on coincidences and I'll start to think that you believe I'm dumb. I got a list and that's high up on Things That Piss Me Off."

You nod and choose your words carefully. "I don't have much going for me in the employment department and Clemont brought me in to protect the girl, too." That much is sort of true. Eliminating her drug dealer, Thomas-not-Thomas, is supposed to help with that. "I thought I could get a few free meals."

"Make sure Clemont pays you more than a few meals, Jesus."

"What's he paying you? You called him Mr. Clemont. Sounds pretty formal. He's not a friend?"

"Friend of a friend. The friend of a friend called me in to help. I grew up in Chicago and my name came up as someone who could help deal with a gang problem. I live in Los Angeles, doing security gigs for celebrities." He catches the surprise on your face. "Yeah, I know. We're a long way from Hollyweird, but no matter where you go, the problems are all the same. Mr. Clemont's got lots of problems. He brought you in to solve the problems I refused to solve for him."

The snow falls heavier now and the city seems to settle, muted under the fresh white blanket. The streetlights light up the snowflakes and in a few hours, this dirty stretch of town could look pretty, at least until morning. The silence stretches out until you have to snap it. "What do you want to know, Chill?"

He shrugs. "You don't show up in a Google search, or maybe you do on page eighty-six or something. There's a lot of Jesuses in the world."

"I imagine you got a lot of hits on the well-known, formerly Jewish magician."

The big man looks grim. "Beware the blasphemer."

"Looking up Jesus is like looking up John Smith. I actually met a John Smith a few months back. The dude looked exactly like I imagined all John Smiths should look like. White guy with an alligator on his shirt and a stick up his ass."

Chill laughs a little, lets that settle down and then looks at you as serious as a knife in the eye. "You asked me what I want to know. I can probably guess quite a bit, but the main thing I need to know is, who am I teaming up with? Are you a good guy?"

"I think I just had this conversation with Willow. I gotta tell you, man, you aren't my type."

"You, either, man. I'm gay, but don't believe the hype. I'm picky. You're cute, but too petite for my taste. "

"I'm both insulted and relieved."

Chill laughs again. "So? How about it? Good guy or bad guy?"

"I told Willow I'm a good guy. You seem like a good guy. But here's the thing: those two pieces of shit that walked in Sam's diner an hour ago and grabbed Willow by the hair and threatened to kill her? Those guys think they're good guys, too. I'm not sure there are good guys, except in bad movies for simple people, maybe. I've seen things. I've seen guys who were supposed to be good do stuff that turned my stomach. Guys with stars and bars."

"I just hang out with stars in bars and babysit them," Chill says, "but I think I got your flavor. Go on."

"What do you want me to say, Chill? Clemont called me in and I just happened to be here when the shit went down and I burned one of the sinners with holy water. What else is there? I'm righteous. I haven't done anything else for him yet." (Except the little matter of putting a bullet in Thomas-not-Thomas, the turtle with an ankle holster.)

Chill nods and looks at his shoes.

"But you aren't up for any illegal shit." It's a statement, not a question, but Chill takes his time answering.

"I'm 37 years old, Jesus. The illegal shit is supposed to be behind me."

"I'm not 30 yet. I got a few more years of stupid left in me."

"It's the testosterone overload, you know."

"I know. What do you want done?"

"Just like that?"

"Can't be worse than what I just got out of."

"What did you just get out of?"

"It's a long story. It'd take up a whole book and it's cold out here."

"How about I do my thing and watch the girl? I provide security and when I need back up, I'll just call the police. You say you're not the bad guy, but when shit goes down, you're not the type to call the police, am I right?"

"Yeah. I'm Batman."

Chill's chuckle sounds like it could come from a little Macy's Christmas elf. "The guys that came in heavy tonight went down easy, but the Lone Wolf and his sidekick will be back, and maybe not alone."

"I read you. I was hoping I'd get the job of watching Willow."

"I have a feeling you might get distracted and she'd get you out of that nice suit."

You nod. "Willow is distracting, but I never take off this suit. I'm too pretty in it."

"You are." He smiles again. This banter between a couple of guys just bullshitting? You've missed this. Everyone in Group is so bare-their-soul earnest, they think the earth turns on the axis of their every conversation.

Then it comes to you. "Chill, I don't want to mow your lawn, but, you're solid gay, right? Not iffy, even when you see a girl as hot as Willow?"

"Solid. No offence, but pussy gives me the heebie-jeebies."

"Excellent. Okay, then you can babysit my future wife and the mother of all my many, many children while I work for her dad and take care of business."

Chill nods. "Is Willow in for the night?"

"All locked in. I even checked behind the shower curtain and under the beds before I left."

"That must have been quite a challenge, getting away from her bed."

"Please. A girl like that, you don't go near the bed until the third date. Respect!"

"Righteous."

Chill turns and opens the door to the diner for you. You step in out of the cold and stomp your feet to get the slush off your shoes. Chill waves goodbye.

"You aren't coming in?"

"You're on your own with Mr. Clemont. What he asks you to do, I don't know and I don't want to know. From here on out, my favors begin and end with protecting the man's daughter and your future wife. Favors weigh heavy, man. The guy who brought me in? I owe him a *ton* in favors, so I couldn't say no.

You taking care of this for me so I don't have to do some sketchy shit for Clemont, though? Now I owe *you* a favor."

"Cool."

"Probably not."

Chill lets the door swing closed. He pauses for a moment on the sidewalk, raises one hand and makes the sign of the cross, blessing you through the glass. The big man tucks his Bible under his arm, turns and the night swallows him.

It's warm in the diner, but you feel dead cold and alone.

ROPE

After locking the door, you find Samuel Clemont making a fish patty for himself in the kitchen. The counters and stoves are built shorter so he can reach everything. You feel taller. Then your shoulders sag when you consider that Willow sees you the way you see this Oompa Loompa kitchen.

Clemont scrapes the burnt fish patty off the grill with a blackened spatula and dumps it on a stiff bun beside a pile of french fries on a chipped plate. "Shoulda set up shop in New Orleans. You burn your food in the Big Easy, you just call it Cajun and nobody complains. Just add hot sauce." He bites into his sandwich and grimaces. "I grew up in Maine, so I hate fish. Ate too much of it when I was a kid. Sick of it. This halibut is about to turn. Might as well eat the profits. Still better than most food I ever had as a grunt."

"Is the Marines where you learned to cook?"

His laugh has a cutting edge. "Hell, no!" He drops the fish sandwich back on the plate. "Though, that would explain a lot."

While Clemont focuses on the fries, you look around. The M4 Carbine is propped against the wall in a corner beside a table with a box of rounds. Clemont snaps his ketchup-stained fingers and waves you over to a stool by the counter. "I talked to Paulie again. He said you'd come."

"It sounds like you've got much bigger problems than Willow's drug dealer."

"I thought Gillie could take care of these guys. Apparently, I was misinformed, so I guess people *can* change. Should have seen what he did back in the day. Gillie's still bad ass, but inflexible about what else I need done. Since you've already shot Willow's supplier, I guess you're up. You pass the test. You can help me with the Lone Wolf and his sidekick."

"Maybe Gillie's got the right idea — "

"You like Gillie? Kinda faggy, huh? I wouldn't tell him that if I were you, Gee-Zuzz. He'd pop you like a little boil on his ass."

"Is that a short joke? I suspect you used to be taller but you're probably shorter than me now. It's hard to tell with you sitting all the time."

His laugh is a seal bark, but you can tell you scored a point by hitting back. You've run into crusty old guys like this. Clemont comes off tough and gristled, but he's really testing your skin for thickness. He wants to see how long it will take before you tell him to go to hell.

It would have already happened, but he is your future father-in-law. You can be polite and appear to have all the social graces. Tia Marta taught you how to look like you were in love while waiting to strangle the life out of her. You can keep your temper on the chain and never let it show. You'll wait. When the time comes, he's not living with you and Willow and the kids. You'll remind him of what an asshole he is as you drive him to the cheapest old age home you can find.

"You owe me one coffeepot. Gillie cleaned up your mess."

On the other hand, why wait to frost his nuts since he's trying to bust your balls? "From what I gather, you want me to clean up a much bigger mess. And you already owe me a chunk of change. The man at the address you specified is dead."

Clemont digs out a cigarette and lights it. He must have had the habit a long time because he cups his hands around the lighter's flame, as if he's still out in the field, bracing against a stiff wind. "You were supposed to get the money and the drugs from the premises. Paulie told me you were good."

"Paulie's right, but I don't have X-ray vision."

"You botched the job."

"If you had dealt with me directly instead of going through Paulie, I'd have had more details, like knowing where to look for the cash. After I shot him, there wasn't a lot of time to hang around and tear the place apart brick by brick."

"Excuses. From where I sit, you screwed up."

"You're always sitting. It's different when you're standing up and walking around, taking care of business. The place was a front. Maybe the guy did business there, but he was cagey. He even gave me a false name."

"What name did he give you?"

"Thomas LeClerc."

"And he didn't even live there anymore?" Clemont looks genuinely surprised.

"A lot of drug dealers don't want anyone to know where they really live. I knew a guy in New York who had a dozen apartments and houses, weed growing in every one. You take a walk and see windows with black out curtains, five will get you ten."

"Uh-huh. So I'm out my money and you want yours. You're going to be disappointed when you find out how the world works."

"I've seen how the world works and I'm beyond disappointment, Samuel. The only light I see is in your daughter. How did an angel like that come out of a guy like you?"

He smiles. "Her mother was a peach."

"Must have been."

"How's this? You double down on the job and keep the Lone Wolf out of here and I'll get you your money. Gillie and I disagree about possible solutions to the problems I've acquired, but a Cuban dwarf might do."

"You've been talking to Willow."

"She called."

"What'd she say about me?"

"Says you don't do drugs and I should ask about your gun."

"It's a SIG Sauer P220 and you already know why I carry it. What did you tell Willow?"

"That you're the shortest bodyguard I could find through my old military connections and she shouldn't count on you being around for long."

"That's hurtful." You flip him the bird and he smiles wider.

"The local gang is giving me trouble. You're a troubleshooter, Jesus. Troubleshoot."

"If those guys are in a gang — "

"They aren't exactly. They're a faction out of the exurbs and they think they're on their way up. They want to be part of the core business and be in the big time downtown. The gang calls themselves The Victorious."

"Sounds like a boy band."

"The Lone Wolf and his burnt buddy had a meeting with me last week, when they started the hustle. If they can do well by the gang, they're not simple foot soldiers anymore. They want to move up the chain all at once on my back."

"So they're trying to make their bones. Guys trying to make bones are dangerous."

"I got my M4 and you got your SIG. Why didn't you go for the P226? You'd have fifteen rounds instead of just nine."

"I hit what I aim at and I like my rounds to have more punch. Chill wanted to bring in the cops to deal with those guys, right?"

"Yeah."

"What did you tell Willow? How much does she know?"

"About the drug dealer you killed, she knows nothing. She's been a good girl lately."

You wait for him to spill more and he stares at you through the smoke. He's the first to break the pregnant pause, so you win. "All Willow knows is those guys tonight came for protection money."

"Keep her in the dark. Here's what you say if she starts looking at you funny: if you call the police, they ask a lot of questions, make arrests and then the bad guys get out on bail. Then they come looking for you. Restraining orders aren't bulletproof. You can have 911 on speed dial, but cops are for after the fireworks are done and blood and brains are smeared all over the walls. No matter how many times you paint, blood and brains always show through. Cops show up late. They're for after-the-fact problems. They're less useful before the fact."

"Sounds about right."

"In my experience, it's exactly right."

"In your experience," he says and lets that hang out there a little longer than you like.

"Let's focus on the real problem," you say.

"I need to discourage these guys so they don't come back. Ever."

"We discouraged them pretty well tonight. They might even get hang dog depressed for a while, what with the burning, scarring and pain."

"Guys like this?" Clemont says. "The Victorious is a *gang*. If it spreads to them beyond the Lone Wolf and his sidekick, the rest of the gang will get involved. That's when things get tricky. You beat 'em senseless and if you let them wake up after the beating, they come back for more, but harder next time. They're used to intimidating people and when they run into somebody who can't bend, they have to come down even nastier just to be sure everybody on the block gets it. We've got to get the Wolf and his pal dead — not connected to me — and nip this thing in the bud. They're seriously bad."

"What do you know about the Victorious?"

"They've been around a while. A few years ago, there used to be a barber down the street. He didn't want to pay protection. They made him drink that blue stuff used to clean scissors."

"Barbicide."

"Yeah. How'd you know?"

"Getting my hair cut is one of the few things that relaxes me. I like the scalp massage. The barber got very sick I assume?"

"Killed him. Took some time, though."

"So you want a cost-benefit hit?"

His head comes up. "A what?"

"You got that M4 and Chill, but you've also got a business and a daughter. You're vulnerable. The gang no doubt have a place they hang out. What you want is to make them feel vulnerable and off balance so they get distracted with bigger problems — AKA me — instead of coming after you for protection money. Maybe they come after me or maybe we can blame a rival gang. That's a cost-benefit hit."

"Right! That's exactly what I need! Blaming a rival gang. Could that work?"

"Only in theory, for a short time. I've seen it tip upside down. It's a lot of death and destruction. I'd have to hunt Wolf and Mr. Birthmark fast before they got to you. They might have already swallowed their pride and called in reinforcements from The Victorious, though if they can't handle a simple protection scam, they might not want to share that information. After what happened tonight, if I were them, I'd just come right back and firebomb the place."

"So hit them fast, before they get reinforcements."

"Downside: they might get me first."

"What's your price?"

"Money's no object?"

"Within reason. Look around. I'm trying to build a legacy here for Willow. I've got too much invested in this place. Do you know how much it costs to custom fit a kitchen for wheelchair height?"

"Uh-huh."

"I was thinking you could take care of this for me for a few thousand dollars."

"My suit is worth a few thousand dollars and you still owe me for the first hit."

"Then a few thousand dollars more," he says.

You sigh and wait for him to come out with it but he's still under the impression you're an idiot. It's time to let the old guy know you are not going to let him drive this bus. "Sam. As the man who will be your future son-in-law, let's not throw feces, okay? We are not monkeys at the zoo."

His eyes narrow but he's still not going to give.

"Let's spray some air freshener," you say. "You get me to hit a drug dealer to keep him away from Willow. You figure you'll take care of a protection racket problem, and pay my fee, by having me steal all of said drug dealer's cash on hand. That hangs together in theory. Almost."

"That was the plan. What's the loose string?"

"I mean, sir, that I don't believe a word of that story. That story — pardon me for honesty in the face of death and disaster and family discord — sucks a big fat clit."

PLAY IT AGAIN, SAM

"What gave me away?" Clemont asks.

"Those guys came in way too heavy for a protection job. You can't give up a hundred or two a week for protection? The math is bad. My expenses alone would cover the cost of paying these gangster wannabes. You could easily slide the gang a little money, or move, or even call the police if principle really is more important to you than your own neck. The hanging string is that you aren't going to risk your daughter no matter how much of a hard ass you want to make me think you are. You're not an idiot — at least I don't think you are. *Yet.* I'm reserving judgment depending on what you say in the next couple minutes."

"Shit," Clemont says, admitting defeat with a chagrinned look.

"So try again."

"All I care is to find someone to take care of the problem. I'd do it myself but..." Clemont gestures at the spot where his legs are not.

"If I was supposed to feel sorry for you now, you shouldn't have acted like such an asshole before. This isn't a favor. You're asking me to clear out a wasp nest. You ask me to kill again, you gotta tell me why I'm doing it. I'm not in the army anymore and I recently made it my policy not to kill people for no good reason. Getting rid of that Vicodin dealer to protect Willow was a good cause. Killing the dealer so you could pay the gang protection wasn't so righteous. I need another righteous reason."

"Keeping the Victorious out of my business is a good cause."

"There might be other solutions than going at The Victorious all *Call of Duty*, so don't give me the good soldier bit, Samuel. After 9/11, I signed up to kill OBL in Afghanistan and got stuck in Iraq instead. I don't follow orders blindly, especially since we haven't fallen in love with each other's undeniable charms yet."

Clemont smokes and thinks and takes his time capitulating. You wait for him to catch up with you at the finish line.

"I guess..."

"Start at the beginning."

"I knew a guy who knew a guy."

"Good start. Go on."

"You know the Scorpion?"

"The car or Mac Gargan, sworn enemy of Spider-Man?"

"Oh, sweet Christ. The *pistol*."

"I'd be more intrigued if the Victorious were actually led by the Marvel Comics character dressed up as a big scorpion, but go on."

He takes a long drag on his cigarette and, as he speaks, the smoke piles toward the ceiling. "The Scorpion is a nasty little machine designed by the KGB. The guy who knew a guy got a shipment of Scorpions. He had Russian connections. All these handguns had been sitting in a warehouse along with lots of ammunition."

"The ammo is still good after all this time?"

"Cold war issue. Keep it dry and it's good forever."

"How'd it get into the country?"

"Container ship. The container was marked 'Machine parts for dishwashers.' The ports are hit and miss. It wasn't much of a risk. After 9/11, they upped security everywhere except where it counts. One of these days a freighter sent by Pakistan or Saudi Arabia is going to blow up in a harbor and destroy all of New York or Boston. Everyone will wonder, how'd that happen?"

"You're scaring me. Talk to me about the guns to calm my nerves."

"There was this guy I knew named Harry. Harry needed a safe place to keep the shipment until he could find a buyer. He started talking to a few people to feel them out to see if they had the scratch for the buy."

"Who did Harry contact?"

"I don't know who all he talked to exactly. Somebody in a militia in the midwest, a religious bunch in Georgia who are getting ready for the race war, some Minute Men in Texas and Michigan."

"Hold up," you say. "The Texans are trying to keep Mexicans out, but there are Minute Men patrolling the northern border in *Michigan*?"

"Yep. Trying to keep out the one Canadian who wants to live in the U.S."

"*Heh.* Okay. And Harry talked to the Lone Wolf and his scabby little friend?"

"Yeah." He looks gray.

"So if the Wolf gets the Scorpions for his gang, he's a hero and he moves up to the big time."

"That's my complication. There's a group up from Florida that wants the shipment, too."

"Who?"

"They call themselves the Recipients."

"Recipients of what?"

Clemont shrugs. "Christ, I think generally. In this case, guns. Harry said they're a mix. Most of them would consider themselves religious folks, but they're determined to get the Scorpions. Getting ready for The Fall."

"As in next autumn or the fall of God, Satan, the Empire? What?"

"Satan or Obama, maybe. I'm not sure they make those fine distinctions. The Recipients are pretty hardcore churchy and they're willing to pay. These guys repping for the Victorious? They don't want to pay anywhere near a fair price."

66

"Hm. Well, I'm against that on principle, even if they hadn't grabbed Willow by the hair. It's that exact thieving attitude that makes a few drug deals go wrong and gives all the everyday, peaceful drug deals a bad name."

"I need to deal with The Recipients. They talk the end of the world now, but they're still making vacation plans for next year on Disney Cruises," he assures you. "Convictions are slippery things. You ever see the TV show *Hoarders*? That's mostly what stockpiling guns really is. They aren't dangerous. They're hobbyists who want to play with my Scorpions on their compound's gun range. No big deal."

"Sure. That worked out so well for Koresh at Waco."

"Take my word for it. The Recipients aren't any more of a threat to anyone than the Amish. In fact, they're just like the Amish. They just want to be left alone."

Bats beat leathery wings against the walls of your stomach, trying to escape. If your future wife weren't in danger, you'd already be out the door, after you lit the place on fire.

Clemont seems to read your thoughts. "The way you talk, I thought you were more flexible. A tough guy. You're sounding like Gillie."

"It's not a question of being flexible. It's a question of dealing with crazy people who act off their politics instead of their principles, especially when both are nuts. You deal with the right people, they won't come knocking later. This is America. The only color anyone should care about is green. Business is America's religion. People who make money their god, I understand. Money means freedom. Religious nuts aren't about making choices. They're about cutting everybody else's choices down."

"You and I care about the green and we can make some," Clemont says. "Focus on that."

"But the people you're dealing with *don't* focus on the green. Doing things for love, I understand. Doing shit jobs for money, I understand. Doing things because you have to? I've been there plenty. Cults and compounds? That leads down a road that ends with hateful bullshit and little girls burned in churches. The most successful gangs and mob organizations stay low profile and keep the peace in their neighborhoods so they can do a profitable business."

Clemont shrugs and you can see the responsibility fall from his shoulders. "The Recipients are who I'm doing business with. The choices customers make isn't my end, anyway." He looks at his cigarette as if it holds all the answers. "This is all Harry's fault. I was just a storage guy. Harry wanted a safe place to put washing machine parts. I had a place. Harry had opening talks with too many people."

"What could go wrong there?" If you roll your eyes at him any harder, you might sprain something.

"He imagined a bidding war, as if the shipment was real estate and the Recipients and the street punks would sit there all civilized. I told Harry this isn't some fancy auction house, bidding back and forth with ping pong paddles with numbers on them. Harry thought he could up the price by setting up a little friendly competition."

"What happened to Harry?"

Clemont stares at the ceiling for some time. Finally he admits, "The Lone Wolf killed Harry to let me know that there would be no goddamn auction. These people don't play that way. They want an ass load of Scorpions. You said you understand doing things because you have to. You gotta do this. Before he died, Harry told the Lone Wolf who to go to for the guns. Me. Me and Willow are in the crosshairs."

"I see. Valid."

"Fix it so I can sell the Scorpions to the Recipients unharrassed and Willow's safe. The Recipients might shoot a few gators out in the swamps, but what kind of damage do you suppose a street gang like The Victorious might do with that kind of firepower? I say no to the Wolf and he — or maybe the whole gang now — will kill me and Willow. You, too. Actually, you first."

"I get it."

"Gillie didn't get it. He thinks the way out is to move to Alaska."

"Can't be much colder than Chicago."

"I'm guessing the wheelchair access in Alaska sucks and I don't want a polar bear to eat me on my way to the mailbox."

"So just tell both groups where to find the shipment and you're done. Walk away...say sorry. Roll away and let the Wolf and the Recipients fight it out."

"That leaves too much money on the table. I'll make five times my money back with this deal. No way. Life is too expensive." He glances again at where his legs should be.

You give Clemont a slow nod.

"When can you get the deal done so the Scorpions are off the table?"

"The Recipient guy is coy," Clemont says. "Didn't even give me a phone number. He said he'd call me. The bigshot wannabes gave me a phone number, though. I'm damned if I do and dead if I don't make the call. Neither party thinks I have the guns yet. I've been putting them off, saying the container is still in transit. I've been sitting on the shipment for over a week. You want to ship something scary, do it during the Christmas rush and there's even less chance of getting caught."

"The Wolf's impatient. He must have guessed you're stalling."

"Yeah, telling him I'm out of stock isn't going to get it done any longer. The Minute Men I could blow off. They're a bunch of paranoid patriots with binoculars. But the Wolf? He killed Harry. We should have killed The Lone Wolf here tonight, but Gillie is too pure for that job. I'd have murdered those two idiots myself tonight. I had those assholes in my sights, but I couldn't do that in front of Willow. With what she's been through..."

"Making Willow an accessory to murder would be bad form?"

"I'd be more concerned about her sobriety. Staying calm and clean...it's a fragile thing." He looks away and studies the ceiling. "I get this deal done, I'll be able to send Willow to a nice rehab out in Colorado."

"I got the picture. I'll help you solve this problem for fifty percent."

"You're dreaming. Me and Harry set this whole thing up. You're late to the party. Ten percent."

"You just lost Harry and now you've got a partner back. You pay Chill out of your half. Fifty-fifty and Willow never finds out you're an arms dealer."

Clemont barks out a big belly laugh. "Willow doesn't know about you killing her drug dealer, but she *already* knows her daddy's an arms dealer." His eyes are steady. You believe him. The Queen of the Giants has a darker side than you had guessed. You try, too slow, to rearrange your face so he doesn't see how much that pains you. You wanted Willow to be pure and you wanted to be pure for her. You should have known she couldn't dress as well as she does and still manage to live off tips.

Sgt. Devin, AKA the Devil, was one of your combat instructors. He warned you that true warriors see the world the way it is. You saw Willow through a gauzy lens. You took her uptown-labelled clothes as a sign that she had fine taste, a perfect match for your preferences for double-breasted Armani suits. You focused on her Jimmy Choos and your Tanini Crisci shoes. The Devil was right: you are an idiot. But you're also a knight. It's your duty to save the Queen of the Giants.

Clemont lights a fresh cigarette off the dying nub of the old one. "Look, kid...I got screwed over. Willow understands because she was by my hospital bed and watched while it happened. The wheelchair is a bad deal, but I could have accepted that. It was the low payout that got me into this. It's a free, capitalist country and an ass load of guns is part of being free and capitalist. Nobody's holding back on buying oranges, iPhones and sneakers just because they get 'em from slave labor. Willow's no different. She doesn't want to know where the money comes from, but she doesn't turn it down, either."

You've been down this road before. Family is family and daughters accept whatever their fathers do. "The deal is *sixty* percent or I walk and you can deal with the crazies on your own," you say.

"Sixt— ?"

"I don't see any other job applicants here and I've got the experience you're looking for. You're going to give me a thousand up front just for expenses and the phone number you've got for The Victorious wannabes."

He soaks that up and smiles. "You sound like you got a plan."

"Not yet, but I will. I always come up with something."

"'Cuz you're *experienced*, huh? New York, mob-type stuff? Does Willow know you're a hit man, not just killing her drug dealer but — hey, how many people have you killed?"

Just like that, he's got you. You sigh. "Forty percent and you keep your mouth shut. I'll tell her my history, but just let me tell her in my own time. Till then, I'm just another bodyguard for hire. And whatever deal you got going on with Chill, pay out of your sixty percent."

Samuel Clemont smiles so wide you see the gaps where his bicuspids used to be. He flicks the butt of his cigarette into the sink. "You and Willow won't last a week, anyway. She'll cut you off quick. Or the Wolf will cut you into little bits. Slow."

He may be right. You need to go recruiting. If you're going to war, you need to get help from the Army. You head out, wondering exactly what your cut on an "ass load" will amount to.

HOLLOW MAN

The next day you find Sgt. Billy at his regular hangout down the street from the Salvation Army's men's shelter. His sloped shoulders look thin even though he's bundled in several layers of clothes. It's easier to wear everything you own rather than to carry it. The nights he doesn't make it to a shelter must be brutal this time of year, even with the sweaters he wears under his big coat. Sgt. Billy is one soldier in Chicago's army of invisible men who wander the streets. When you ask him for his help, he's pissed.

"All this time, I *knew* you could speak English! I knew it and you just kept walking by, throwing a few dollars in my hat."

"Easy, man. I'm talking to you now."

"Yeah? And why's that?"

"Got a job for you."

"A job? I haven't had a job in a long time."

"It'll be easy. It will hardly be different than what you do now."

"That doesn't sound like a paying job. If it was, I'd have heard of it already. You want me to put up posters or something?"

"Even easier than that. C'mon, let's go get a sandwich. I'm buying."

He doesn't move. "They won't let me eat inside."

"Then I'll go in and get it and I'll come out and have breakfast with you."

72

A few minutes later you're sitting next to him on his usual stoop in front of an abandoned building. Despite his invisibility, there's something left in him from when he was a citizen. He's grateful and polite. Sgt. Billy wants to know more about you before he'll talk business. When he demands to know where you're from, you tell him New York City.

"You know about the Molemen?" he asks.

"Spider-Man went up against the Mole Man. Or do you mean the Molemen, like the enemies of Superman? I'm not a big Man of Steel fan."

"Don't be an idiot."

"Are they Chicago hip-hop guys?" you venture.

"You are an idiot. I mean the Mole People under New York! People said it wasn't true, but it's sort of true. There were a lot of us under the city. Fewer now. There were books about it. Actually there are more underneath Vegas. I'd live there, but I can't take the heat. Chicago gets cold, but you can get to a shelter or sleep on a vent or whatever to get warm. You get too hot, what are you going to do? Homeless, the cops leave you alone. Homeless and naked? They ain't gonna leave you alone."

"Where'd you serve, Billy?" you ask.

"Korea."

"Wow."

"Not so much. You?"

"Sandy places."

He finishes half his sandwich and folds the plastic over the rest to save for later. He stuffs it in one of his pockets. The coat is tattered and filthy. Sgt. Billy smells like onions so you tell him you aren't hungry and give him the rest of your sandwich. That disappears into another filthy pocket.

"Sgt. Billy, can I trust you?"

"I wouldn't, but I suspect I'm smarter than you." His smile splits the space between his gray beard and his broom of a moustache. His eyes are not unkind.

"You know The Victorious?"

"I know who they are. Assholes."

"Do you know where they hang out?"

"Everybody knows. Nobody says. They hang out at a garage up a few blocks and around the corner, less than a few minutes walk from here."

"How would you like to hang out across the street from them? I need eyes on the street."

Sgt. Billy looks to the sky. He might be counting to ten. "Henry David Thoreau said that it's not what you look at that matters. It's what you see."

"I need you to be a proctologist, Billy. Watch the assholes. Recon-only mission from a discreet observation post. If they move in force or if you see something that looks weird, you call me. You tell me. I'll give you a description of two guys to look out for in particular."

"Proctologist. You're a funny guy, but what you really want is a spider crab." He explains when you quirk an eyebrow: "Spider crabs are covered with algae and detritus. Even sea anemones attach to its shell and a spider crab sits in the sand and the silt of the seabed. Living camouflage. A guy like you in that suit can't hang out for more than five minutes without drawing attention. You go over there dressed like you're going to church and you'll get rolled. I'm your spider crab."

Your eyes narrow. You have to know now. "What did you do after Korea?"

"Married a sweet girl from Texas. Got a degree and taught high school English and sometimes biology."

You nod and clear your throat. "Anyway, you gotta hang out somewhere. Why not for pay?"

"Depends. I can see why you wouldn't like The Victorious. The only people they like is their own people. But I have to know why you want me to do this, Jesus."

"A couple of guys who want to move up fast in The Victorious threatened my future wife last night. I'm trying to figure out how to get rid of them."

"Sounds righteous."

"It is." You hand him one of the disposable cell phones you picked up this morning and show him how to call you.

"What's the wage?"

You hand him a hundred-dollar bill. Sgt. Billy looks at it like he could eat it, but he hesitates. He tears the bill in two and hands half back to you. "Hold on to that and pay me when you're satisfied I'm done, Chief. Give me all that at once and I'm liable to do something I shouldn't with it. Once you pay me, I won't be so useful to the mission."

"Okay, Sergeant."

"This young lady...the future Mrs. Diaz? Let me tell you what you need to know."

He's back in life coach mode. You hold back on a heavy sigh. "Don't tell me anything you don't want me to know."

"If I don't pass it on, what use was the pain? The key to keeping my sweet Texas girl was to keep the drinking to only the weekends or at least really late in the day. If I could have even managed that bare minimum, she would have stuck. A woman in love will put up with a lot. That's why they're better than us. If you find a good one who will put up with you, stick with her 'cuz she's rare."

"How come you couldn't keep the drinking to the weekends?"

"Because, like the poster at the VA says, no soldier comes back unwounded."

"Roger that."

"She deserved better. Drinking's no good when you got kids to watch out for. Parenting and husbanding is tough enough when you're sober. Texas is better off without me. She was *good,* man. If I hadn't been so drunk, I would at least have more memories to cherish." When he stands, you offer your hand and instead, Sgt. Billy salutes you.

Talk of kids and sobriety: Willow called stuff like this synchronicity. Maybe it's just your body reacting to stress that makes your monkey brain whisper, "It would feel so good to get high. You still have a lot of Vikes and ooh, the euphoria!" Maybe it was Sgt. Billy's salute, crisp and unexpected, that triggered your hunger for more Vicodin.

You had planned to go visit Willow and discuss how many kids she wants. Instead, you feel the familiar ache of the hunger that isn't hunger. The counsellors say it's a craving for the kick and the rush of dopamine. Throwing coffee pots and pointing guns at people, wielding the divine power of life and death delivers the same dopamine trick. Maybe adrenaline unlocks the same brain chemicals as dopamine to sate the same needs. To be pure for Willow and lift yourself up above the bare minimum, you're going to have to get past running after these furious rushes and dangerous highs. Batman never gets the girl.

Is your career a solution you fell into because your body got addicted to fear under Tia Marta's fierce tutelage? Does the SIG fill a biological craving to even out that terrifying high? Is the switchblade in your sock the answer to a psychological twist in the branches of your cosmic tree? Is this how God made you, or did He fashion this shit life for you as a challenge to grow out of and overcome?

In *The African Queen*, Katherine Hepburn says to Humphrey Bogart's character, "Nature, Mr. Allnut, is what we are put in this world to rise above." Maybe God wants you to be Charlie Allnut.

When you look at your life, the God and the Devil look like twins on a bender. You may as well ask these questions of a magic eight ball. What you really want to do now is escape questions and doubt and suck down an eight ball.

You push off, heading east. If you don't get to a meeting soon, you might slip, and you are determined not to slip. You're doing this for Willow and all those beautiful little kids you'll have with her.

The counsellors in Group say you should stay clean and sober for yourself first. Alone? You aren't worth that much effort, but maybe your hopes and dreams for you and Willow will pound that mountain road flat.

You go to Group.

FIGHT CLUB

Twelve vets in a mustard-coloured room sit in a circle. You don't care for circles. They demand too much eye contact.

Kyle is the Jamaican nurse who has access to drugs. He says he knows he should switch specialties, but he thinks he can control his addiction. That much, you're almost sure, is true. At the last coffee break he told you he was clean and sober and he deserved his chip. Then he leaned in closer. "But I'm still *selling*, if you're interested. No pressure, mon, but just let me know. On a nurse's salary I got more month left over at the end of my money than I can stand, yeah? If you feel the need, I can hook you up."

The familiar craving gnaws at you, but you turn away and guzzle more acidic coffee to try to drown the Vicodin urge. It's like trying to fight a house fire by peeing on the potted plants.

If this were AA or something, Kyle might have worried that you'd rat him out, but in the VA programs, the code is still in force. Close ranks and be the badass robot. Help each other, cover your buddy and no matter what you do, don't trust the brass. You covered each other when there was sand under your boots. Why should scuffed tile be any different? Vets suffer double the unemployment of civilians and veteran suicides outpace combat deaths. Everybody needs a break.

Official policy is that anybody who sells isn't allowed to stay in group therapy. If you care enough, the group leaders say, you rat out threats to the common sobriety. If you were solid in your commitment to staying clean, you'd rat out Kyle for your protection. Instead, you let Kyle slide. You don't do it just to ignore The Man and official policy or even the desert code. You hold back on dropping the dime because Kyle is a high interest credit card. You should cut him up, but what if you need him someday? What if the drug-hungry tingle comes on too strong and you need a hook up? You keep him around, just in case, even if he could jam you up.

The group leader, Tim, is a swell guy. Everybody says so. He's friendly and smiles at your jokes, but you don't like the former lieutenant. You suspect that to Tim — Smug Tim, in your mind — you've got a life sentence. You're filed under a case label that will never change: Vet with Substance Problems. There's something so mortal and terminal about that. Sure, things are screwed up now, but doesn't anybody ever get *over* the bad shit? To heal, do you have to accept a higher power? The only divinity you know is that feeling you get holding a SIG and pointing it at someone. Will you ever just be Jesus Diaz, and not that cloying thing: "A survivor"?

Talk therapy feels like masking tape on a broken car window. Cover it up all you want, but what's broken is never really fixed and it looks like shit. Slather on the same true confessions, add tears, muted applause and "Thank you for sharing!" Rinse and repeat, as if speeches about weakness and victimhood are a magic spell that, once spoken, fire up a time machine that change history and your DNA.

If you live long enough (which seems unlikely) you don't want to be stuck in a mustard-colored room like this as an old man. You don't want to end your days the same way you now spend them, avoiding eye contact with the survivors and addicts. When you look around the room, you see people who can't get over the past because they are too busy talking about what got them here. They're reliving it, wallowing in it. Everybody says Group helps, but talk therapy never made you feel as good as holding the SIG in your hand.

There are a few others here who have PTSD, too, though, unlike you, they picked up their Post Traumatic Stress Disorder in the desert while wearing a uniform. Your PTSD comes from a basement in Florida. Your captors didn't allow you the dignity of clothes, let alone a uniform.

You feel a headache coming from the horizon and zeroing in on your forehead, so you push those old thoughts away and focus on why you hate Tim. Oh, yeah. Group leader Tim has his shit together. He has a house and he says his wife is a hottie, all sideways smiles and aw shucks. He has a couple of kids and a regular job and he knows where he's going to be next year and the next and the next. He's going to be here, in this room with mustard-colored walls, listening to vets like you and pretending not to judge.

Smug Tim says he "had a little Percocet problem" — coyly — the same way a brainless reality show star might say, "I have the sweetest little dog. Fits in my purse. What breed? It's a Percocet!"

Tim picked up his little Percocet problem after an IED took his right leg. You envy Tim his little problems. The mental scars and emotional stumps no one can see? Those don't fix with a metal leg.

"Good to see you again, Jesus. I was worried about you," Tim says. "Haven't seen you for a few meetings."

His crooked, smug smile has too many teeth. You could fix that. "Been looking for a job," you say.

"Excellent! Did one of our counsellors hook you up with a fresh resume?"

Heh. That's funny. What's your resume going to say besides: Hit man; recently let go from The Machine for trying to steal skim; dropped one boss off a high building. Most recent achievement: shot a drug dealer. Current position: Fugitive from the FBI for questioning in a car bomb case. "Been looking on my own," you say.

"Good for you!"

Excellent! Good for you! Does he mean that or does he go back home to his hottie wife and cute children and laugh about how everybody's so dumb they never catch his irony? Aside from only being three-quarters present and accounted for, what's this guy really all about? If you lose your leg, do you get to be this positive and chipper all the time, too? Maybe you're overestimating Tim. Maybe he's just stupid. You read somewhere that some psychologists believe happy people are delusional and depressed people see the world as it really is. If getting your shit together means being stupid and happy, maybe it would be worth it to get a few more concussions.

Smug Tim rambles on. You look attentive, but you're looking at the poster on the wall behind him. In blood red it reads: Casualties of 9/11, the War on Terror and the Invasion of Iraq: 0.28% were 9/11 victims; 0.55% US casualties in both Afghanistan and Iraq; 4.39% civilian casualties in Afghanistan; 94.78% civilian casualties in Iraq. While he talks, you try to figure out the math in real numbers. If the 0.28% was about 3,000 people, then...damn. Tia Marta was your only teacher. The bitch never taught you math.

You knew some of those casualties: Iraqi, Afghani and American military. Listening to Smug Tim is part of the penance. When the little Muslim kids come to you in the day, they are just daydreams you can unhitch. They aren't scary then. When they come at night looking like skinless, burnt zombies? Different story.

You come out of doing the bloody math in your head. Shattered Crystal is talking. Skulls are tattooed on her knuckles. Shattered Crystal always wears long sleeves and covers herself up, but the edges of more tatts appear now and then at her ankles and collar. As she mows the same psychological lawn again, Tim puts on his listening face — or maybe he really is listening, who can tell?

You watch the sharp end of a yellow eagle's beak dance along the line of the sternocleidomastoid muscle in Crystal's neck. When she turns her head to address Tim, it stands out and ripples.

You know it's the sternocleidomastoid muscle because a buddy in your platoon had his shot out by an enemy sniper one bright sunny day while he was burning shit in a barrel with jet fuel at the edge of the base.

"Sternocleidomastoid. Somehow missed the arteries. It's a lottery wound!" the medic had said. The guy lived, but he was never going to look left to check his blind spot again.

Shattered Crystal was raped by two superior officers in Iraq. Some people put on weight to try to make themselves less attractive to their abusers. Living mostly on table scraps, you weren't given that option in that basement in Miami.

As a tank commander, Crystal couldn't put on weight and get sloppy, either. Making herself tougher, pretending to be another person: that's how all those tattoos started. Then she kept going and the tattoos grew and spread and came together. Trapped, Shattered Crystal figured she would never come back from Iraq. She never thought she'd have to apply for a job at a Denny's with all those scary tattoos.

You didn't turn to tattoos. There wouldn't be much point since you never take your clothes off in the presence of another human being. You didn't get fat, though that sounds like a more pleasant way to defend unwanted advances. Instead, you became another person. There are two of you in one body. To protect yourself, you usually let the smartass with the flexible morality do the talking. He's kept you alive so far.

The question is, who is the real Jesus? You can never trust your brain to answer your questions honestly. You'd have better luck figuring out whether Tim's really happy when you lie to him about your progress.

"Forgiveness." A new voice cuts in on Shattered Crystal's practiced monologue of undeserved shame.

You look up. It's the guy with the salt and pepper hair — you can't remember his name — and he's eyeballing you with a familiar, hyped-up look. The nice guy half tells you to smile back at him and look away. The tough guy in you says stare him down and if he doesn't look away, take him out in the alley after the meeting for "a lesson in deportment." That's what Tia Marta called your beatings.

"Deportment and comportment," Tia Marta teased as she ran the flogger up and down your bare leg. "I'll go a little easier on you if you know the difference, Jesus. It pays to increase your word power. See how your balls jump as I bring my cat-o'-nine up your thigh? That's called the cremasteric reflex. Your testicles are trying to hide from me. Funny, isn't it?"

"What are you doing, Jesus?" Salt and Pepper Guy says. "You got any forgiveness going on in your life? I don't think you do."

"Excuse me, Hans," Tim says. "Crystal was speaking."

Hans! That's Salt and Pepper Guy's name. Hans as in Hans Gruber, the bad guy from *Die Hard*. How could you forget?

"Now I'm speaking, Tim! Now I'm speaking! Crystal's always talking and you listen and you nod but nobody has any answers for us and meanwhile, this guy here," — Hans points at you — "is planning some evil shit. I see the signs! He's got a shadow soul, man! Don't you see that dark cloud? Don't you see the metal teeth in the gears working behind his eyes?"

"Calm down, Hans. We do not talk to each other like that in Group!"

"Talk like what? Tell the truth? Save a soul and maybe the freak's life?" Hans has that shiny-eyed earnest look unique to spiritual gurus, true believers and the terminally crazy. "Jesus! Listen to me, man. To err is human, to forgive is divine."

"I'd like to find it in myself to forgive," Crystal says, "but I'm not good enough. I don't have it in me."

Everyone goes quiet. Hans somehow manages to look even more smug than Tim.

You feel a rant and a lesson in deportment coming on, but you keep cool. There are predators and prey and witnesses. This room has too many witnesses. "I don't believe in forgiveness," you say finally. "I believe in vengeance."

Hans winces. He can't believe you didn't roll over on your back and beg for a belly scratch as soon as he dropped his greeting card wisdom on you.

"Jesus," Tim says. "You know that never works out."

"Works about as well as blaming yourself for being human. When they freed the slaves from those cotton plantations, the slave owners couldn't believe their victims didn't want to keep working because they'd been 'treated well.' We are those slaves. The people who sent us to the wrong country thank us for our service and patriotism but they don't know what patriotism means."

"Forgiveness is the answer," Hans says. "Don't wait for others to be perfect, perfect yourself."

"I'm not doing anything with feel-good slogans you pulled from Pinterest, dude. You want me to forgive so I can move on? Gimme my slice first. Even in the Bible, to forgive somebody, they gotta line up an apology, repentance and restitution. Dick Cheney and Rumsfeld and all those cats restituted fucking nothing."

"Lefty in the house!" some GI Joebot in the circle pipes up. A few others giggle and mutter.

"It's not about left or right. It's about what's *correct*. If I forgive everything, that means it's okay."

"I disagree, Jesus," Smug Tim says. "Forgiving doesn't make it okay, but it might make *you* okay."

"Forgiveness is divine, huh? To forgive what we've lost takes godlike power. Anybody here a god?"

"I've forgiven everyone." Tim taps his artificial leg with his cane and sits back, as if he can beat you with his disability. That prosthesis is the source of his power. He's one of those asshole cripples who believes a one-legged man can never lose an argument because he's always carrying phantom pain as his trump card.

"Tim, if you've really forgiven everyone, maybe you're a living saint."

He smiles his aw-shucks smile.

You struggle to sit still in your seat. "Or maybe you're an idiot coward who gets a lot of approval for announcing he forgives everybody. If you forgive, you're sure everyone will applaud and say, 'There goes Tim, lost a leg and still a good sport.'"

You're making entirely too much eye contact, but you barrel on. "I see that and say, 'There limps Tim. He's the guy with the little problem with Percocets who's still addicted to the idea of being a good soldier. Yeah, Tim can't stand the idea that not everyone likes him. He's *so* impressive, thinking he's like God, but really, he's just desperate for approval. It's pathetic."

The air is hot. Your mouth tastes like bad coffee. You stare him down and he sees what Hans sensed in you.

"Yours is an interesting perspective," Tim says finally.

The circle ripples as the others shift in their seats. They look at the floor. You called him out and all he's got is "interesting perspective"? Maybe he is a good guy full of forgiveness, but he sure sounds like a wimp backing down.

You turn your lasers on Hans, your voice low, slow and reasonable. "Dude, I don't know what your issue is with me, but Crystal was fucking talking and you want to hear somebody who agrees with you, so let her talk. She's in pain because you're asking her to do the impossible. She blames herself instead of giving a guy like me the names of her superior officers — excuse me, *rapists* — so I can make sure they never have the equipment to do that again to somebody else."

"I don't want that," Crystal says, wiping a tear.

You don't believe her. Her voice lacks conviction. You could convince her you should go castrate her attackers in less than the time it takes a hot coffee to cool. All she'd have to do is give you names and a slight nod and you'd do that for her for free. Or just strangle them the same delicious way you strangled Tia Marta. Serve up forgiveness all day and you're still hungry. Righteous vengeance is more filling.

Everyone else is quiet and sitting far back in their chairs, looking at you in a new way. This is the most you've spoken in Group. That was a mistake.

"Check him!" Hans shouts. "He has a weapon on him! I'm sure! Check him! He carries!" He springs from his chair, but Crystal's hand snakes out and catches Hans' wrist before he can come at you. Tim sticks his cane between you and Hans. It's purely a symbolic boundary, but everybody's ex-military in here, all about defending boundaries: the symbolic, the imaginary and the useless.

It's probably Crystal's pleading eyes that break the spell, because as soon as Hans looks in her face, he softens and steps back.

You raise your hands in a gesture to show they are empty. Your hands tremble. Your body shakes from the inside out, but your voice is steady when you say, "The sign on the front door says no weapons beyond this point, Hans. I am not carrying."

"That's right!" Tim says. "This is a *safe* space. We do *not* bring weapons in here."

That idea must be comforting to Smug Tim.

"And we do not interrupt another member's time," he adds. "Sit down, Hans."

Hans throws a defiant glance your way but sits. He apologizes to Shattered Crystal.

You get up to leave and the group choruses with calls for you to stay. "I'm done for this evening," you say. "Got a headache coming on."

"You going to take anything for that headache, Jesus?" Hans asks. You give him a tight grin.

"Your Indian name is Sees Things That Aren't There. I won't forget your name anymore."

Hans smiles, like he's won something. Or maybe you really have given too much away. "You *are* packing, aren't you?" he says.

You open your trench coat and spin slowly. At the conclusion of your 360-degree turn, you come back to Hans's eyes. "The force is not strong in this one."

Crystal bursts out in a giggle so Group is not entirely unrewarding tonight.

"I'm out."

"You don't have to go," Smug Tim calls after you.

"Got a job. Stuff to do," you say. "I'll be back." Then you say "I'll be back," again doing your Arnold Schwarzenegger impression so they don't know if you're serious about returning. That's fine. You don't know, either.

The automatic door squeaks as it slides aside and you gulp in cold breaths to try to settle your heartbeat. The shakes are still there, a tell of your weakness. Hans is probably just crazy, but why did he zero in on you? What bothers you more is what it means. Despite going up against the Lone Wolf and Mr. Bad Birthmark, you're still a bad guy.

This life isn't what you nearly died for: not in the water off Surfside Beach; not in the Miami basement; not in the desert; not in New York. Smug Tim tries to make you run through the past. Like Shattered Crystal, he wants you to tell it, cry over it, make sense of it and maybe even get bored of it. But what's the difference between that and wallowing?

"You won't be back," you tell yourself aloud. "If things are going to change, you have to get things right for you and Willow. It's time to start looking forward, not back," you announce to the whizzing traffic.

Fuck Smug Tim and forget him. He might be mocking you with every optimistic word about life goals, to-do lists and positive reframing.

You hate Shattered Crystal because she's you. Go away, Crystal.

You hate Hans because he was so close to right about you packing heat. What if he's right about evil behind your eyes?

You shut that thought down as best you can. Doubt is for guys with regular jobs.

You hate Group and their politics, their cliques and their phony, self-congratulatory backslapping. Their earnest esprit de coeur exhausts you. You have no mercy for them. That shelf is empty. All you've got for them is distance and indifference.

Heh. Distance and indifference. That makes you sound pretty godlike, after all.

You turn your mind to how lovely Willow is. You think about what a great mother she will make as you step into McDonald's to retrieve your gun. You hid it above a ceiling tile in the men's john.

DOUBLE JEOPARDY

The Super, Miss Iris, acts like a sweet, old woman as long as you're up to date on the rent, which you are not. You slow down as you walk past her door and tread lightly up the metal steps so your footsteps don't echo up and down the stairwell. You need the three s's: shit, shower, and shave. If the military had added another s for sleep, it wouldn't have been so bad.

When you walk into your apartment, there's a fat man in the corner fiddling with an iPhone. You've seen him once before. You can reach for your SIG, but a very tall bald guy puts the muzzle of a sawn off to your head. The only sleep you're in danger of getting any time soon is the long dirt nap.

The bald guy with the shotgun frowns, puts one finger to his lips — his middle finger — to let you know that now is not the time to scream for help, the police, or to engage in witty repartee. Now, you conclude, is an excellent time to shut the fuck up and listen. When you nod your understanding of this unspoken signal, the bald guy smiles and nods back. One canine and a top front tooth are missing from his smile and the rest of his teeth look like caramel corn. The effect is grisly.

"Jesus! How about that? Here you are. C'mon in," the fat man says. "Jesus Salvador! Jesus Salvador Umberto! Jesus Salvador Umberto Luis! Jesus Salvador Umberto Luis Diaz! The burning man! That is *quite* a handle you got there. What was the deal? Insecure? First name, middle and last not good enough for your mother, was it? Or is all that extra nonsense because you come from a huge Roman Catholic family with a lot of old uncles to honor?"

You stare and wait. The fat man doesn't look impatient. He blinks, amiable and avuncular.

"Or maybe it's because you're an only child and your dad had plans for a huge family but your mom said she was going to have one and done? Your dad had big plans and then he had to use up all the boys' names in his head since your mother decided to kill all his progeny while they were still seeds?"

You think of your dead brother Rodolpho. No, you weren't an only child, but you were alone in the world too soon. Rodolpho died in a swirl of red water. Your mother disappeared. Sharks ate your father. You have a long story to tell about how your family suffered so you could live in America. Since their sacrifice landed you in a lousy room with these two, you decide it's best not to get into it. You just shrug.

"You're an eloquent guy, Diaz."

You shrug again.

"Don't overdo it." He gestures toward the only other seat in the room, a wooden chair by the table. Before you can sit down, the fat man holds up a finger to stop you. "One thing. My friend behind you is Lurch. My advice to you is, please, do not piss off Lurch."

You turn to give Lurch the slow scan up and down and he puffs out his chest and smiles again.

"Don't worry," you say. "I'll let the Wookie win."

Lurch stays puffed up but at least that closes his rotting maw. He keeps the sawn off levelled at your gut as he pulls out the chair and turns it backward. He tilts his head and you straddle it, your arms cross the top of the chair.

The fat man sweats even though your room is cold. "I thought you'd be taller."

"I get that a lot. I'm not that short. I just didn't grow up next to a nuclear plant to be a freak like poor Lurch."

Whoever cut the stock on the sawn off did a lousy job of it. When Lurch hits you in the right kidney, there's an extra sharp edge to the blow. The pain makes you forget your headache.

The effect, as Tia Marta taught you, is called the Gate Theory of Pain. Got pain? A fresh new pain from somewhere else can block the original pain signal. Lurch's savage blow eclipses the sun. You swallow your cry. The fat man is patient while you get your breath back.

Tia Marta was a master of pain, but Lurch could give her a few tips. The right kidney is a little lower than the left to make room for the liver. Lurch located your right kidney with such great accuracy, it's clear this isn't his first rodeo. When you wipe away tears to clear your vision, and glance back, his ugly teeth are back on display. Unlike the Lone Wolf, he isn't jittery, either. Violent people who look placid are scarier than using a rattlesnake for a condom.

The fat man leans forward so you're eye to eye. Under your jacket, at your side, you still have the SIG in your waistband. It would be satisfying to shoot Lurch in the kidneys so he gets a feel for what the pain is like, but only a desperate fool would try it. You are enough of a fool to give it a try, yes, but you aren't quite that desperate yet.

"Your landlady, Miss Iris? I had a good conversation with her."

"I bet."

"Don't be angry with her. After I paid your rent, she let us in and was very cooperative ."

"Thanks."

"You're welcome. Miss Iris told me lots of things. You were behind on your rent quite a bit. I paid up till the end of the month. I expect that after our business is concluded, you'll want to move on."

"What business do you and I have? I hear the real money is in coming up with new iPhone apps."

The fat man smiles. "Miss Iris said you were a smartass. How long have you known our friend, Samuel Clemont?"

"Not long."

"How did he get hold of you? Does Old Sam have connections to the New York mob scene? Or do you two have military friends in common? Or is the big black fella a friend of yours?"

They seem to already know everything.

"Chill's a friend."

"Uh-huh. And Samuel's girl?"

"Who?" It would be bad form to give them Willow to use against you.

"Willow Clemont. The tall blonde girl you walked home. Don't tell me *she* slipped your mind. Nobody forgets a girl who looks like that. I've got pictures."

The future Mrs. Diaz is already in the crosshairs. "She needed walking home, that's all."

"Uh-huh." For the first time, the fat man glances at Lurch. "How about that?"

"I didn't catch your name," you say.

The fat man smiles. "I didn't tell you. A guy like you with too many names and a guy like me with none. I like that balance, the yin and the yang of it."

Time to pretend you aren't just a pawn. "So you're from the Recipients and you want the guns."

You see something in his face that passes quickly. What was that? Confusion?

"You're a little brownish man playing in a game where you don't even know the stakes," he says. "You have no idea the trajectory you're on. I see the big picture. That's the hand God dealt you in the big poker game. That's not my fault or my problem. Even better, you're going to help me because I'm appealing to your basic instincts. You want to live, I'll bet."

"That would be good."

"I'll let you live as long as you do as I say."

"What's the magic word?"

Lurch hits you in the right kidney again in exactly the same spot. This time, you fall to the floor gasping as the pain jangles up and down your back. Your jaw drops wide. All you can do is writhe, succumb to your screaming nerves and wait.

"There are people coming, Jesus. A little bunch. They're very important. You're on the floor gasping for air, looking like a landed carp and I'm up here, working on a whole other level."

You manage a nod. It would be churlish not to agree.

"When more of my people arrive, they're going to want everything that Samuel Clemont has. We know there's a local street gang who wants the Russian shipment. Old Sam's partner, Harry, shouldn't have looked for more buyers after he spoke to us. That was rude."

He waits until you can speak again, studying you as you moan. He looks like a nerdy kid examining an unfamiliar insect whose wings he's just yanked off.

When you can speak, you're feeling cooperative. "I don't know where the shipment is. He's afraid the locals will try to get it before he can sell it to you."

"Good. So we're really on the same team. Simple solution: show those gang members we're serious people and do it right away. We are still prepared to pay what we offered. If Clemont deals with these other people for fear they'll kill him and his daughter, we'll kill him and his daughter. You and the black fella, too, of course. *Heh.* Your death. A mere afterthought. How does that feel?"

"Like any average Tuesday evening." The pain is so bad, you wonder if you'll piss blood, if you dare to try to pee again. Ever. "Clemont already hired me to deal with The Victorious."

"Samuel can only give you a carrot. Now that you know we're very firm about getting the shipment, you have the extra motivation of the stick. A young criminal such as yourself often loses track of key priorities."

You croak out a couple of lines from *The Untouchables*: "That's the Chicago way. Here endeth the lesson." If you were in better form, your Sean Connery impression would come out better. The key to the impression is to pretend you have loose dentures, but your breath is too shallow as yet for the forceful delivery required.

The fat man laughs politely. "We'll call Samuel soon. We'll expect his immediate cooperation. We expect that you'll convince him of all that's at stake. You do understand, right? I don't want Lurch to break a sweat making you understand."

"I get it."

"Clear as glass?"

"Like glass dropped on concrete."

"Excellent. Hey, where'd you learn to speak English?"

"Florida."

"Huh. Of course. Well, my compliments. Even when you cry, you don't sound Hispanic."

The fat man hauls himself out of the chair with a soft grunt and crouches beside you to examine your face as you work through the pain.

The knife in your sock is handy. You could stick that in his eye, taking time to dig for the brain, but Lurch has that sawn off pointed at your groin.

You close your eyes to the agony. The SIG springs into your hand by magic and you double tap Lurch in the face twice before he can cut you in two...You open your eyes. Nah. That doesn't happen, but magic would be useful.

The fat man straightens with another grunt and steps over you on the way out the door. "We'll call soon. Leave him his gun, Lurch. He'll need it to deal with the Wolf."

Lurch keeps his shotgun trained on you as he bends and tucks the PS3 console under his arm. He backs out of the room and, peeking around the corner, stage whispers, "*Bang!*" and disappears.

Their footsteps echo off the metal treads of the staircase as you try to get up. Pain is such a small, inadequate word for all the work it does. They took too much stuffing out of you to risk it. All you can do is crawl to the window and peer out, your breath pulled and pushed through gritted teeth, hissing.

On the street below, the fat man waddles out to a black Ford F150 where he waits for Lurch to open the passenger door for him. The F150 is indistinguishable from every other truck of its kind. It's too far to see the license plate even if the high angle allowed you to spot it. The vehicle sports an extra antenna from its roof with a foxtail tied to the end.

You hold the bruised spot over your right kidney and watch Lurch and the fat man pull away from the curb.

Once they're gone, you roll over and bang the back of your head against the radiator. You experiment with banging it a little harder, but the Gate Theory of Pain doesn't seem to be working in your favor today. The fat man has you in his fist and Lurch has your PS3 and *Lego Batman 2*.

You let the Wookie win.

OUR MAN IN HAVANA

A lot can happen in six minutes. Only six minutes ago Willow packed a bag while Chill tore off in his SUV to lure away anyone following her. A black muscle car peeled off after him, so you felt pretty confident Chill's decoy manoeuvre worked. You took Willow's keys and headed for her yellow hatchback in the parking garage behind her apartment.

Confidence. Silly mistake. Six minutes can feel like just a few seconds.

Six minutes from now, Willow will run to your side, screaming for you not to shove your attacker's own blade up into his throat. You're so angry by then, you want to kill your attacker as if he's a zombie: push the blade through the floor of his mouth, through his tongue, into the roof of his mouth and past the palate's bony resistance up into his brain pan. The long blonde will have her way. The mystery of why you will spare him will interest you almost as much as the fight did. But that's six minutes from now, proving that six minutes can also feel like an ugly hour.

He comes at you from behind, out of the shadows, just as you turn Willow's key and pop the car's hatch. Your attacker could have killed you easily if he had kept the job simple and walked up and shot you in the back of the head. However, a flash of dirty white bandages and a splotch of a birthmark tells you it's the guy you scarred forever with a scalding pot of coffee. You thought of him as the skinny guy. Then he was Mr. Bad

Birthmark. Now he's Scarface. If he hadn't taken his burns so personally and came at you with a knife — you figure out the blade is actually a bayonet in the next few seconds — Scarface could have killed you and then probably killed Willow. Or kidnapped her and demanded her father give up the arms shipment before killing her horribly.

Instead, you hear your assailant step in a puddle three steps away and that's just enough warning for you to slip sideways. Instead of puncturing a lung and taking you to the ground to gut you like a pig, Scarface slices the air.

And you're living in the now.

This guy is tall but skinny in the lumpy way skinny guys go once they get too old to eat anything they want. Once he loses the element of surprise, you surprise him by grabbing his wrist and following his momentum. You smash his wrist on the lip of the hatch again and again. The bayonet goes into the trunk. You drive a knee into his side.

He grunts and twists away with strength that rises from fear and desperation. He tags you with a glancing punch to the jaw, but you're already turning away from the blow and, when you spin around, you whip the back of your hand into his nose. It doesn't crack but it stuns him enough for a follow-up left hook to his neck. You throw your hip into it for oomph. The work that goes into putting heft into that punch shoots searing pain from the spot over your kidney where Lurch dinged you less than an hour ago. So far, that's the worst pain Scarface has inflicted.

You're not sure what startles Scarface more. Maybe it's because he had the advantage and suddenly things are going so badly, so quickly. Fights are like that. Maybe it's the agonizing pain in his larynx that paralyzes his speech and muffles all his other senses. Scarface is stunned and breathing heavily, with eyes like shiny pie plates. Maybe he looks so scared because you're laughing.

As he falls backward, he drags you down by your coat, his dirty hands clawing at your lapels. As you go down you lead with your knees and come down on his balls squarely. His eyes bug out and you see the whites all around the perimeter of his irises. You'd think that would end it, but a fight like this doesn't end with a somebody ringing a bell three times and saying, "Okay, you got him."

Scarface shrieks and the fight goes on, though it's pretty much just wrestling after that and you're on top pinning him. When this fight is over, he knows he'll be over. The pull of his hopes and dreams are still, surprisingly, bigger than his pain. Even with his last conscious moments a misery, he fights to keep the pain going as long as possible. A smarter guy would have given up earlier.

You'd forgotten the animal joy of knowing you're going to win. You don't feel that often nor enough. You could have kept that winning feeling if you had just killed him then.

Guys never get knocked cold as easily as they do on TV unless they're hit with a ball peen hammer. You saw that once, back in Havana on the Hudson. You'll never forget the wet crunch and the way the guy crashed stiff, like a tree felled by one swing of a god's ax. It made you sick, but that's the sort of thing that, even as you watch mesmerized, you know you're going to wish you hadn't seen it. Before the struggle with Scarface is over, you wish you had that ball peen hammer.

It ends in an awkward scramble on the ground with short, little punches. Scarface tries to poke your eyes out. He manages to scratch your cheeks a bit, but he's fumbling and weak. You grab a handful of hair and lift his head into an elbow smash. When his eyes roll up, he really does look like a grasping, barely sentient, flailing zombie. You don't feel the pain over your kidney anymore. That will come later. Victory's euphoria eclipses pain better than the Gate Theory of Pain ever could.

You could finish him with the SIG, but he made it personal and so, stupidly, you do the same. You could cut his throat with the switch in your sock, but instead, as he gasps for breath, you drive the heel of your palm into the sweet spot, just in front of the ear where his jawbone meets his skull. His head is turned and flat against the concrete. There's no give in a concrete floor to lessen the blow.

Scarface sleeps. His bandages are torn away and you can see the mess you made of his face. He'll die ugly, but he'll go to hell in his sleep. When you stop hitting him, all you hear is your heavy breathing and the distant squeal of brakes and a car door. You listen longer, waiting for static from a police radio and urgent voices summoning backup. However, you hear no sirens and see no red, white and blue lights strobing doom.

You stand and retrieve the bayonet from the hatchback. The back door to the apartment building bangs behind you. That's got to be Willow. Best to have this done before she arrives. Before you can turn with the bayonet in your hand, you hear someone moving fast in the shadows and grit under fast footfalls.

You're still breathing hard and waiting for your heart to come down from its full tilt gallop. "Willow?"

The silhouette of a large man appears from out of the shadows. "Shit!"

You recognize that voice. He's twenty paces away, but you can feel where he's aiming, a spot over your heart. It's the Lone Wolf, his right arm in a sling. His trigger and middle fingers are buddy taped and straight out in a splint. In his outstretched left hand, a little .32 catches the light, shining silver.

"I told Skeet not to take you on alone! That idiot! When he wakes up, I'm going to tell him 'I told you so,' every day for the rest of his stupid life."

You both slide a glance to the guy at your feet. All Skeet's resources are focused on breathing. Nothing else works. A quickly spreading stain darkens the unconscious man's pants at the crotch.

"That's supposed to be you on the ground."

"Didn't work out."

"Yeah."

"I guess Chill lost you."

"Hard to crank the wheel fast enough one-handed. He lost me going around too many corners. I can still shoot, though."

You gesture at the .32. "Are you good with that? I mean, even with your left hand?"

"Sure." He points it at your head.

"Are you sure? It's important. You're a little far away. If you're going to shoot me with a peashooter, I'd rather you not take all night killing me. I got places to be."

He lowers the gun again. Either the guy has Attention Deficit Disorder or he's toying with you. That's okay. You're playing for time while Willow sneaks up in the shadows. She's silent, so either she's wearing high heels with felt on the soles or she took off those come-pump-me pumps.

"His name is *Skeet*? I've never known anyone named Skeet."

"There's that actor guy. No relation," the big man offers.

"I figured. I've been calling him Scarface, you know, like they called Al Capone."

"Dude! We are in Chi-fucking-cago! You don't think I know who Al fucking Capone was? I've seen the movies, man. I *live* here. Shee-it!"

"There's an interesting story about Capone you won't find in Wikipedia."

"What do I care?" He raises the gun.

"Quick story. Do you know why they called Capone Scarface?"

"Because he had a scar on his face, you *fucking* moron." He's about to pull the trigger.

"He got the scar in a fight over a girl. I think he was pretty young, still a bouncer at the time. He said he got the scar in the Lost Battalion in France during World War I, but he never served."

"Uh-huh." His first shot misses, but you feel the bullet's breath.

You were just stalling, but it is true he's a bit far away. Not so far away you can reasonably expect to reach behind your back and nail him between the eyes by whipping out the SIG. Most gunfights go down within six feet, up close and personal, not twenty paces. Old-fashioned duels settled disputes at ten paces, though duelling pistols sucked then and it was a one-shot deal. You could dive for it, but still, your best hope is Willow. This isn't some John Woo Hong Kong action flick where the hit man moves in precise slow motion choreographed dance sequences while everyone else has the reaction time of a three-toed sloth trying to figure out the safety on a machine gun.

Yellow phosphorescence catches Willow's blonde hair as she crouches low, still moving, still silent. *That's my girl.*

"Told you, you'd miss at that range." *Please come out into the light and keep your focus on me.*

As if moving by your unspoken command, the big man does step out of the shadows and takes just two steps closer. Pride came before a fall for Scarface Skeet. You? Odds are excellent you're still screwed.

"The interesting story a lot of people don't know about Capone was what happened to him in San Francisco."

The big guy spreads his feet wider, aiming carefully. He won't miss this time. *Hurry, Willow!*

"The guards at Alcatraz said they treated Capone just like any other prisoner. They got him for tax evasion, of course, but did you know about the couple of guys he killed with a baseball bat? Those same guys had served Capone as assassins during the St. Valentine's Day Massacre and he wound up beating them to death at a cocktail party with a Louisville slugger. Imagine being that second guy, waiting for your head to be caved in, watching the other guy getting his head beaten in first."

"Probably felt a little like what you're feeling now."

"Heh. Good point!"

"Still boring, though," the Lone Wolf says. He pulls the trigger again, misses and you hear the ricochet behind you. "Talk faster." He is toying with you.

C'mon, Willow!

"Though the guards treated him the same, to the other inmates, Scarface Al was a celebrity. So you know what some of them wanted to do?"

"Take him down. Make their bones like I'm about to do with you?"

"One of the other inmates came at Al with scissors. Al was still tough, though, even without a bat. He was still street. Al put up his hands, blocked the attack and the scissors went into his hand, between his fingers."

"I should go dump Skeet at an emergency room, so hurry up and finish the story. Places to be." You can feel the spot he's aiming at, like he's pushing a finger into your forehead.

"The funny thing is, Scarface Al? He took his time and beat the shit out of that inmate."

"So? Not much of a story."

"Well, I thought the funny part was that the guards watched the beating go on. They let Al Capone off the leash. They watched, laughed and applauded as it happened, so anybody else who got the idea to go after Capone and make trouble, they'd get the message. Al beat that guy like a rented dick at a porno convention."

The guy chuckles.

She's only one car-length away. She's stealthy, but stealthy is too slow and what you need is firepower.

"Do you know the moral of the story? The moral of the story," — talk slow, give her just a little more time — "is I'm going to beat you down. I'm going to beat you down so hard, you won't feel safe when you crawl up your own ass to try to get away from me."

"You talk pretty."

"Thanks."

His next shot pops as you drop to your belly, using Scarface Skeet's body for cover since he's the only cover you've got. The Lone Wolf lines up the shot that will kill you when he detects movement behind him. Willow tries to hit the big guy in the face with a bright red fire extinguisher but he's a half-step too quick and shoves her back into the side of a car. The car alarm blares immediately, jolting you as you pull your SIG and snap off two rounds. Your first shot goes wide. The second catches him in the meat above the knee. Wouldn't it be sweet if you got him in the femoral artery so he'll bleed out beside Scarface Skeet? He shrieks like a girl with her nipples caught in mousetraps.

The Lone Wolf goes down on one knee and fires at you but you can't throw shots back his way. Instead of doing the sane thing and running, Willow comes at him again. You fire two more rounds, deliberately wide, just to keep him interested and distracted. All the power of the SIG Sauer P220 is reduced to that of a New Year's noisemaker because you're terrified you'll shoot your future wife.

She swings the fire extinguisher again. The big guy is still firing your way instinctively, but his aim sucks worse than ever since his cheekbone is caved in with her first strike. From where you lay prone, the big guy looks quizzical as he turns to look up at Willow. She bashes his handsome face again.

When he's laid out, Willow stands on his forearm and wrist with both bare feet to pull the .32 from his hand.

She looks your way, half her face hidden behind a curtain of mussed hair. If Wonder Woman were blonde, and did her fighting in a tight cream jacket and skirt, she'd look like that.

Scarface Skeet lets out a long groan as you lean on his stomach to get to your feet. "Took you long enough." You try to look casual and cool, but your heart is hammering against your ribs, trying to get out and run away. You're shaking. It seems no matter how many times people shoot at you, you don't get used to it.

"I had to be quiet and the bastard *still* heard me at the last second!" She turns on the Wolf's unconscious form and spits. "That's what you get for taking *me* hostage, fuckface."

"Thanks. Um...if there's a next time, and we should make sure there never is...all I'm saying is, next time, move a little faster."

"I wanted to hear the end of the story, too. Any of that true?"

"Sure. It's all true. I like to travel."

"You went on vacation in San Francisco?"

"Sure. Took the tour at Alcatraz. I'll take you sometime. You've got to have a crab sandwich with sourdough bread at Fisherman's Wharf, though. That was the best part of the tour."

She blows her hair out of her face, a beautiful woman with a shiny .32 in one hand and a fire extinguisher in the other. "Can't wait for the sourdough bread," she says. "I, uh, have a hard time picturing you on vacation taking a tour of Alcatraz."

You tell a lot of lies for a living. It's galling when someone suspects you're full of shit when you tell the truth. Still, her skepticism shows how smart she is. She *should* think you're full of shit all the time because you usually are. Maybe you can change that. "You got me. I was in San Fran to drown a guy in a bathtub."

She laughs and snorts, not taking you seriously.

The car alarm blares on. It's an old alarm that runs up and down annoying scales. Of course, no one's coming, but you shouldn't hang around, either.

Your hands are still shaking when you grab the bayonet. You should shove the bayonet through Scarface Skeet's brain. For some reason you can't explain — a distant memory of something terrible on a Cuban beach — you stop to grab Scarface by the jacket and drag his limp body to prop him into a sitting position against a concrete pillar. Somehow, it doesn't seem right, murdering the guy while he's having a therapeutic nap.

You place the tip of the bayonet under his chin. It's sharp. A trickle of blood slips down the blade as you brace yourself and take a deep breath for one brutal and efficient zombie-killing shove.

"Don't!" Willow screams, her voice cracking.

"He came to me." You promised you'd beat them all down so far they'd never get up. Bloody and piss-stained, Scarface Skeet is a rabid dog. Even with Willow as a witness, you've got to put these thugs down.

A worn memory fires up. You'd rather leave that memory alone.

Willows closes her warm hands around your trembling, cold mitts.

"Don't," she says again, softer. If she'd screamed it again, or tried to order you, you would have done it. Instead, she's asking.

"He came to me," you say again, your voice far away now, weaker, emptier and scared.

Gently, she takes the bayonet from your hands. "He's helpless. We won. Don't be that guy. Stay with self-defence. Be the bodyguard. Don't be the killer."

You stand and step back and Willow smiles. She cups your face with her warm hands and you close your eyes.

You're not living in the now anymore. You're a kid on a Cuban beach. The way the sun is slanted, you're sure it's early in the morning, just past dawn. You shake as terror washes over you. You taste cold saltwater.

You open your eyes and she's staring back, still gentle and forgiving. With Willow, you're the hero. Without her, you are six minutes to Cuba. Without Willow, you are your father.

ARMOR OF GOD

When you close your eyes, your father, Marco Diaz, is not dead. He stands barefoot in cool sand yelling to you as you swim. He tells you to keep your fingers together as you practice your front crawl. You want to quit, but he yells, "Just a few more minutes!" He said that at least thirty minutes ago, too.

You swim, fighting the waves, and, when your father goes quiet, you pause to make sure you haven't swum too far. You pop your head up and scan the beach.

Marco Diaz is no longer watching you. His hands are planted on his hips. A hunched, older man wearing a white shirt and long pants pulled high on his belly stalks toward your father. He yells something. You don't know the words but recognize English and anger. The man has something in his hand. It flashes in the strengthening sunlight.

You blink. You're back in a parking garage in Chicago. Willow cups your face gently.

"Will he live?"

"Huh?"

"Scarface. Will he live?"

"Yeah, though he might not want to for a little while."

"I hated him before," Willow says. "I feel sorry for him now."

"I doubt he'll take his beating as a life lesson, turn things around and get right to work on curing cancer."

"You never know," Willow says. "People can change. And if you're not good at something, you probably shouldn't do it. He's not good at whatever it is he did before you, uh...?"

"Racked him up?"

"Yes."

"His name is Skeet."

"Really? He didn't have much of a chance then, did he? The Lone Wolf is bashed up, but he's breathing fine. We should go before he wakes up. He might be, you know, annoyed." She pulls at your elbow.

"You sure? If we wait around for them to wake up, they'll be a lot easier to beat up the second time around."

She doesn't laugh. As you climb into the car stiffly — your hurt kidney reasserts itself for attention — you decide Willow must be one of those beautiful optimists you hear about. She seems so hopeful. How did she get that way? She's the opposite of her father. If that pattern holds true and your kids turn out so different from you, maybe you should find hope, too. From her heights, if she knew your depths, you'd never have a chance with her.

But how different are you from your father? Not different enough, obviously.

Willow wants to talk. "What are you thinking?"

"I was getting kind of emo over Skeet and the Wolf. Don't worry. I think it's passing." You drive, your mind in a fog, criss-crossing the city to make sure no one follows you. The safe house sits on a quiet, well-to-do suburban street, so it's hard to pick out which two-story family home is a family with kids, which is the marijuana grow-op and which is the meth lab. In this economy and with the huge mortgages in an area like this, might there be a few that are all of the above?

When you open the hatchback to grab Willow's bags, you are astonished to see you took Skeet's bayonet. You leave it in the trunk and the garage closes automatically behind you.

Chill opens the back door and gestures you in. Instead of the .357 Magnum, he's got a shiny Ruger Super Redhawk Alaskan in his fist. The .357 must be reserved for impromptu Bible readings. He reads Willow's face. "Any trouble?"

"Trouble doesn't bother me," you say. "I bother it." It sounds like someone else saying it, a tin line from an old film noir. Fine. That's the best you can manage for now. You're afraid that when you close your eyes, you'll be back in the surf, seeing the hunched man stalk toward your father, something flashing in his hands as it catches fresh sunbeams.

"The skinny guy and the Lone Wolf came after Jesus," Willow says.

"Was it bad?"

"They wanted to know if I'd heard the good news about Scientology, so yeah."

Chill looks at the scratches on your face and nods. "When you were done, did they need to be taken away in a coroner's truck or an ambulance?"

"Tupperware."

When Chill frowns, babies cry and strong men grow weak, but Willow ruins your tough guy act. "Jesus let them live."

"Really?" Chill brightens. "Respect!"

You're worried that, just when you had decided you liked Chill, he might try to high five you, as if you'd shown good sportsmanship in an especially brutal little league game. To your relief, he tells you he's going to go check on Willow's dad.

"You stay here and recuperate tonight. I'll check out of my hotel and bring my stuff over in the morning."

"I thought you were staying here," you say. "Who's place is this?"

"My uncle's house," Willow says. "He's out of town."

Once she disappears into the bathroom, Chill eyes you, looking pensive. "Samuel told me to murder the Wolf and Skeet."

"You had the good sense to say no, Chill, so I have to deal with it."

"Mr. Clemont will want to know why the Victorious wannabes aren't dead, Jesus."

You simplify, since you don't quite understand why you held back, either. "I couldn't make his daughter and my future wife an accessory. He'll understand. Tell Samuel I held back for the same reason he didn't shoot them when he had the chance."

"That would make for tension in the family."

"Damn right. What did Clemont tell you about the Recipients?"

"He claimed they were a harmless cult. I told him that was an oxymoron and if I killed any reps from The Victorious, that'd make me an omnimoron."

"Like me?"

"Yeah."

"The Recipients know who we all are, Chill. If I don't take out the wannabes, they'll kill us all before Clemont can pay me enough to skip town with Willow."

"That's inconvenient. What do you want me to tell Samuel? As you'll recall, my policy is I don't know and I don't want to know."

"Tell him I'm working the problem, but he needs to get the shipment out of storage and get the deal with the Recipients done. I need them off my back."

"I'll pass it along. I'm sure Mr. Clemont will be suitably reassured."

Willow walks into the kitchen and pulls a glass from a cupboard. "So guys...how big is Dad's arms deal that we're in this shit this deep? Is it World War III? Should I go hide in the attic?"

You and Chill turn to her together and chuckle nervously, morons in stereo. "I'm supposed to keep you out of that," Chill says. "I don't know —"

"And he doesn't want to know," you finish.

"And your father doesn't want you to know anything about this, either," Chill says sternly.

"It's an accessory after the fact sort of deal," you add.

"Nobody knows where you are and unless the neighbors turn you in, Anne Frank, you're safe," Chill adds. "We just have to stay here and don't so much as look out the curtain."

"Safe. Huh. Great! I'll just go hide in the attic and start working on my journal."

In a sweet gesture only gay guys and Europeans can pull off without feeling and looking like idiots, Chill leans in and kisses Willow on both cheeks. "You're safe, girl. Guaranteed. Just stay off the phone, stay inside and keep the curtains closed."

You're suddenly aware again that you're in a small room with giants. You step back and lean on the counter, trying to look taller, more casual and less battle fatigued.

When Chill's gone, Willow checks the cupboards and finds tea bags and a tea kettle and a couple of chipped teacups. When Willow offers you tea, you accept. You were taught never to turn down tea from a lady. Old habits, even when ingrained under duress, still hold.

"It's just you and me until I can get my iPod recharged," Willow says as you join her in the living room.

"You talk," you suggest. "I'm an excellent listener." More old habits.

"I have another idea."

You smile. Maybe you won't have to wait long to feel those long legs wrap around you. She forgot her iPod charger, but did she remember to throw in a pack of condoms?

Instead, Willow Clemont wants conversation. She wants you to talk. You can tell by the way she sits up straight with her teacup in her lap that this is the job interview part of the introductory dating period.

"I could talk all night about how much I love your eyes. You have kind eyes, Willow. I like that in the future Mrs. Diaz."

"You don't have kind eyes, Jesus. That's why I need to know more. For starters, I'm guessing your parents were Catholic."

"The raving kind. Lots of guilt."

"And did you inherit their sense of guilt?"

"Pass. Next question?"

Willow bestows a patient grin, but the tolerant yet strained kind of smile is loaded in the next chamber. "Where did you learn to fight? In the military?"

You didn't mean to let out that long sigh. Her eyes are still kind, but the rest of her face isn't so sure about you.

"I knew this guy, back in New York. Used to tell this story about how to handle a cop if he stops you. Long story, short, dude's stopped by a cop in Texas. He's got a chopped up body, a shovel and a couple of hundred pounds of marijuana in the trunk."

"True story?"

"Guys bullshit. Who knows? All stories are true mixed with horse shit until neither is both."

"If I give myself a headache, I bet I'd understand what you just said."

"Well, you know. Good stories are all Irish fact. Even if it's not true, it ought to be."

She nods for you to continue.

"So dude's stopped by a cop and the dude has incriminating things in the car. But he's also got a skunk in the back seat."

"Why would he have a skunk in the back seat?"

"I forget what he tells the cop. I just remember that the dude has like, squeezed the skunk juice all over the car and, the stench is so bad, there's no way the cop is going to stick around to ask questions. He talked about how it was just another day at the office to escape heinous criminal prosecution with just a skunk and a smile. No interrogation, no arrest." You give her your best smile.

Her eyes narrow. "Are you saying you wish you had a skunk right now so you wouldn't have to tell me anything about you?"

You smile wider. It doesn't work. She doesn't laugh or snort.

Instead, Willow stands and removes her jacket. She's wearing a matching cream blouse and skirt with no slip. She unbuttons two buttons from the top of the blouse, pauses for drama and sits down. "You were my knight in sh...tarnished armor tonight, Jesus."

"Technically, you saved me," you point out.

"Still, I appreciate you helping me and my dad out. I'd like to show some appreciation."

"I'm down," you say, too quickly.

109

"But," she sits and crosses her legs, "I don't go to bed with strangers."

You take her in, slow. She's taken the time to apply fresh lipstick that paints her lips cherry red. Through the thin fabric of her blouse, you can make out the dark circles of her erect nipples. She crosses her legs again and you picture her in nothing but the high heels.

You spill your guts.

CONFESSIONS OF A DANGEROUS MIND

"Marco, my father, was the one who first taught me how to fight," you begin. "He was a boxer when he was young. They taught me stuff in the military later, but...Dad was more serious about it."

"More serious than the army? My God, what did he do to you?"

"It wasn't like that."

"How was it?"

"In Cuba, there was a man who came after my father. It was the only time I saw my father in a real fight. He taught me things until we left Cuba. After that...he didn't make it all the way here."

"I'm sorry."

"Don't be. If he'd lived, I probably wouldn't have loved him so much as I do now."

"Dads aren't so bad. You've probably noticed my dad is a little crusty, but I love him."

"Crazy."

"Maybe. What about the man who attacked your father? What was that about?"

You ignore the question. "It's been a while since I was in a fight like that. Scarface Skeet almost got me. If he hadn't made a little mistake at the very first...well, if you make a mistake at the beginning of the fight, it's like buttoning up your shirt wrong." You glance meaningfully at Willow's cleavage. "You start off wrong, you may as well unbutton the whole thing and start again. Scarface should have made a run for it. I probably wouldn't have chased him. I just wanted to get you someplace safe. That's my first priority."

"What did your Dad teach you?"

"The military's policy on hand-to-hand combat makes a lot of sense. Only do it as a last resort, as in just long enough to get to your gun and reload. If I'd gone with that tonight, I not only wouldn't have scratches on my face, I wouldn't have broken a sweat. Also, they say if a fight is going too well, it's an ambush. If I'd just shot Skeet immediately, I would have been out of there before the Lone Wolf doubled back."

Willow gives you a look that might be disappointment so you barrel on, "If the fight is fair, you haven't planned properly. Standard Army manual cliches, all true as far as I know."

"With the gun and without the sweat and scratches? That wouldn't have been so brave or noble."

"I didn't want to be brave. I wanted to win. And you stopped me, so you made me noble, Willow."

"That's kind of sexy."

"I wanted to cut Scarface open just to see the gears inside."

"Not so sexy," she says. "Tell me about your Dad and Cuba and the man who came after him."

You imagine helping her out of that shirt and slipping that tight skirt down her legs slowly, worshipping her with your eyes and lips and tongue.

"Dad taught me the basics. Jabs. Uppercuts. How to throw a hook without wrecking your shoulder."

"How do you do that?"

"The trick to a good hook is not to miss what you're trying to punch. Hitting the target is important. If you pretend the target is a couple of inches behind your opponent's nose, for instance, you hit harder. Keeping distance just right is good. A lot of guys can wail on somebody, but it takes skill to make the other guy miss and waste energy."

"You saw your father fight?"

"Just the once, on the beach. He won, but it wasn't really an even match."

"What happened?"

You clear your throat and have a sip of tea. It felt great when you were sure you were going to beat Scarface Skeet. Maybe that's how Marco Diaz felt, too.

"I learned the most important stuff from those few minutes on the beach. An older man — a guest at the hotel where my father worked — went at my father with a steak knife from the restaurant."

"My god!"

"I was out in the water and by the time I got to shore, it was almost over. The most important stuff is that the guy who hits first almost always wins. Also, you have to deal with the weapon before you take down the man. My dad took the knife away from that tourist like it was nothing. The guy was a bit older, though. Maybe he thought he was going to scare my father, make him run away. Now that I say that, the fight was over so quick, that's probably what was on his mind. He didn't really come to kill. You pull a knife or a gun, you better mean to use it. That was the other man's mistake."

The silence stretches out and when you don't fill it, Willow asks, "What are you not telling me, Jesus?"

You ignore her question again. "The real fancy stuff is what Dad taught me later. It was about fire and water. If you fight like water, you flow around the opponent's attack and go for a body blow or tune up his face. If you take the fire strategy, whatever your opponent throws at you, you burn him. So, like, he tries to kick you? Don't just block it. Break his fuckin' ankle...excuse me."

"I grew up with a Marine for a father. He invented swearing. I don't mind. In fact, tell me more about your family and later I'll tell you how much I like to talk dirty in bed."

"Show, don't tell."

She stares into your eyes and smirks as she opens another button on her blouse. "What happened to the man?"

"I was coming in from swimming. It was very early in the morning and there was no one else around. Only I saw the fight."

"From what you say, it was a short fight."

"Yes. My father took away the steak knife. Then he held it in his fist as he boxed. The jabs were a.... death by a thousand cuts sort of deal."

"Your father knifed a man to death in front of you?"

"Not exactly. As I came out of the water, I was screaming and crying. I ran up to my father as he held the man by the neck. My father slapped me to shut me up."

You touch your cheek, surprised. "I'd forgotten that. I remember him slapping Rodolpho once, too, but that was it. Before the beach, I didn't really think of my father as a dangerous man. He'd taught me boxing, but fighting and being the kind of guy who can...well, which was the real him? The father I knew was a pretty placid, often funny guy, but inside, there was something else waiting to come out."

"What happened to the tourist?"

"He bled, but he was still alive. His white shirt looked like it had big, red flowers. Years later, I was somewhere traveling and saw this ugly shirt with poinsettias on it and this familiar feeling came back. I felt...I thought I might throw up. My father wore a white shirt that day, as well, but his shirt looked more like some art an old girlfriend of mine used to like. The artist had a funny name. Klimt, maybe?"

"So you're saying you were a little kid when you watched your father stab someone to death?"

"No. I'm saying he stabbed him enough to make the old man want to die. Then my father dragged him out into the water and drowned him. I guess he was a mess and wanted the outgoing tide to take his sin out to sea."

Her jaw goes slack.

You shrug. You try to make your shrug look casual, as if you've told this story a hundred times. As if you're bored of it. As if the mind fuckery wasn't such a big deal. "But that wasn't the real fucked up part," you add.

For the first time, Willow cuts her eyes at you and looks skeptical. "Jesus. How could that possibly be the *un*fucked up part?"

* * *

You close your eyes. You can still see Marco Diaz wade back to the beach shirtless. He looks back toward the floating body as if he expects the old man will come back to life and come after him again.

You run at him and throw yourself into your father's arms, crying. Without hesitation, he pushes you back a step and slaps you again. "*Silencio!*" The shock of the wet slap makes you hold your breath.

His face softens a little and he gives you a begrudging, grim smile. "*Mijo*," he says. "Dry your tears." He cups your face in his big hands. "It's okay."

"What was the man screaming?"

"It's nothing."

"He tried to kill you for *nothing*?"

Marco Diaz makes a disgusted sound in the back of his throat. "Something about me and the man's wife. He was confused and crazy. A misunderstanding. He didn't want to talk. I bet he stayed up all night rehearsing his speech to me, like I was a child. The man was a fool."

"Why? Why did he do that?"

"*Sh. Sh.* It's nothing. The man was very bad. He came after me with a knife. I had no choice. *He* came to *me*. I had to defend myself. I didn't want to die. I don't want to lose you and Rodolpho and your mama."

"B-but, what he said — "

"Quiet, now." Marco Diaz, your beloved father, stares you in the eyes and tells you to keep his secret. "If you don't keep this a secret, I'll have to go away and I'm not willing to do that, *mijo*. I'll do anything to keep me and my family together. You see that corpse floating out there, Jesus? Would you rather it was me?"

"No, papa!"

"Would you rather it was *you*?"

Your eyes go wider but you don't speak, can't speak. You don't know your father at all. He is transformed into someone, some *thing* else.

"Then be quiet now. Don't tell anything about this to anyone. We will never speak of this. It was self-defence and that's all it was. *He came to me.* Don't ever forget that much. Whatever his reasons, *he* came to *me*."

Tonight, with all that blood...it triggered something you thought was dormant.

Smug Tim says that by using a technique called Flooding — reviewing the worst things we experience over and over — we can get bored of the bad memories. Instead, you suspect the memory of the Cuban beach is *more* entrenched in your memory now because you've reawakened some cruel brain cells that make the scene fresh. They've been waiting to be rediscovered.

"Your father slept with some tourist's wife while they were on vacation?"

"My father was a handsome man. My mother, Maritza...I think she must have suspected him, not of killing that guy, of course, but sleeping around. When he died...her reaction made more sense to me later. Anyway, just before we left Cuba, my father sold America to her on the basis of the usual stuff...opportunity, promises of riches, awful, overpriced hot dogs and beer in a baseball stadium. The clincher was that he came home one day from his job at the hotel all puffed up with some stupid story about how we should move to America because he had pride and wanted to be treated better."

"Doesn't that make sense?"

"There was some nonsense about buying my brother Rodolpho and me baseball caps. The Cuban police would have picked him up in a minute if the man's wife had told them she'd slept with the help. I guess she kept her mouth shut and got sympathy and all the inheritance."

Willow stares at you differently now. Her eyes are wet.

"Is all this conversation still sexy?"

"No. It's just sad. I wish I had a cigarette."

"I don't want the future mother of my children smoking. Could it be sexy in a sad way?"

"Or a Thai stick. Thai sticks are — you ever tried them? It's a citrusy taste and makes me feel light and breezy. Thai sticks are a sweet high."

You let that go. Instead you say, "I left a couple things out."

"What else could there be?"

"Walking back along the beach, my father held my hand. He never held my hand, not since I was very little. He didn't think it looked right. Wasn't manly enough. That morning he held my hand tight and I looked back toward the corpse. He yanked me to him and told me not to look back. Then he did the weirdest, creepiest thing. He sang. My father had a lovely singing voice, but this he sang just loud enough for only me to hear. He sang, 'That could be *you*. That could be *you*!' Like some kind of sick show tune. I know guys have weird battlefield reactions and euphoria and whatnot, but he sang that to me as we walked away."

Willow shakes her head, disgusted now. Not what you were going for. "That better be the most fucked up part because this is awful and — "

"Exhausting, yeah."

"No," she says. "I'm still with you."

"Would it be sexy again if I told you I kept my father's secret until now?"

Willow's eyes narrow. "Is that a fact or an Irish fact?"

You stand and cross to her. You kneel at her feet and take her hand and kiss her palm. You hold it to your cheek.

Willow stands and drops her teacup and what remains of her tea to the thick, white rug. She pulls you to your feet to lead you upstairs.

At the doorway to the master bedroom, you hesitate. She doesn't know all your quirks yet and the time is inopportune. "I am pretty banged up. I won't be able to get my shirt off without screaming, so I'll have to leave it on, okay?"

"Whatever you need, Jesus. I'll do the work tonight. I'll make you scream, but you'll forget the pain."

"That's called the Gate Theory of Pain."

"What?" She opens her blouse.

"Never mind." You slide the fabric of her shirt across her skin, down and away. "When I first saw you. Oh, man, I can't tell you."

"When I first saw you, I had no idea," she says. "I didn't know at all. And now, after all that's happened, you're my Lion's Mane Jellyfish."

You slip behind her and feel the weight of her breasts in your hands. It feels odd and...unfamiliar...to reach *up* to cup her breasts. Then, "Um, what?"

"Lion's Mane Jellyfish. They are massive, freaky jellyfish that have been swimming or floating or whatever...don't stop that with your hands.... That's nice. I like it slow and gentle...at first." She sinks back and leans against you, lets her head sink back, gives you her throat.

"Lion's Mane Jellyfish have been around the Arctic Ocean since before dinosaurs. I saw a picture of one on Facebook. They have all these tendrils and they grab passing fish and pull them in. The fish never see it coming. They're swimming...yeah...they're swimming and — more! *Rougher now*, Jesus...mmm...oh, god, I can't wait! Um...the prey never see the jellyfish coming. They get stung. They're pulled in. They get eaten. By the way, I *really* enjoy getting eaten, Jesus."

"I'm starving, Willow. Feed me."

She straightens and turns and bends to kiss you, her tongue finding yours. She squeezes you tight. Your body aches, but that's going away as your blood heads south. Willow pulls her head back, but grinds against you as she reaches for the small of your back and pulls your SIG from its home in your belt holster.

Willow holds up the pistol for a moment, studying it. "Boys and their toys. I don't need one of these to blow your brains out." She smiles, winks and slowly, tortuously, runs her long pink tongue across her upper lip. Her lips are full and moist and painted red. She tosses the SIG on the chair and turns her attention to your tie, unknotting it.

You stop her hands at the second button of your Oxford shirt and shake your head.

"I can feel muscles under that shirt," she says as she unbuckles your belt and tosses it aside. "That'll do for now."

You kiss the fingertips of her left hand while she slowly rubs your hard on with the heel of her right. You move to her nipples, kissing them each delicately. She presses against your mouth, urging you to suck harder. Flicking your tongue across her aureolas wins low, approving moans. Except for the high heels, she stands naked.

Her skin is hot against your face and her heavy-lidded gaze is only for you as you slip your hand down her belly and between her legs, teasing and stirring. Wet and panting, she leans against you, her knees buckling, spreading her legs — an insistent invitation. You kneel to serve.

For the second time tonight, you watch with pleasure as you make someone's eyes roll up to the whites. The future Mrs. Diaz's eyes roll back like a slot machine as she gasps and writhes under your tongue. You want to do that to her every night and every day for the rest of your lives and you tell her so.

"That sounds delightful and impractical. Ooh..." she wriggles. "We'll get dehydrated."

She pulls you up, then pushes you down on the bed and you let her take your pants off. "Mm," she says as she whips off your boxer briefs, eyes widening. "I have plans for that!"

When Willow pulls at your tie — forgotten and hanging around your neck — but you stop her as she reaches for the buttons of your shirt again.

"Please?" She wraps your silk tie around her hands and wrists. She raises her arms behind her head as she sinks into the bed, stretching back, her legs spread wide. "I promise I won't hurt you. And I'll never bite unless you beg me to."

You kiss her and tease her clit until she stiffens. You stop just before she's about to go over the threshold.

"Cruel!"

Willow grasps your cock and slowly licks her lips again, studying your reaction. She doesn't move her fist. She smiles and watches your face as she flicks the tip of her tongue up and down the shaft. She treats you like a lollipop with long slow licks, her gaze locked with yours. Finally, you have memories you want to keep. She makes you slick until you shake with lust and potential, but just as you think she'll give you relief and envelop you in her hot mouth, she pulls back and smiles wider.

"See? I can be mean, too!"

You chuckle and rise to unwind the tie from her fists.

"Still no shirt off?" she pouts. "Doesn't seem fair. Here I am, your buffet."

You raise the tie in two hands, a question. She nods her understanding and leans forward. You gently place the tie across her eyes and knot it firmly behind her head. Willow straddles you and, blindfolded, she unbuttons your shirt with nimble fingers.

When you flip her over onto her hands and knees, she stretches back like a cat, her heart-shaped ass in the air. You tease her and, when she pleads for more, you give Willow the only mercy you ever want to give anyone.

Soon, she's on her back again, her legs straight, her toes pointed. One side of her face is hidden under a fall of long blonde hair again, just like it was after she bashed the Wolf's chiseled cheekbone flat. Your dream comes true when she wraps her long legs around you and pulls you tighter to her.

You are desperate. You are fire. Willow is oxygen.

She urges you in and urges you on. She moans louder, meeting each hard thrust as the pace quickens. Willow is the most beautiful woman in the world and, for a change and for tonight, you are the luckiest man.

In the end, you both are savage addicts. Vicodin highs, feral sex and serrated violence: These are the only ways you know to live in the now and make the world go away.

"I want you to only wear heels and never anything else," you whisper in her ear.

"I can't wear the high heels *all* the time, Jesus!"

"I'll carry you." You turn out the light by the bed, before she can think to remove her makeshift blindfold.

"You can't," she says beside you in the darkness.

"I'll carry you like a secret."

A KISS BEFORE DYING

Chill has a coffee ready for you when you come downstairs at 11:30 a.m. Grocery bags are spread out over the kitchen table, as if he's preparing for a siege, which you guess he is. He hands you a travel coffee mug and the keys to his SUV. "The boss wants to see you. I'll protect Willow until you've sorted out this mess."

"He's putting a lot on one guy, don't you think?"

"Yeah. Long as I'm not the guy, I'm good with it. She sleeping?"

"Yeah. She'll be sleeping in." You can't resist a wolfish grin and strutting a bit on your way out the back door.

Chill raises his coffee mug in a mock toast and rolls his eyes. "Get your ass over to the diner."

"I'm going along with my ass if that's okay," you say. "It's all attached."

"Long as you don't get it shot off, yeah. You've had the gratuitous sex and violence. Be careful. I expect it's mostly violence from here on out."

Samuel Clemont sits in his wheelchair with the M4 Carbine across his lap. He knows that you and Willow stayed in the safe house last night, so he's probably guessed the rest. Better he think about you and Willow in bed than you and his only daughter fighting the forces of evil in a grimy parking garage. He locks the door behind you and rolls on your heels to the kitchen.

121

"Chill told me you ran into trouble."

"Let's not live in the past. That was the Wolf. I'm more worried about the meeting I had with the fat guy who paid my rent."

You sit across from him at the kitchen's small table. He offers you nothing so you hold the travel mug in your hands and concentrate on the heat seeping through to your palms as you watch him eat. He's cooked a thin steak for himself, so rare it's bloody, and slapped it on a thick slab of Texas toast made gray with juice from the meat. The grease of the shiny hash browns unsettles your stomach.

"What's in the shipment besides Scorpions?"

He stops chewing and swallows hard.

"Your daughter's in serious danger and the Recipients know who we all are, so let's not dance anymore and get down to it. An anonymous fat man, who keeps a monster named Lurch as a pet, came to see me yesterday. You said they were like the Amish. My right kidney is so bruised, it disagrees. Vehemently."

"Never mind them. I expect you'll take care of The Victorious for me fast so I can do the deal with The Recipients and reopen the diner."

"Well, smell you! Ha! Look, these guys have scoped you out thoroughly and they don't screw around. The Recipients threatened all of us. These are not people you should be doing business with."

"Too late for that. Willow won't move outside for sunshine and fresh air until this is over, so, yeah, we'd all like to get this sorted out before she gets scurvy. I'm holed up here protecting my business. Chill's watching Willow. You are in charge of solving the Wolf problem. If you'd killed him and his pal last night, you'd have made some real progress and the fat man would have no reason to give you more motivation."

"I don't need more motivation. You've held out on me. This can't be just about Scorpions."

"Why are you making this complicated, Jesus?"

"The anonymous fat man I mentioned? He's secretive, but his face did some interesting things when I mentioned the Russian guns. What else do you have to tell me?"

Clemont puts his fork down and sighs. "There's a bit more to the story."

"Better give it all to me this time so we can both make sure Willow stays safe."

"I told you I had a business partner."

"Harry."

"Yeah. Harry got the shipment and I paid him off. It should have been that simple."

"Wait. *You* paid him off?"

"Yeah."

"Up front, in advance, the whole deal, paid 360 degrees? You said before that you 'put money toward it'."

"Yeah. So?"

"See, that kind of pisses me off, Sam. I thought I was just dealing with a guy who owned a diner who was willing to store some guns for the hardcore dealer. The way you described it before, you were just the storage guy, the tube."

He shrugs and points at the grill. "Gotta justify at least some of my income to the IRS."

"I must have been blinded by your daughter's beauty."

"Could be you're just not as smart as you think you are. Nobody's as smart as they think they are."

You take a long, deep cleansing breath. That was the first thing Smug Tim taught you. You squeeze your shoulders to your ears and wait for the muscles to relax. It still doesn't help. "How long have you been an arms dealer, Sam?"

"Since I got blown up and my country failed to pay to get me back to a normal life. Technically, I've been an arms dealer since I was busted down a rank for bringing a pistol back from Iraq after my second tour. They took the pistol, but when I went back I got more and started selling them at gun shows to make up for the loss in pay." For the first time, you see sadness creep in, prying off his mask of anger. "It wasn't for spite. I had bills. Then just before the end of my third tour, I got blown up. Then I had more bills."

When you start to feel sorry for him, you remind yourself he hasn't been straight with you.

He lights up a menthol cigarette and blows smoke at the ceiling. "I had no problems moving rifles and small arms. Ever since Obama was elected, the gun biz got crazy good. The NRA keeps saying the president is going to take away all their guns so the country's gone nuts. Obama hasn't looked sideways at gun laws. Mitt Romney passed more gun control laws than Obama. Romney passed an assault weapons ban, but that doesn't matter to the gun nuts. Since Obama came into office, the diner's done worse but the gun business is better than ever. Remember that shooting in Colorado? The one at the midnight showing of the Batman movie? Applications for gun permits went up fifty percent right after."

"Keep going."

"Anyway, crazy as shithouse rats, some people. They buy more than they can afford and then bury them somewhere, ready for the race war that never comes. If they're so sure of the fall of civilization, they should buy more seeds and learn to become farmers, not fighters. And The Victorious? If they get hold of the shipment, cops and civvies alike are going to be running and screaming everywhere. Chicago will be Tombstone, if the Earps had six shooters and the outlaw cowboys had machine pistols."

He looks away for the first time and studies the floor, his lips a thin line. "Partners in crime. I thought Harry and I were solid. Like brothers, you could say. He was a funny guy. Could tell a great story. You remind me of Harry, actually."

If Samuel Clemont had given you a wink just then, you would have really liked him. Instead, you search and find the hint of a smile at the corner of his mouth. That's the closest you'll come to being friends with the man who would have been your father-in-law. But he only has a few minutes left to live, so what does it matter? Of course, you don't know that yet.

Clemont shrugs with one shoulder, looks at his cold steak and grimaces. "The only way Willow and I can get away from the diner life is a big score and this is big. I tried to play it down before, so you wouldn't be too greedy, but, after last night's incident in the parking garage— "

"You're killing me, man. Spill!"

"The fat man called. He wants to meet at an abandoned warehouse tomorrow night. His people are coming from Florida and he's not going to be put off anymore. A firestorm's coming."

"Just do the deal with the Recipients and I'll figure something out to keep the gang off your back."

"It's already negotiated. When you failed to kill the Wolf and his sidekick last night, he decided you're too soft. A liability. The fat man says I can split up the shipment so The Victorious will get their Scorpions after all."

"But, what are The Recipients getting if The Victorious are getting the Scorpions?"

He sighs. "Mines."

In the sand wars, you thought it was a terrible thing to be ignorant of what you were fighting and dying for. That's one of the reasons you were so anxious to leave the military and get out of the desert. Now you wish you didn't know what you were fighting for. What might The Recipients do with ordnance that heavy? Stage another Waco, Texas where the FBI kills another bunch of women and children in a cult siege? This problem just graduated from worries about the Chicago police, ATF and FBI to an anxiety attack with Homeland Security. This is the kind of homegrown, terrorist-level douchebaggery that could get you stuck back in Cuba, jailed forever in Guantanamo Bay with no salsa music.

Returning to Cuba in chains would be so ironic on a cosmic scale it feels like it's *bound* to happen. The man who would be your father-in-law is right. You aren't as smart as you thought you were.

When the lock turns and clunks in the front door, that thought is confirmed. It's the Lone Wolf, limping but purposeful, coming through the front door. You whip out your SIG as you slip to the kitchen's doorway, already lining up your shot on the big guy.

You shout to Clemont to hunt cover, but when you glance his way, his rifle is pointed at your head.

"It's about time you showed up, Wolf! You're late! I've been stalling this little Cuban asshole for what feels like days! I'm tired of telling him what he wants to hear!"

Of course. The Victorious will get the Scorpions. Your reward for trying to keep Willow pure is delighted vengeance for the wannabes. The Recipients get the mines and the Wolf gets you.

You aren't *nearly* as smart as you thought you were.

IN THE LINE OF FIRE

What's coming isn't impossible, but the scene is so unlikely you have to question if you're really seeing what you're seeing. The left side of his face is bandaged where Willow smashed in his cheekbone last night. He looks like the guy from *Phantom of the Opera*, if the Phantom ran around carrying makeshift explosives. The Lone Wolf stops in the middle of the diner carrying two wine bottles and a longneck: Three molotov cocktails in the hollow of his shoulder sling.

"Hey, baby, I'm home! Did you miss me?" The Lone Wolf looks like a zombie who rose from a hospital bed and stumbled here to eat your brains.

"The Wolf wants *you*," Clemont says. "If he gets you and the Scorpions, all my problems go away. Thanks for pissing off the Wolf so bad you changed his priorities. He wanted the whole thing, too — mines and all — until I offered *you* up. Now everybody can be happy with what they get and Willow and I will still get that big score. I'll tell Willow you said goodbye."

You watch as the Wolf flicks a silver lighter under a rag fuse.

"I don't think so," you say. "I think he means to make sure nobody gets the shipment."

Willow's father laughs derisively, but from his wheelchair in the kitchen, he can't see what you do. The Lone Wolf lights the first fuse, smiling wide. The first bottle arcs over the counter, shatters and bursts in the middle of the kitchen. Clemont stops laughing and starts screaming. One of his shirtsleeves is on fire, which explains why he misses you with his first shot.

Frantic, he wheels back from the flame, heading for the doorway to take a shot at the Lone Wolf.

The Wolf throws the next bomb straight to the rear of the diner and you throw yourself backward to dodge the next torrent of flame. Willow's father rolls in your way. You tumble over him and you're both knocked to the floor. The wheelchair clatters and you and Clemont land awkwardly on the hard linoleum. Your SIG skitters out of your grip and away. Crimson, yellow, orange and blue vines of flame race up the walls, chewing through the building's guts. Old construction materials and years of cooking grease strengthen the fire to a roar.

"You will not be selling anything to those Nazis!" the Lone Wolf bellows, coming closer. "Harry wanted to keep the bombs away from them! I'm going to make sure they never get them!"

Nazis?

A smoke detector beeps its jangling alarm from the ceiling.

"You hear?" Wolf screams above the alarm. "*Nothing* to white supremacists!"

"We had a deal!" Clemont looks shaken and confused.

"Harry told us the plan, cracker!"

You struggle to rise and get your pistol, but Clemont manages to hold on to his rifle. The muzzle hovers an inch from your face. Clemont holds the weapon awkwardly, one-handed with his burned arm, his free hand cupping the wound. He grits his teeth against the pain. Despite his screaming nerves, he's still got you locked.

"I'm going to burn alive in here, Jesus, but," he aims between your eyes. "I'll save you that, you sonofabitch."

"The fat man will be on the war path if they don't get those mines. I can still protect Willow. Chill can't do it all alone. Not now. Your daughter needs another bodyguard. Me."

Clemont hesitates a second and sometimes a second is all it takes to change everything. His eyes flick to the Lone Wolf, whose rictus grin is visible in the pass-through. With his good arm, the Wolf raises the last bottle bomb above his head, ready to give you a foretaste of hell.

The M4 booms. The wine bottle shatters and the Lone Wolf screams as the liquid flame rushes over him.

You rip the carbine from Clemont's hands, denying him a second shot. You rise, pointing the rifle at Clemont's head as he pulls himself away from the reaching flames.

It would be best if The Lone Wolf teleported into Lake Michigan and then directly to a hospital burn unit. Since he doesn't have that technology, the next best option, would be to stop, drop and roll. Instead, he runs back and forth in a panic, feeding oxygen to the flames. Not all mercies are tender. You raise the rifle, squeeze the trigger and drop the Lone Wolf with one shot, cutting short his agonized wail.

Clemont's pant cuffs are alight at his knees, but maybe he can't feel anything below the waist because he's focused on tearing off his smoking shirt. Tattoos wind around his body. The dragon wrapped around a burning cross is ironic because in another minute the dragon will look like it's spewing real fire. The letters WC on his upper arm must stand for Willow Clemont. The spiderweb tattoo at his elbow is a lesser known indication that he's killed a black man and he's proud of that fact. The swastika across his belly is also a strong sign that you've made a terrible mistake. The quicker you shoot him, the faster you move on to living in the now, that happy time when you aren't supplying explosives to white supremacists.

Clemont screams for your help and beats at the flames, swearing at his useless stumps. Sweat pops out on your forehead. The tiny kitchen is an oven and the hot air is a giant hand, pushing you backward.

"Where are the mines?"

"Fuck you!"

"Tell me where the goddamn shipment is or I'll leave you!"

"It's in a truck parked at East Wesley and North Main! In a parking lot! Get me out of here!"

The flames climb higher. "Where exactly?"

Instead of answering you, Clemont pulls a set of keys out of his pocket and throws them at you. "You've got it! It's a white panel van at East Wesley and North Main! It's a regular child molester wagon! You can't miss it! Okay? Now get me out of here!"

You have just enough time to grab Willow's father and drag him to the rear of the kitchen. You don't.

Instead you use that precious time to give him the middle finger and back away. "You pointed a gun at me! You were going to give me up to the Wolf! You were going to kill me! I save you, you'll do it again and we both know it. I don't forgive, Sam! *I do not fucking forgive!*"

He curses you. If the venom of spewed hate alone could kill, you'd be in flames along with Samuel Clemont. He shrieks in pain. His hair is on fire. Samuel speaks in tongues. He's still screaming gibberish as you retrieve your SIG from the floor. By the time you give him the double-tap, his death is a microscopic mercy.

We're on the same team, the fat man had said.

How can you ever be pure for Willow now? Samuel Clemont has stained your soul. You'll have to keep this secret from Willow, too. People in love aren't supposed to have secrets, but killing your future father-in-law makes the short list of crimes you have to keep to yourself. Willow's father has cursed you forever. You'll never be the good guy. Your best hope is to find a way back from evil to less bad.

Eyes watering and coughing, you crouch low to get under the smoke filling the diner and rush for the back door. You still have hope right up until you smack into it. The exit door is locked.

No, *not locked!*

Through the tiny wire window, you see a big Chevy parked with its front bumper kissing the door. The door is worse than locked. It's blocked by a couple of tons of metal.

Worse still, Skeet, half his face bandaged, lies slumped on the hood with a shotgun across his legs. With visible effort, he raises his head and his hazy gaze finds you not more than a few feet away on the wrong side of the door. He grins. Hatred shimmers in its purity and righteousness through Skeet's broken face.

The ceiling caves in behind you as a black cloud reaches for you like a choking claw.

You're living in the now, but probably only for another few minutes.

GET SHORTY

"Hi, Skeet!" you shout through the door. "I feel a curious burning sensation! You should tell your mother 'cuz she'll want to see her doctor about it!"

Scarface Skeet smiles back placidly and flips you off. You can't goad him into coming in after you. You're not even sure you deserve mercy so there's no sense wasting the rapidly burning oxygen on him.

The diner's walk-in freezer might buy you a little time. You whirl and burst through the freezer door and slam it behind you. The light is still on and it's chilly in here. It's about the size of a large walk-in closet.

When you were a Military Policeman, you envied firefighters. They dealt with fewer drunks and getting girls was easy. You called them basement savers and bucket heads then. You could sure use them now.

In the movies, a firefighter in full gear would arrive. You'd thank him, raise your pistol and ask politely for him to give you all his gear so you could make a clean escape. That would work if you were Tom Cruise. The script would allow for the rest of the firefighting crew to be incredibly stupid and blind once you got to the safety of the sidewalk.

You need cavalry. Chill's too far away. Willow's with Chill. God never answers your prayers. You only have one ally left in the city and you hope he's not too drunk to answer your call.

The phone rings and rings. You imagine Sgt. Billy's old, arthritic fingers scrabbling for the phone, searching through filthy pockets filled with moldy sandwiches.

"Yeah?" Salvation. Maybe.

"I'm trapped in the back of the diner. God Eats is on fire!"

"Yeah?"

"The only way out is through the back door and a guy has blocked it with a car! He's sitting on the hood with a shotgun!"

"Yeah?"

"Can you help me?"

"Who is this?"

"Sgt. Billy — !"

"Relax, son. Grow a sense of humor. I'm on my way. A couple of minutes." He still has the cell you gave him to his ear as he runs. His breath is short and fast already. Is "a couple of minutes" really two minutes? Or is that the generic two minutes, meaning five or maybe ten?" No smoke is coming in around the cold locker's door, but you resist touching it. If it's hot, you're already fucked and if you're dead by fire, you don't want to know that. Smoke inhalation would have been kinder. You loosen your tie and try to slow your rapid breath.

You look around the locker. Boxes of beef burgers, fruit, vegetables and milk sit in an array on the shelf. Unfortunately, there's not one asbestos suit or oxygen tank to be had. You've got nothing else to do so you hang up on Billy and call 911.

"911. What is the nature of the emergency?"

"Imminent fiery death." You give her the nearest cross street since you have no idea what the address might be.

The operator tells you someone else has called in the fire but asks you your name. "Salvador," you say. "Salvador Dali."

"Is there anyone still in building, Mr. Dali?"

"Yes. One person in the back of the diner in the cold locker...soon to be the hot locker."

"Who is this person?" the operator asks.

The light over your head fries out.

"He didn't live long enough to figure that out." You hang up.

You call Sgt. Billy back. *Ring. Ring. Ring.* Nothing.

You call him again. There's no voicemail on a throwaway phone. You wish you'd sprung for a full cellular plan. You could be leaving a message, telling Willow how sorry you are that you failed her. You'd tell her Sam is dead and promise to say hello to him if you saw him on the other side. Instead, you go to the locker door and listen for a scream or a shout. You need to hear something soon. The words of some forgotten army trainer come back to you again. "Every minute, a fire doubles in size." The diner isn't that big.

You pace. It's four strides, back and forth.

Some things would be better not to know, but it's too late for that. You wish you hadn't seen those tattoos. Did Willow's father go full Nazi after his desert war, or was that from before? He couldn't have gotten into the military with those tatts, could he? Maybe. Samuel Clemont had been a lifer, but maybe he could let it out and be himself later in life.

From experience, you've seen officers look the other way on lots of heinous acts. Plus, after 9/11, some behavioural restrictions were lifted because the brass was desperate for bodies to fill uniforms and body bags. You knew a couple of white supremacists in your unit in Iraq, but by the time they got to Afghanistan they seemed to be cured of their hatred for blacks and reserved all their bigotry for Muslims. It's hard to stay a racist when you serve alongside the same people you were taught to hate. Some guys managed to stay true to dumb and hateful but most of the rest conceded that people of the cool and colorful persuasion serving their country and saving their lives were at least "some of the good ones."

You try the cell again. Again, no answer.

Where is Willow now? You could call her and say goodbye, but you don't want to hear her answer when you tell her Samuel is dead. Besides, she must have known her father was a hateful racist. People don't get tattoos to hide them. She knew he was an arms dealer. Did she...could she know he was selling arms — no, *explosives* — to Neo-Nazis? You're all for capitalism, but there's a common code, even in a world where "Never again," clearly means nothing. If you don't have a code, you're the bad guy. You've already been the bad guy. You're supposed to be beyond that by now. So much for therapy. Fuck you, Smug Tim!

You're still a guy who carries around a SIG Sauer P220 and a switchblade in your sock. You want a bottle of Vicodin more than ever. You could chug that back, be set alight and not really mind. You'd just lay on the floor sleepy and quietly burn to death watching all the pretty colors. Or you could crack open the locker door and let the smoke take you.

There's a crash from the front of the diner. It's really only been a few minutes, but old buildings like this? The insulation is probably old newspapers and ancient Sears catalogues. You put your palm to the wall of the locker. Beyond that wall, you're sure, is another wall of flame. The locker wall is so hot to the touch, it's uncomfortable to hold your bare palm against it for more than a few seconds. The air feels thin as you push it in and out, beginning to gasp. Is the oxygen burning away, or is this panic? If this is just overwhelming panic, it seems like a reasonable time for it to kick in. It feels like you're drowning again.

The weight of the SIG in your palm is reassuring. That's a better option. Take fate in your own hands, close your eyes, put the muzzle in your mouth, pull the trigger and see what comes next. You were always so sure someone else would kill you. Big Denny De Molina or one of his crew would step out of the shadows, put a muzzle to your head and say, "Big Denny says hello."

That would be better than this. *Nazis! Nazis with a plan,* the Lone Wolf had said. Nazis with *mines.* Lurch and the fat man are going to blow something up and that no doubt means the deaths of innocent civilians are on you because you couldn't stop The Recipients.

Something else falls and crashes beyond the freezer's walls.

Too late for hope now. People have told you you're a funny guy all your life, but you'll never be a stand-up comedian like Louis CK, Joe Rogan or Joey CoCo Diaz (no relation). You'll never get the chance to make the world a better place, with laughing crowds applauding and loving you. You'll never see France, or Spain or the Vatican. You really wanted to check out those cool castles in Scotland, hang out in pubs in Ireland and wander around London, too. You'll never see Hollywood. You wanted so much more for yourself. You wanted to be an optimist like Willow. You wanted to be hopeful for the human race, despite the daily news that smacked the shit out of that idea every fucking day. Like the old dude in *The Matrix* said, "Hope is humanity's greatest asset and its greatest weakness." Something like that.

If you shoot yourself right away, you don't have to torture yourself with all the things you never became. You always felt you were meant for bigger things and the profession of hit man was just something that happened to you, not something you chose. If you got another chance, you tell yourself you'd make better choices. Then the quieter voice in your head that you don't listen to enough speaks up. "I'm about to die and I'm still bullshitting myself. Lots of people start out bad but make it to good."

You cross to the locker door and touch it with your bare palm. Hopeful. It is too hot. Sgt. Billy is too late. Death by fire. You sure didn't see that coming. You could douse yourself in cold milk when it gets really hot in here, or will the fire eat up all the oxygen and leave you gasping on the floor until flaming beams crush you from above?

The SIG feels heavy: like a secret kept; like a love denied; like the memory of a disappointed friend you are forced to carry to the end. Good news: the end is here. What's the real rule on suicide? Is that something that really pisses off God? If so, He doesn't understand your problems. Screw Him.

Something shifts and falls against the wall behind you. That must be the bathroom ceiling caving in. Where are the firefighters? Even if they save you, how much better off would you be? With a couple of bodies out front and your record, you may as well burn. You can't talk your way out of the murder investigation back in New York, anyway. Either way, you're dead and Willow's far away. Sometimes clever just isn't enough.

You can't even say you had a good run. You raise the SIG to your mouth and scrape the muzzle across your teeth painfully, chipping a canine, as Sgt. Billy drives the hulking Chevy through the back wall of the diner. He takes out the back wall and the door to the freezer, missing you by inches.

Sometimes clever isn't enough, but brute force often does the job. It's still too late to make it to good. Now is the time to be a badass.

THE FUGITIVE

When the Chevy bursts through the freezer wall to the inferno that was the diner, heat and billowing smoke pours over you. Sgt. Billy throws the Chevy into reverse and squeals back out of the fire, nearly running you over twice. The late December air feels like a welcome dip in a cold pool during a heatwave. Fresh oxygen feeds the fire and stokes it to a raging blast furnace that pushes you out of the hole in the rear wall in a swirl of smoke.

Sirens run through discordant scales out front and a crowd has gathered in the back alley to watch the flames stretch up. They are a motley crew of a few teens with scraggly beards and a dumpy woman pushing a stroller. The crowd stands still, wide-eyed and slack-jawed, all eyes on you.

A small child in the stroller sits forward to get a better look at you. Dressed in a pink snowsuit, the little girl peers at you with huge blue eyes.

You stagger out of the flaming building toward them and lean heavily against the old Chevrolet's fender, sucking the crisp air into your lungs between raspy coughing jags. The air is so cold, it cuts. When you're sure you can speak without throwing up, you shout to the alley's assembly, *"Ta da!"*

Only the little girl claps. Tough crowd.

"Again! Again!" she squeals and only then do a few of the teens have the grace to chuckle at your peculiar spectacle. Following the little kid's lead, you get sporadic, confused applause from the slack-jawed onlookers.

Sgt. Billy leans over, pops the passenger door and beckons you in as he guns the engine. "You comin', Chief?"

You tighten and straighten your tie, bow to the crowd and jump in the car. You're still coughing and choking on smoke. Sgt. Billy rounds the corner and slides away just as a cop car turns and powers down the alley, lights blazing and sirens stuttering a staccato warning. If the cop thinks to pursue the Chevy, he won't have any time because, as you glance back, a ladder truck turns after him to attack the fire from the rear of the building. The alley is blocked.

A shotgun sits on the floor of the back seat. "Where's Skeet?"

Sgt. Billy pulls over and turns off the engine. "What is a Skeet?"

"The skinny black guy with the shotgun! What'd you do with him?"

"That fella is in the trunk. Sorry I took so long. It was a real oven in there, huh?" Excited and pale, his breathing is very shallow.

"How'd Skeet end up in the trunk?"

"How do you think? I put him in there. I walked up, grabbed the shotgun and smacked him in the forehead a few times with the stock. It's enough to discourage anyone. He didn't have any fight in him."

"Good thinking. Between his beatings, he's not going to be able to work a cash register for a long time. Hey...he was armed. Respect! You are still a soldier, man!"

"It wasn't like that, dumbass." His eyes narrow. He looks pained and even more pale.

"How was it?"

"I'm an ancient homeless guy. What, you think I tried some bullshit Rambo stuff? I stumbled up and told him I was having a heart attack."

"Wow. That's more good thinking."

He winces. "I wasn't faking, you asshole. I'm an old alcoholic. You think I run every day to stay in shape?" Sgt. Billy takes his pulse, pressing two fingers into his neck and gives you a worried smile. "It was only a couple blocks, but I'm not up to this shit. The job was supposed to be recon only, you dickless fuck!"

You jump out, run around to his side and rip his door open. In a couple of minutes you have him lying across the back seat. Then you're behind the wheel and headed for Mercy Hospital. You push the accelerator as hard as you dare, slaloming through openings in traffic.

"What's this all about, Chief? You said you were doing this to protect your lady."

"I am."

"My left arm hurts bad. I'd like to know what I'm dying for."

"Hold on. We'll be at the hospital soon. I'll get you to Emerge. We're going to take some corners pretty fast in a second, so let me know if you hear any screaming from the trunk."

"And if you don't?"

"Then I'll take those corners a little faster. I'd love to have a chat with Skeet instead of dealing with all this macho bullshit. It would be great to get some answers."

His breathing comes faster now, but Sgt. Billy still manages to ask you the dreaded question. "You one of the good guys, Jesus?"

You hear something dark in Sgt. Billy's tone and you risk turning the rearview mirror down so you can glimpse him. He holds the shotgun. It's pointed at your head. You take his questions more seriously. "I got into this to save a young woman named Willow, the tall blonde I told you to look out for. Her father hired me to kill the man who was dealing her drugs to help her stay clean and sober."

Sgt. Billy emits a tight chuckle. "Only one drug dealer in all of Chicago, is there?"

"I followed her to a couple of meetings. I sat in the back and listened to her talk about her struggle to get past the pills. She wants to quit. Her dad wanted me to cut her supply line so I cut it."

A horn blares to your left and behind you as you weave in and cut off a slower car about to cross an intersection. You lose traction on ice, slide and fishtail as you turn a corner and blow through a red light to more blaring horns and narrow misses.

"And?"

"Then the dad had another job for me. He's got some guns and stuff to sell. He told me to somehow keep his gun shipment out of the hands of the local street gang. He told me they killed his partner Harry. Now I think that's not true."

"So you got me to watch the Victorious's headquarters. Nothing came of that."

"The hell it didn't. If you hadn't been so close by, I'd be bacon."

"The Victorious get the guns?"

"No, but I know now where the shipment is." You flash your lights and honk a warning and a pedestrian caught halfway on a crosswalk sees you speeding toward him. He scampers back to the sidewalk and cowers behind a light stand as you flash by. You don't know the city well, but the hospital must be close.

Sgt. Billy wheezes as he speaks. "Why the fire?" You can hear his pain.

"Willow's father's partner Harry warned the Lone Wolf — the guy from the Victorious who set the diner on fire — that there was more than guns to the deal. White supremacists wanted explosives."

There's the hospital. You take the exit going the wrong way and your tires lose traction in the slush for several feet before the brakes bring the Chevy to a shuddering stop. You jump out. "Somebody get a doctor!" A nurse smoking near the entrance drops her cigarette and runs inside, you presume for a gurney. You pop the back door open, sure that the man who saved you from an awful death is dead.

Sgt. Billy is pale as paper, but he's still got enough strength in his right hand to level the shotgun at your head. "You're telling me you're a hit man who's helping a guy get explosives to Nazis?"

"You put it that way, it sounds bad."

"Make it sound better." He's too weak to hold the shotgun much longer. His aim falls to the center of your chest.

"Sergeant, I'm telling you my father-in-law-to-be played me but I'm going to make everything okay."

"How?"

"Not a clue. I haven't had a lot of time to think about it."

"It's always something with girlfriends and their daddies. Are the doctors coming soon?"

You look back. A security guy is eyeing you, but no help appears to be on the way. "Could we get some help over here? Guy's having a heart attack!" The security guard nods and waves to someone behind him through the glass.

"Willow's father thought he had a deal with the guy from The Victorious to get the guns and kill me, since I pissed 'em off so much, beating the shit out of Skeet and all."

"I get that. I'm kinda pissed at you, too."

"I get that a lot. The Lone Wolf was told about the Nazi side of the equation by Willow's Dad's business partner."

"Harry."

"Right! All I know is the white supremacists have some kind of plot to carry out with the mines that even a badass gang member wouldn't approve of."

"The business partner who warned the gang and soured the deal... Harry. Where is he?"

"I don't know. He flew the coop with a bunch of Willow's Dad's money."

He lowers the muzzle. The shotgun points at your crotch. "If I pulled the trigger right now and made you a eunuch, do you even know why everybody would be better off?"

Pounding feet and a gurney with a screeching wheel come up behind you.

Sgt. Billy points the shotgun at the floor and offers it to you. "Take it. Where I'm going, I won't need it."

You take the shotgun gently and hide it under your trench coat.

"You're not all the way a bad guy, Jesus. I knew that when you bought me a sandwich."

"Thanks."

"You don't operate out of malice. You're just a complete idiot who can't see the forest for the blonde."

"Thanks."

A rough hand pulls you away. Two orderlies, two nurses and a doctor have finally arrived.

"What? Were you guys on a coffee break?"

A black nurse pushes you farther back. "We're swamped in emerge. What happened?"

"He's a homeless guy named Sgt. Billy. He thinks he's having a heart attack."

"What's his last name?"

"As far as I know? Billy."

"Sir! Can you hear me?" one of the orderlies asks.

"Of course, I can hear you! I'm right here! My chest feels tight. Feels like a car is parked on my chest and it hurts like hell. Excuse my language, ladies, but I'm not fucking deaf!"

"Sounds like a heart attack," the doctor says.

"Gee-zuzz fuck, of *course* it sounds like a heart attack! Please excuse my language, ladies. This is my first heart attack."

A nurse titters and tells him to relax as the orderlies yank Sgt. Billy out of the back seat and on to the gurney. "You're feisty. We'll get you inside with some warm blankets, hook you up to a monitor and get you straightened out."

You walk beside him as they roll him toward the entrance to Emerge. "Jesus," Sgt. Billy says, "you aren't seeing the big picture."

"People keep saying that."

"Then *listen*! The father-in-law's business partner who took off with the money?"

"Yeah, yeah. I don't know where he is!"

"Oh, hero. You're too close to see it. You've already met him, you big dope."

"Um...oh." Your scalp heats up. Willow's uncle is out of town and you slept in his bed last night. Harry was Samuel Clemont's business partner, the man he said had been "*like a brother*". Thomas-not-Thomas! The man you left dead in a coffee table was Uncle Harry. You've killed Willow's dad *and*

143

her Uncle Harry. Fortunately, you don't think she has any more family you can fuck up.

Sgt. Billy watches you work it out and whispers, "Moron." He slides a glance at the surrounding crowd and says, "The nurses here are cute."

The nurse who is the least attractive by far titters her approval.

Once inside and down the hall away from the entrance's cold draft, the doctor pulls his stethoscope from his neck and shushes everyone so he can listen to his patient's heart. You take the moment to pull out your half of the ripped $100 bill you owe Sgt. Billy. Before you can put it in his hand, you're denied your grand gesture. The old man stiffens in pain. His eyes go wide as he inhales with a wet, ratcheting sound. You know that sound. You've heard it a few times: The death rattle. He's starting to drown in the mucus stuck in his throat.

The medical team moves with real urgency now and rushes Sgt. Billy into a trauma room and pulls a curtain. You wave goodbye with the ripped bill. "Sorry.... I swear, Billy. I'll look more carefully from now on. All homeless guys look alike, but I'll look more carefully, I promise. I'll see the difference."

"Sir?"

When you turn, a security guard is already taking you by the arm and you have to stiffen and hug the short stock of the shotgun under your armpit so he doesn't see the muzzle at the hem of your trench. He's a large white guy with a kind face who doesn't walk so much as lumbers like a bear. His huge paw is less than an inch from the weapon under your coat. You're not the religious type, but now would be a good time to rediscover a childhood prayer as he escorts you toward the Emerge entrance.

"It was nice of you to pick up a homeless guy, sir. You're a good Samaritan. A lot of people wouldn't have done that."

"Sure. Had to. He saved my life."

The guard looks at you curiously. "Oh? How's that? You smell of smoke, sir. Was that man in a fire? You pull him out? We'll need to make a full report."

"Long story. To tell you the whole thing would take a book."

"You can't leave your car in front of the ambulance bay. Can you park your car in the parking structure across the street and come back and we'll take your information? You can fill us in."

Once you're outside in the cold air, he lets go and you step back. He's the older sort of rent-a-cop who depends on his size and authority to stop trouble. When trouble does find him, he's the body type to grab hold, wrestle anyone to the ground and sit on them until his buddies arrive with handcuffs. However, looking him up and down, you know this for sure: you can outrun him.

As you and the guard approach the Chevy, a weak but repetitive thumping comes from the trunk. Skeet is awake. "You can have the car, amigo."

"Pardon me? What did you say?"

"The car. It isn't mine. I borrowed it." You open your coat a few inches so he can see the shotgun. "And this." Before he can say anything, you toss him the Chevy's keys. "There's a very unreasonable young black man in the trunk. Could you tell him for me that he should rethink his career choices?"

You back away. The rent-a-cop, wisely, does not move. His gaze isn't on your face, but on the shotgun bulge under your trench. When you get to a corner you yell to him, "He needs medical attention badly! Multiple concussions — and at least one that he deserved. Maybe not. It's still...muddled. His name is *Skeet*! Tell him to change his stupid name, too! And tell him I'm sorry! At least about some of it!"

You turn and hurry on your way. You're even farther away from righteous than you thought.

THE HARDER THEY FALL

It's the logistics that slow any mission. First, you have to get as far away from the hospital as quickly as you can without attracting attention. You want to hold on to the shotgun, so you can't very well grab a cab or a bus or the El. In crowded quarters they'd smell the smoke on your clothes first and spot the bulge under your jacket next. After 9/11, Homeland Security isn't catching many terrorists, but the whole "See something, say something," can really cramp a hit man's style. You search for a good car to steal.

You're pretty desperate to get your style back after old Sgt. Billy spotted the worm in your tequila so easily. You tell yourself you weren't seeing things clearly because you were too close to the action. You wanted to believe Samuel Clemont's cause was just so you could be a hero to Willow. Clemont said you aren't as smart as you think you are. When events happen fast, that can make anyone dumb. At least, that's what you tell yourself.

Heroism is a problem. It's like signing up to kill Osama bin Laden and ending up serving in the wrong country all over again. If Smug Tim were here, you could punch him in his smug face. That would make you feel better, but he would probably give you that same smile, wipe his bloody nose and say something like, "We are doomed to repeat the same painful lessons over and over until we learn the intended lesson." That guy is a longwinded new age Magic Eight Ball.

146

Waiting for dark to finally creep over Chicago takes a couple hours of zig zagging through the city. You spend that time trying to figure out how to tell Willow that her father is dead. She can never know how he died. You can never tell her how you dispatched her Uncle Harry, the tricky yet noble arms dealer, Thomas-not-Thomas. "Dispatched" is such a good word for what you do. It affirms your image as a modern day Musketeer. It also sounds like you're sending the people you kill somewhere. Most of them end up in Hell probably, but if you make a mistake, maybe they're getting to Heaven faster.

Your Drill Instructor believed in Heaven and Hell (yes, as real places) because he wasn't instructing anyone in the ways of murder. Your DI's motto was, "Kill the enemy and whoever may be standing beside the enemy and let Allah sort them out." Not much of a motto, and too long to put on a bumper sticker or a t-shirt.

And you hate killing civilians. Killing the wrong people makes your stomach ache.

Your cell rings. It's Willow. "Jesus?"

"Hi, baby. I've got some bad news."

"Dad's dead."

"Uh. Yes."

"I know."

"What —?"

"I'm in a car with Lurch and another man who says he has no name."

You grit your teeth. Someone else is listening and you can guess who by his heavy breathing. There's something new in Willow's voice, too. Something thin. That is the sound of creeping terror, like a knife at her throat.

"The fat man is listening then," you say. "Anyone else would say Lurch and the fat man. Go ahead. Tell him he's fat. Friends take friends aside and let them know."

She barrels on. "The man with no name says to find the shipment and call him at dawn. He'll tell you where to come to get me and deliver it."

"Tell the fat man to let you out right now because I don't know where the truck is. Samuel is dead and he's the only one who knew. It could be anywhere in the city."

There's a fumbling sound, a roar and a cry. You recognize the fat man's voice. "If you don't know where the truck is, the girl is useless. If the girl is useless, I'll drop her out of the car right now, but I won't be slowing down to do it. In fact, Lurch! Speed up!"

You made a tactical error there. "I know where the truck is. I've got the keys in my pocket. Don't hurt Willow. You're going to get your way."

"You're sure?"

"I'm sure. And if you hurt her, I'll be coming after you. You know that. Then I'll get my way."

"Less drama, more motion. On your way. We'll be ready for delivery of your shipment by dawn. I'll call you and tell you where to go. I'm sure I don't have to tell you —"

"You have eyes everywhere. No cops, no tricks. We'll meet in some empty lot or something you've already scoped out and we'll do the exchange and I'll be on my merry way with the future Mrs. Diaz."

The fat man clicks off.

Of course, his plan for you and the future Mrs. Diaz isn't quite that neat. He'll shoot you and Willow, perhaps by testing out one of those handy Russian-made Scorpions on your skulls.

You race to the safe house, now known as Uncle Harry's house. It's past eight and the lights are off. The front door is an open mouth. It's knocked out, not in, suggesting Lurch snuck into the house somehow, was in a rush, and made a mess on his exit. You leave the shotgun on the front porch and pull the SIG, checking angles around corners before slipping inside. Your pulse pounds in your ears. You yell Chill's name. The house is still warm. You just missed the excitement.

You run upstairs first. All of Willow's belongings are gone. You doubt Lurch worried she wouldn't have a change of underwear and toiletries. That was the fat man's move to make sure no trail was left for you or the cops. You grab your small pack from the back of the closet and throw it over your shoulder as you rush downstairs.

Chilli Gillie is face up on the kitchen floor, a big knife stuck in his gut. There's so much blood, you have to step carefully, so you don't slip, slide and fall on him.

"They're gone," he says.

"I know. They called me. I thought you'd be dead."

"I'm working on it," Chill tells the ceiling. "No rush."

A cell phone is on the floor, just out of his reach. You're pretty sure it's Willow's. You scoop it up and use it to dial 911. "I'm a huge man and I've been stabbed," you say. "Hurry. I'm bleeding out. Lights and sirens all the way." You give the operator the address and snap the cell shut. You've dealt with enough stupid questions from people in authority today.

You put the pistol away and crouch beside him.

"Don't touch the knife! Don't pull it out. Cuts both ways. Leave it."

"I know. I promise. I won't."

Chill is already putting pressure around the wound with his vest so it looks like he's holding a fake knife. However, all the blood messing up the fancy purple lining is scary and convincing.

"Looks like they got you in the spleen. You can do without that. You'll be okay." *Unless the blade sliced open his colon and shit is spilling around inside, filling his guts with blood and filth.*

Chill looks up at you, but it's as if he's looking through you. "I've been laying here...waiting and thinking."

"Any ideas where they took her, Chill?"

His breath is shallow and rapid, just like Sgt. Billy's was. "Dunno."

"Who was it?"

"Big bald guy with zombie teeth. Could have killed me with his breath. Fat guy was here, too. Laughed at me."

"Say anything useful?"

"Nah. Just...a prick. Asked if I voted Democrat and laughed more."

"The fat man has no name. The muscle was Lurch. I've met them. They're Nazis."

Chill's eyebrows shoot up. "Nazis? Shit. Didn't see that coming when I made breakfast this mornin'. If I'd known, I would have had sausage and eggs instead of oatmeal." He looks down again at the knife. "I've been stabbed by Nazis."

"It's...yeah..."

"Took me by surprise twice then. Don't like him...the Lurch. First clue he was in the house was the knife in my vitals." He sounds so weak and fading.

Sirens call from the distance that they're coming fast. People still always have too much time to think about what waits for them and, no matter how fast the paramedics speed, all ambulances are way too slow.

"How can I find Willow?"

"No idea, man."

"How did Willow know her dad was dead?"

"The cops called. They didn't want to tell her over the phone, but I took the phone and talked to a detective. Got it out of him. The cop didn't want to say on the phone, but he said two bodies were in the diner." Chill takes a few breaths before he can try another long sentence. "They weren't absolutely sure, but a burnt corpse by what was left of a wheelchair...." He winces at the pain, but continues. "Until you walked in, I assumed the other corpse was you." His eyes shift to the cell in your hand. "Told the cops we were in Cleveland and we'd come as soon as we could. Was going to stay here and hole up until I figured out who to go hunting to avenge you."

"Thanks for the thought. How did Lurch find you?"

"As soon as Willow hung up with the cops, she called for drugs. I told her not to, but she was crying about Samuel and she said she needed a fix. Half an hour later..." Chill's eyes shift to the knife protruding from his gut. "I didn't know what to say to her. When she found out about her dad...said she'd be alright as soon as she got her high and jumped to her happy place."

The sirens are getting very close.

"*Run*, man. Po-po's coming. Jesus be nimble, 'cuz they'll be quick. It's a nice neighborhood. They'll assume I'm white...so they're coming as fast as they can." He gives you a half-smile, grimaces and closes his eyes.

"Chill, what do I *do*? Is there someone you want me to call?"

"Wish I could talk to Harry. Don't know where he ran off to. Told him I'd take care of his niece. Messed that up, I guess."

Uncle Harry is a John Doe at the morgue. Then it hits you. "Wait. *Harry's* the guy you were doing the favor for?"

He gives a slight nod. "He told me Samuel was in some deep shit. I told him to skip town and not to come back until the drama had blown over. Said he and Clemont had a falling out. He couldn't even talk to his brother anymore. He was a mess on the phone, broken up about her and Clemont. He was drinking more and losing it. Harry wasn't sure, but he thought someone might be following him, too. But the main thing was I keep Willow safe. Damn it! This screws up my perfect record, too."

Harry was right. You followed him quite a bit actually.

"Harry said he had some money hidden for me, too, money he took from Clemont. Figured he'd stop his operation by taking out operating money...and if I'd just do this one sketchy job, we'd be square. I told him I guard celebrities, not waitresses on the edge of an arms trade. He said I owed him one, which I did."

He gasps and, by his face, you guess there's a stab of regret mixed with the stabbing pain. "Man, I *told* him I was out of the deep shit. I should be back home, making sure Sandra Bullock gets from her limo into a restaurant safely. Shit!"

Thomas-not-Thomas was Chill's friend. Now you've got *another* secret to carry to the grave. The way things are going, you won't have to haul that weight long.

"What do I do, Chill?"

Before he passes out, he manages three more words. "Get the girl."

As Chicago's finest come in the front door, you disappear out the back and over the fence. You forgot the shotgun by the front door. You left Chill to die among strangers.

Inventory: you've got Willow's cell phone, a stolen car parked around the block, the keys to a truck parked across town that's loaded with Scorpions and Russian mines, and a burning love for the future Mrs. Diaz that's only a little bit brighter than your glowing hatred for Lurch and the fat man. You've got the SIG and a switchblade and no idea how to get the girl.

THE HUNGER GAMES

The first time you saw Willow Clemont in person, she strode up the sidewalk toward Thomas-not-Thomas's front. There was plenty you didn't know then, like the fact that it was a front. That was crucial information. You didn't know Thomas-not-Thomas was Willow's Uncle Harry or that he was Samuel Clemont's business partner or Chilli Gillie's friend. You didn't know anything about arms deals and Neo-Nazis or the softness of Willow's lips. Maybe you would have found out more, except, after spotting Willow, in particular her legs, you began following her around Chicago instead of the target.

Paulie had sent you the address of the target, a man the client had identified as Willow's drug dealer. Paulie sent you a picture on your phone, one for the target and one for Willow. Paulie didn't tell you her name. He'd labeled the jpeg file only "Total glamazon." The rule was that you could take out the target at that address. "Sooner is better," Paulie said. Cash and drugs awaited. "Exterminate the roach, but make sure the glamazon isn't anywhere near when you do the job. That's solid."

During the week before Christmas, you did follow the man around sporadically in a rental car. You broke into his car when he was at the movies. His registration papers listed him as Thomas LeClerc. He was almost as cagey as the anonymous fat man. In Thomas-not-Thomas's business, dealing with The Victorious and getting bids on mines from white supremacists, he had plenty of people to fear. No wonder he used a front in a scummy neighborhood and commuted back to his life as Uncle Harry in Evanston.

You checked under Thomas-not-Thomas's seats, the glove box and the trunk. Finding no drugs in the car (which was terribly disappointing) you had nothing else to do but to see the movie, too. He saw *The Avengers*. The previews weren't over before you sat directly behind Thomas-not-Thomas. You could have just slit his throat then and be done with the job, but the movie was really too good for that. Harry laughed and rocked in his seat, just like you, when The Hulk slammed Thor. It made you want to leave the target alone and tell Paulie to find another assassin. But there was the promise of money and drugs. Your meagre funds wouldn't last forever. Just driving around in a rental was costing you more for each day you didn't walk up and put a bullet in the target.

After New York, you wondered if you were getting rusty or soft. The hunger for an escape into a sweet high ate at you, though. Mostly the target stayed home. Except for Willow, Harry had no visitors at the scummy address, which, for a drug dealer, didn't make a lot of sense. Harry had been a cautious target dealing with dangerous people. You watched him meet the fat man — no Lurch then — in a tea room in The Loop. They looked like they argued, but that only made sense later.

After your high-profile mess in New York, you wanted to pull off an elegant hit. You considered following Thomas-not-Thomas around in a stolen car and running the target off the road. However, unless there's willful vehicular manslaughter or a bridge involved, a death within city limits on residential streets wouldn't pass a coroner's cursory glance. Also, you might get hurt.

When the target ventured out, usually he drove to the bar where you finally shook his hand on Christmas morning. Harry had a pattern and loved that bar too much. Patterns reveal weaknesses. That's what gave you the idea to make it look like an accident. The drunk driving angle was so obvious, you thought that was the only way to get him. You considered breaking his head with a baseball bat and then somehow driving him into a light pole, but that was way too complicated, with doomed shades of *The Postman Always Rings Twice*. If it didn't work for Jack Nicholson, it wouldn't work for you.

Then one night after Harry left the bar, you struck up a conversation with Chinese Rick about alcoholism. You told him you had a handle on sobriety but you missed hanging out in bars. You told him the model plane hobby didn't get you out of the house and away from your bitch of a wife. You asked him to keep the Cuba Libres coming — you'd pay — but not to put any alcohol in them. Chinese Rick thought you were crazy, but kept his judgments to himself after you tipped him harder. Chinese Rick didn't blink when you sat down and got social with one of his regulars, Thomas-not-Thomas.

If you hadn't hesitated and gotten so fancy about the mission, you wouldn't be in this deep now. Maybe you would have figured out more in advance if you hadn't switched your recon to the glamazon. You had to know her name. It was her long legs that made you want to follow her at first. Her shape was pleasing, of course, and her long blonde hair made her look innocent and wholesome. Her look was too girl-next-door for you to believe she could be a serious druggie.

When you followed her from the target's house to a meeting, you slipped in at the back. The air turned blue with cigarette smoke, surely a rebellion against city ordinances, but such rules are unreasonable to expect from a bunch of addicts. The usual cast of people who had gone through addiction's gauntlet came forward and shared their stories.

They were the same stories that are repeated across America several times a day: the cop who hit his wife when he drank so he turned to pills; the son who stole Dilaudid from his aging father (making the old man suffer more back pain so he'd have his fix); the mom who didn't think she had a serious problem because they were all prescription pills; the young mother who wanted to quit because another baby was on the way; the young father who tried to commit suicide after his toddler got into his stash and almost died.

And then there was Willow. That's how you first heard her name. "Hello. My name is Willow and I'm an addict."

"Hi, Willow!" everyone replied. There are armies of people in church basements and rec centers and library multipurpose rooms across the country, doing this ritual, making time sacred, fighting the hunger.

"The first time I took drugs was in high school," Willow said. "My father was away and my Mom was sick with cancer and I started by taking some of her drugs. The first ones made me sick, because I didn't know what I was doing. I thought I'd get high and instead I threw up. I think it was something to help my mother with hormone levels or something. I threw up all over my bed. Got it out of my system before I grew a dick, though."

Everyone burst out laughing, you included. You peered at her from between the heads of people in front of you, yearning to get a closer look.

"Then I got hold of some of her pain meds and my pain went away. It was great at first. People call it a crutch, but everybody's got a crutch and I needed a powerful one to lean on. People who would call us weak? They've got cigarettes and fried food and coffee and chocolate croissants and Honey Boo Boo and true crime and unanswered prayers and football."

The room got unnaturally quiet then. Willow did not waver. "The people who judge us? When they win they call it smarts, but lots of it was luck. They were lucky to be born into the right family. It wasn't their intelligence or hard work that saved them from breast cancer. My mother had breast cancer and she was the hardest working, smartest woman I ever knew."

She spoke as if lit by a spotlight, her eyes just above the crowd. You had the eerie feeling she wasn't really talking to the crowd at all. She spoke as if to the ghost of her dead mother, floating above her fellow addicts.

"The people who judge us, the ones who don't want a methadone clinic in their neighborhood or who scream at you at a family get-together...they don't know our struggle. They don't know our hunger. They don't sympathize with our sadness because the taste for pills just happened to miss them. The straight edges? I think they're like those screaming personal trainers you see on TV angry at fat people. They were born skinny and think they've earned something. They've got their addictions. Lots of people call this a journey to sobriety, but since I quit pills, I'm more aware of all the addictions around me. Love, hate, judgment, self-righteousness...those are addictions, too."

She gets a smattering of applause from the uncertain. Some around the room nod. A few more look worried about where Willow's speech is going. This isn't the usual rote "sharing time" about condemning her former lifestyle and wondering what she was thinking. This is *Look into the Existential Abyss. We May as Well Party*. But then Willow takes her defiance out of its dive.

"Nothing is as good as that first hit," she said. "After that? I'm tired of all addictions. They aren't healthy. Getting high feels more and more like another job. When I talk to people at these meetings, there's something I notice. We talk about our addictions and how good it felt early on. Later, getting to feel good gets to be more of a chore. It's a shit job on top of your regular shit job that costs you too much money. For me...well, you can get high, but you can't get to happy. It's like I can eat but never feel full. Does anybody know an addict who uses daily and looks happy? I don't."

The room resonated with the group's murmured agreement.

"I try every day not to use," Willow said. "I've already got a shit job. I don't need another one."

"One day at a time!" a woman called out.

"I know that's true," Willow said. "But some days, I look at my phone and I want to make that call and go get some candy, you know?"

"We know!" the same woman called. "Don't do it!"

"I know. I'm trying. The thing about candy is, you can't have just one. So I'm trying not to make that call. If I start, I know I'll take more and things will get out of control again. After my mom died, I was dog shit for a long time. Mom wouldn't have wanted that for me. I have to go without the candy. Vicodin. Percocet. Poppers. I have to stop but I'm tempted every day. Kind people and my family are trying to help me. I just know that I can't stop at one pill, so I have to make sure I don't start at one pill. I'm working on that. Soon, I think I can be confident in my new life. The really key thing for me is, if you love yourself enough and if you love other people enough, no matter what the cost, you'll ask for help. I'm asking for help."

It was like she was speaking directly to you, telling you to make her life easier by killing her dealer. She said she wanted to quit. You heard, "I can't quit cold turkey, please help me."

The group applauded her all the way back to her seat. You slipped out at the next break, but for a moment before you left, Willow's gaze met yours, through the crowd and across the room. In that second, you felt a new yearning and you wanted to sate that new hunger. You desperately wanted to substitute your old needs for Willow. You wanted to be pure for her. You wanted to kill the man who gave her all that dangerous candy. If not for Willow, you never would have returned to Group at the VA and sat still to listen to Smug Tim's dull cliches about getting past the past and forgiving the unforgivable.

The Vikes you found behind Thomas-not-Thomas's toilet tank were Willow's stash. He hid it from her, trying to help his niece quit.

Harry Clemont gave you a nostalgic story about journalism school. That was probably all lies, a well-rehearsed cover story. Or maybe that part was true and he was lonely, getting drunk in a shitty bar on Christmas, and trying to connect with a dangerous stranger. Maybe he thought he was making you feel better about being there with him, a fellow drunk who'd been kicked out by his ex.

Thomas-not-Thomas stole money from his brother Samuel Clemont to get away from a deal with white supremacists he wanted nothing to do with. He called in Chill to protect Willow. If you'd gotten to know Harry, you're pretty sure you would have liked him. He told convincing lies. He may not have been a civilian — as a gun runner, he was in your war zone — but Thomas-not-Thomas was a gun runner with a conscience.

He was a better man than you, but you didn't know that yet.

The bag of Vicodin is still in your flop, hidden in the bottom of the chair in the corner. If you can find Willow, you can both keep each other clean and out of trouble. You're almost sure. If you can't find Willow, you want to eat every pill and then go find more.

Where to begin to look?

Your superior officer when you were an MP, Lt. Mathers, was a real bloodhound. To find a missing person or an AWOL soldier, he would run down family first. That doesn't help you much. You've shot and killed Willow's known relatives.

That leaves known associates. Chill said that when Willow found out Samuel was dead, her hunger overcame her quest to be clean. She called someone, but it must have been on the landline back at her uncle's house because when you check her cell's most recently used numbers list, all you find is calls back and forth to the diner.

Several contact numbers are listed on Willow's cell: her hair salon, some names you don't know with area codes that aren't local and Connie's Pizza.

The light cast up from the cell lights your face as snowflakes kiss the screen. Then, a spark of hope. You find a telephone number that reads: Candy.

SOME LIKE IT HOT

Your superior officer in the Military Police was a tricky guy. On your first meeting, Lt. Chuck Mathers slid it in sideways that he was Eminem's long lost uncle. The last time you saw him, he confessed that was bullshit, but he said that little detail got him laid and made young idiots like you listen more carefully.

"The little details are a rabbit's warren and you have to keep an eye on them if you're to find your way and get rabbit stew." Mathers was a smart MP, an antidote to the gorilla-busting-heads-in-a-bar cliche. When a grunt was in trouble after beating up his girlfriend, Mathers always knew when to go soft and when to go hard with the questions. Mostly he let bad soldiers talk, playing down the cause and consequence of their crimes. He gave bad soldiers rope until they hanged themselves.

"Getting information and confessions? It goes easier if they like you. They won't like us when we're done. In fact, they'll hate us later, but so what?" he said. "Weeds hate the hoe."

Going into a strip club to break up a fight, Mathers went straight to the biggest man first to let the others know the chaos they revelled in was over for the night. Mathers could be up on adrenaline from the bar fight arrests one minute and in the next switch gears to talk a sad guy who was AWOL into coming back to base. He'd go gentle, avoid unnecessary drama, and cut the dude the needed slack to get him in off the ledge. He began every shift with the reminder, "Have a plan A and a plan Z. Strong peters out by 30. Clever lasts."

Mathers's lessons come to mind as soon as you see Willow's candy girl, Liberty Montano, walk into the coffee shop. Dressed like a starlet out of the '40s in a floaty, feathery white jacket, she wears a black beret and teardrop-shaped sunglasses that make her look vaguely like a cute, huge-eyed alien. She spots you immediately from your description on the phone and plops into the booth seat across from you.

You're drinking a regular decaf to keep your nerves from jangling too hard at the thought of Willow at the fat man's mercy. The double espresso Liberty told you to order for her is still hot and ready.

She isn't what you expect from a drug dealer. She looks like a college girl and you tell her so.

"I *am* in college, moron. It's the only way to afford the tuition. I'm working on an MBA, though I've probably learned more in my off hours." She slides her sunglasses down delicately. She sports two black eyes. Your best friend did that to you not long ago in New York. You wince in sympathy.

"Lurch's work?"

"Swift." She rolls her eyes as she slides her glasses up.

"Have you known Willow long?"

"A while. We've partied a few times. Interesting girl. When she comes into money, I see more of her. She jumps on and off the wagon, weeks at a time."

"Do you like her?"

"Sure. As much as I like anybody. She's a client. Most of the job is schmoozing, so you know...." She sips the espresso, frowns and reaches across the tabletop to the sugar. She dumps a steady stream into the small cup and stirs the thick mixture into a brown sludge.

"Help me out here," you begin. "Lurch gave you a couple of black eyes to get you to give up Willow?"

She gives you a curled lip. "He punched me in the face before any questions, just to get my attention. He got it. The wide guy asked all the questions. Lurch has got the Bond villain thing going on. It was brutal. In the exquisite. They convinced me pretty quick that when Willow called, I was to tell her I was on

161

my way with her medicine. They went instead. Took the pills, too."

"What number did the fat man give you to call?"

"He didn't. They waited with me."

"Shit. How long was that?"

"Most of today. Like, from around noon."

"What was that like?"

"Excruciating. First Lurch smacked me around. Then the fat one gave me a lecture about the history of the Civil War. Then they noticed I had Netflix and they forced me to watch *Toddlers and Tiaras* with them. Made me wish they'd get back to the beating."

"But they knew she'd call you?" You wonder how long Lurch and the fat man followed Willow to figure out Liberty was her supplier?

"I told them Willow hadn't called me in a couple weeks or more, but they were sure she'd call and she did. They knew all about her. The wide one said her dad just died in a fire. Poor kid. Sounded like the dad was an asshole a lot of the time, but still…. Easy trigger for candy lovers."

"I know a bit about that subject."

"Then you know that whether it's peanut butter cheesecake or Vikes, anything that happens that's good or bad means you deserve a reward, so people call me for pills. There's a reason it's a booming business. There's no bad time to get high and, when your dad dies in a fire, that's a really good time to get about as high — "

"As satellites, yeah. But how'd they know about the fire so quick?"

"Back when I was sampling the product, I'd occasionally watch stars go nova on the other side of the galaxy and talk with shamans in a jungle made entirely of mushrooms and patrolled by giant jaguars. However, despite these amazing experiences, I don't have any answers for you, Jesus. You want wisdom? I say, keep calm, bang a gong and call the cops." Montano shrugs and drinks her sweet caffeine sludge.

Plan A is a straight plea for mercy for Willow and vengeance for herself. "I need to find the fat man and Lurch. They've got Willow. I'm worried they'll do worse than a couple of black eyes."

"Yeah, and when you find them, I'm sure you'll give them each a stern talking to."

"I might even get very cross with them, yes."

"I don't know where they are, Jesus. They didn't leave a forwarding address. Like I said, call a cop if you're so worried. Just leave me out of that noise."

"Cops aren't an option. Willow's my mission."

"I'm not a helpful option, either. I'm thinking of taking some time off to travel. California's warmer and, after meeting Lurch, I'm not scared of mud slides, earthquakes and radiation from Japan anymore. Hollywood might be a good move. It's Vicodin Heaven, especially for all those poor rich stars who aren't allowed to eat food. It's all pills and booze for fame whores. They live on wine spritzers, adoration and Roxy, knocking back 30 mg at a time to hasten the cozy slide to has-beens on *Where Are They Now?*"

"How did Lurch and the fat man track you down?"

She shrugs again, hiding behind those cartoonish sunglasses, as readable as Sanskrit.

"Who were Willow's friends? The ones she partied with? Did she have a best friend or"— this kills you a little — "anyone special recently?"

"So I should give you client names? I don't think so. Besides, the only guy I ever met through Willow was her uncle."

"Uncle...?"

"Harry."

Damn. He used his real name around his niece's drug dealer. If he'd used his real name with you, maybe he'd still be alive. Mm, no, you still would have shot him. The hit was address-specific, not name-specific. If you'd done more of your own recon, instead of relying on the lie Samuel told Paulie, you'd have figured out Liberty Montano was Willow's dealer. You'd have killed this annoying girl instead.

"Harry is such a jerk. A real bloviator. He broke Willow's cell once, as if she wouldn't know my number by heart. You don't touch a girl's cell. He was always trying to keep me away from Willow. He even came to me in person once. Relatives don't get it. I don't have to call anybody. People come to me.

"Last I saw Willow, I sold her a big bag of Vicodin. Ever since she came into money, she's quite the hoarder. Her drunk asshole uncle — who was *driving* her, by the way — comes up and takes that big bag of Vikes right out of her hands. He told her he'd hold them and if she really wants them, he'll give her a little at a time because he's worried her kidneys will shut down because she's such a greedy gobbler. Some people don't get irony. The *drunk* kept trying to get his druggie niece to go to a meeting! Naturally, from my perspective, he's spreading out the time between my sales. Right in front of me. Galling."

"So...you didn't think Willow was going to quit?"

"Oh, sure. It's just a question of time. Girls Willow's age either don't do pills or try it once and throw up. The ones that stick, girls like Willow? They quit when they turn thirty, get married, have kids...whatever gives them that life-change mojo. Willow will take door number three. She's just a smart girl going through a tough time that makes her dumb. She won't be a customer forever. If it weren't for her mom...you know about her mom, right?"

"The cancer, yeah."

"Terrible thing. Without that and her dad ending up in a wheelchair, she'd never be calling me for medicinal stress relief."

"But," you persist, "you sound sure about Willow being able to kick?"

"Some go for the full Marilyn Monroe, too, I suppose, though there's compelling evidence that Marilyn Monroe's death wasn't suicide. It was murder. Did you know that?"

You shake your head. "I'm more of a JFK assassination buff."

"*Hmph. That* one? No way Oswald acted alone."

"Okay, but about Willow — "

"Seen it a hundred times. Willow will be okay if she can just stay away from trauma and drama. I'm going to miss her. And, not for nothing, by your questions, I obviously know her better than you do."

"You're making me sad."

"People make themselves sad. There's only one way I make people happy. You want to buy some happy? If not, I'm making travel plans. I was hoping for some more money for the road west."

You're missing something, but what? You better be missing something, or you and Willow are dead at dawn. To live to see past sunrise, you have to choose the battleground and that's going to be whatever hole the fat man and Lurch have crawled into with the future Mrs. Diaz. But the fat man was so cagey, he wouldn't even give Liberty Montano a cell number. He was so smart, he found Willow's drug dealer and waited for the call from Willow he was sure would come.

You prepared several stories to tell Willow's candy dispenser. You'd prepared lies to convince her to help find Willow before dawn. But Plan B, C, D, and E won't help because Liberty Montano *has* no information.

How could the fat man be that all-seeing? How did he know about the fire so quickly that he could instantly jump on the opportunity to grab Liberty? How long had he been following Samuel and Willow around, gathering data? He must have done more recon than you did with Uncle Harry/Thomas-not-Thomas.

You watched the target, not just to find your opening for the hit, but to make sure Paulie's mission for you wasn't just a trap to get you arrested by the FBI or murdered by your former associates from New York. It took you a week to convince yourself that Paulie was legit and not setting you up so Big Denny De Molina could walk up and decapitate you with a shotgun blast. The last time you saw Big Denny, you both stood in a burning house and you never want to see him again.

Wait. When you met the fat man in your apartment, he called you "the burning man." *And there it is.* When we're rushed, we're dumb.

The fat man knew you threw the coffee pot in the diner to scald Skeet. The fat man knows so much, you have a clue how you can find Willow. He must have eyes on the street, just like you did when you hired Sgt. Billy for the job that killed him. The homeless blend in with the streetscape so well, they may as well wear concrete camouflage. The fat man hired an invisible man.

The candy dispenser must be a whiz at reading faces. "You've got an idea."

"Yeah. I do."

"That's impressive because I'm useless."

"Yes. No. Uh...you gave me an idea."

"By being useless?"

"Yeah."

"Okay."

"There is something you can do for me," you add as you stand to leave.

"What? For free? The coffee isn't that good."

"You'll want to do this." You point under the table at a canvas shopping bag. "I swung by my apartment on the way here. It's that big bag you were talking about. If pleading, negotiation and torture wasn't going to work, my last resort was to buy the information from you with all those delicious Vikes. There's a bit less in there, but still a lot. Take it. Willow and I are going on the wagon. We won't wait until we're thirty. We're quitting cold turkey. We'll do it together. Weaning is not an option."

She gives you a pitying smile. "I've heard that before. I doubt it'll work. You can't make that decision for somebody else, and you did say letting go of the happy pills was your *last* resort. It is your girlfriend's life on the line, right?"

In that moment, you aren't sorry Lurch punched her in the face a few times. "It's for real this time, Liberty. No more pills."

"What makes you think it's real? People stop, sure, but nobody kicks in one shot."

"It's not one shot. We've been playing around growing up for a while. Besides, in the next few hours, Willow and I will probably have several near-death experiences. I hear they're life-changing. That should give us that mojo you mentioned."

"Good luck," she says. "But, dude? You wanted my opinion about Willow. I got one for you, too. I look at you and I see a guy who doesn't quit cold turkey. You've got the stink all over you. Whatever your drug of choice is, you're not the type to ever stop chasing that high."

"Sounds less like a prediction and more like a curse."

Liberty Montano sips her espresso sugar sludge and stares in your eyes. Her smile is not kind. "You? You're a Marilyn. Maybe they'll make it look like suicide, but you are definitely *so* Marilyn."

FROM DUSK TILL DAWN

As you head down the street from the cafe, you pause to check over your shoulder. It would have been helpful if you looked in a window and caught Lurch's uniquely Frankensteinian silhouette in the reflection. Instead, you stay watchful and find, to your disappointment, that no one follows you. Dawn is hours away, but you still have to get to the truck filled with Russian mines and Scorpions.

With no one to catch in the shadows, you wonder, what would Lt. Mathers do? The lieutenant was not universally loved, but he taught you to think clearly in difficult circumstances. You want to rush to the truck to make sure it's waiting where Samuel Clemont told you to find it, but finding Willow is your highest priority. The Nazis have her and could be killing her, or worse, right now. You want to run in circles with your arms over your head as you scream long vowel sounds. Instead, you prioritize your emotions and make a mental note to lose your fucking mind later.

There's no time to wait for your tail to show up. You've got to go to them. You have a hunch you spotted the person who followed you between the diner and Willow's place. You grab a cab and head that way.

God Eats is an empty hulk. The front of the restaurant's shell is still intact, but beyond the yellow police tape, lies a ruin. You tell the driver to drop you off down the block and walk up the opposite side of the street. You hike the collar on your trench coat against the settling cold. A police cruiser is parked in the mouth of an alley nearby. A van marked *Fire Investigation Unit* stands next to where the diner's front doors once stood. A klieg light casts a bright white shine down the ashen throat of the dead building and you glimpse two flashlights bobbing at the rear. The dead neon sign that had flashed "God Eats." is not lit. *Hm. God Eats. If He's Hephaestus, the God of Fire, He sure does.* (Tia Marta skipped a lot of important subjects, but the classics interested her.)

A few blocks on, you expect a darting shadow to slip in from behind, slitting your throat and stealing the keys to Samuel's panel van. Instead, in a narrow alley across the street from Willow's apartment, the man who followed you sits on a mattress of cardboard, his back resting against a garbage can. He rubs his gloveless hands together as he watches her building. Ezekiel, or at least the homeless man with Ezekiel 25:17 emblazoned in white across his black hoodie, doesn't see you coming until it's too late to run.

You promised Sgt. Billy you wouldn't think of all homeless people as a wandering mass of lookalikes. You'd take them as individuals, not clones hiding behind similar beards and identical masks of bewildered distraction. How often had you passed Ezekiel in the street, never suspecting that he was looking back with more than a casual interest? When you saw him in the street after kissing Willow the first time, the bastard even asked you if you knew someone was watching over you!

He's no poser. You can't fake that homeless look without layers of Hollywood makeup, daily humiliation, persistent lice and dejection. They hired him just like you hired Sgt. Billy. Both sides needed invisible observers.

"The fat man sent me," you say. "You can stop watching the apartment."

Ezekiel looks up at you warily, his eyes wide. You give him a reassuring smile and offer him a hand up.

Instead of taking it, he squints and says, "What's the code?"

"Morse?"

"That ain't it."

"Damn, the fat man is a smartie, isn't he?"

"Smarter than most."

"Got a name?"

"Daniel. Just Daniel."

"So, you know you're an accessory to kidnapping, Daniel Just Daniel?"

"One, you ain't a cop. Two, do I look that ambitious to you?"

"Do you know who I am?"

"Jesus Diaz. I'm supposed to keep an eye out for you."

"What did the fat man tell you about me?"

"I don't ask what I don't need to know. Keeps me from accessorizing kidnapping." He smiles. "I was outside the diner watching when you nailed that dude with the pot of hot coffee. I don't know much about your particular *who*, but, the way you did it, I can guess *what* you are."

"You caught the show, huh?"

"Hells, yeah. That shithead almost knocked me over when he come screaming out of the place. Threw himself into a snowbank."

"The fat man has the girl."

"Mm. Willow Clemont. The fat man told me. She's a tall girl. A looker. Saw you smoochin' the other night. If it were me getting kissed like that, I wouldn't have been in such a hurry to leave. What's wrong with you?"

"That question has baffled experts."

"I see it. It's in your aura. You got a lot of yellow in your aura. That's fear. Not judging. I can see you're worried about the tall girl. And red. You got a lot of red. At the right time, that's passion. This is the wrong time, so I see it's a lot of mad. You're a real angry man. You need more purple, guy. Violet is royal and divine. Clears out all that bad shit."

"Thanks."

"You say that, but I see more red lighting up your chakras. Dangerous for your karma."

"What's the fat man's name?"

"Dunno. Didn't say."

"Where is he?"

"Didn't tell me that, either."

"I need to know where Willow Clemont is before they hurt her."

The man shrugs and looks away. There is no defiance in that look. "Sorry, Jesus. I can't help you, but I would if I could."

"How come you can't?"

"You've met Lurch, right?"

You nod. Daniel is a pawn, not a douchebag white supremacist. He's more afraid of Lurch than he is of you. Plan A: Keep it nice, but make sure he knows you aren't going to stop asking until he tells you something useful.

"True story," you say. "Tony Jacob was a kid I knew in Union City. He would go into the city to snatch purses. His theory was that the farther away from home he was, less likely he'd get caught. Like married people? They figure if they go to another country, they're temporarily single and adultery doesn't count."

The man bobs his head.

"Despite Tony's awesome theory, he did get caught one day. He grabbed a purse off a lady in Hell's Kitchen and ran. An off-duty cop — big, brawny ox — was out jogging, spotted my man Tony and chased him down an alley. He dropped the purse, but this cop kept coming after him. He was a young cop from the neighborhood, cocky and badge-heavy."

"I know the type."

"I bet you do. So, this cop runs down Tony, tackles him and gets him into a double arm bar, his foot planted between Tony's shoulder blades."

"So?"

"So the cop's in a back alley and he doesn't have a cell phone. He's got no back up and no friends. Tony struggles hard and he can't drag him out to the street. The cop can't let him go, either. The cop holds him, just barely, but can't do much more. Tony's on his belly, but it's a standoff."

"What did the cop do?"

"He calls up the alley. He shouts for help. He asks passersby to call the police. They're New Yorkers. They pretend they don't hear him. They gawk a little and they keep walking. The useless wrestling continues, but the cop still can't get anybody to help haul Tony off to jail. Time goes on and the cop sees his only option is to beat the shit out of Tony until he cooperates. He beats on my buddy until he begs for his life. Just then, a few of the local toughs look down the alley and see this cop kicking the poor innocent citizen's ribs in. He's the local badge-heavy cop, remember, so naturally, they recognize the prick. Next thing you know, it's the cop on his belly in a double arm bar and Tony is wheezing down the alley while the cop begs for his life."

"So your buddy got away to steal again another day? Nice story."

"Well, not quite. Up the alley, Tony spots the lady's purse beside the dumpster where he threw it. He bends over and somebody said later that, when he bent over? There was a series of crunches and clicks. One of the gang beating the shit out of the cop said he heard it from more than a dozen feet away. Like a sack of wet bones shifting and clicking. Next thing you know, Tony's on the ground sucking wind again. A bunch of his ribs cracked and his lungs got punctured when he bent over. Tony was dead before the ambulance arrived."

"Hard way to go. Why'd you tell me that, Jesus? Are you the cop in this story?"

"My point is, you should tell me what I need to know because I'm more trouble than I'm worth. All red through my chakras and all. I am Captain Relentless. I won't stop, so help me."

He looks at you, but shrugs. "I can see you're serious, but I got nothing for you."

You're going to have to reach deeper into the alphabet. Plan B: The Not-so-veiled Threat.

You crouch on one knee, so you're eye to eye with Daniel. "Another guy from the old neighborhood. Gayle Ott. Funny name for a guy. *Gayle* Ott."

"You're named after a God."

"*Heh.* That's been mentioned to me once or twice. Anyway, we called him Otter."

"You called a guy named Ott, Otter? Y'all got imagination."

You sigh, trying to picture violet swirls of divinity cleaning away your reds and yellows. Holly Go-lightly from *Breakfast at Tiffany's* had mean reds, but her mean reds and your mean reds are different. Yours end with somebody getting shot in the face.

"Otter worked in a drug supply chain, delivering things. It was a non-prescription sort of deal, operating somewhere between a meth maker and the meth dealers. Otter shorted the count. He kept a little back and sold the extra little bit on his own. He said he only did it once, but thieves are like pedophiles. When they're finally caught, they all say that the time they were caught was the first time they stepped over the line. It never is. The boss wanted Otter punished, of course, but he also wanted to know who Otter sold the stuff to. His customer needed a mild tuning up, maybe a couple of black eyes, for instance, so they'd remember who it was proper to do business with."

"So what'd you do?"

"I threatened to cut off his toes, one by one. Pulling off a sock and a shoe was almost all that was necessary to convince him I was serious. He told me what I needed to know without the need for too much violence. Two toes later, problem solved. You take the little toe, nobody misses it much. Take the big toes and your balance is all messed up for life and you walk funny. Most guys start with the little toes, but that's just sadistic, dragging it out like that."

He gazes back. "I could scream rape. People are around. I'm not worried about a guy in a suit who talks to me in a public place. I'm worried about waking up to a monster with breath like death. Worse than all the guys I know from the shelters. Lurch is...I've never met anybody like Lurch. He doesn't talk. He's the kind who just breaks things. No offense, but he's like...movie monster scary."

Daniel Just Daniel is smart and isn't scared of you. Maybe even figured out that you've never cut off anyone's toes. Big

Denny De Molina told you Otter's story, but apparently the magic of persuasion doesn't translate when you tell it.

Plan C: Get biblical.

"Ezekiel 25:17," you say. You grab Daniel by his jacket and pull him up as you stand and slam him against the wall. You pull the SIG out and dig it into his crotch. "The path of the righteous man is beset on all sides by the inequities of the selfish and the tyranny of evil men. Blessed is he," you say, your voice rising with the rhythm and flow of the words, "who in the name of charity and good will, shepherds the weak through the Valley of Darkness, for he is truly his brother's keeper and the finder of lost children."

Daniel struggles and makes a half turn as if to run. You catch him by the shoulder and spin him back. You place the muzzle of the roscoe at the tip of his nose and the man goes crosseyed. You whisper, "And I will strike down upon thee with a great vengeance and *furious* anger those who would attempt to poison and destroy my brothers! And you will know my name is the Lord when I lay vengeance upon thee."

"I got the fat man's cell phone number. That's all I got."

"That'll do."

Daniel gives you the cell number and you make the SIG disappear under your trench coat again.

"You sure know your Bible," Daniel says. "Should have expected as much from a guy with a name like Jesus."

"The Bible I don't remember much at all, but I love Jules."

"Who?"

"I know movie dialogue, especially everything Quentin Tarantino ever bestowed upon us. Blessed be the Tarantino. May peace forever fall upon Saint Tarantino. It's one of the best scenes in *Pulp Fiction*."

"Fuck," Daniel says.

"Blasphemer."

"The fat man is going to send Lurch after me. Lurch will kill me twice."

"Not if I get him first."

"How are you going to get a thing like Lurch? His name is *Lurch*, for Christ's sake!"

"No problem. If all goes according to plan, in a couple of hours, you're going to make a phone call for me, Daniel. You'll never have to worry about Lurch again. Willow will be safe and no one will get Medieval on your ass as long as you do exactly as I say."

"And what if I don't?"

"If Willow's hurt or dead and you could have helped me save her and you didn't? That would make you a true bad guy. After I get Lurch and the fat man, then it'd be suitable for me to hunt you down. If you don't help me and I find them anyway, maybe I'll fail. With my last breath, I'll make sure they know you helped me."

You give him a moment to work it through.

"Okay," he says. "A phone call."

"I'll throw in $100 for your happy help and genial cooperation." Evil is a mystery, but capitalism he understands. You give Daniel Just Daniel the other half of Sgt. Billy's torn hundred-dollar bill.

THE NIGHT OF THE HUNTER

Daniel does as he's told and joins you for a cab ride to the truck. Maybe it's the torn bill. Maybe he's still thinking of what the cold muzzle of a heater feels like at the end of his nose.

The cab smells like burnt cabbages and sweaty feet. You give the cabbie an address that's a couple of blocks from your actual destination. His dirty ID card on the dash has an unpronounceable name you can only guess is Egyptian. For a cabbie on the graveyard shift, he's mercifully uninterested in chatting. Instead, the guy plugs his white earphones back in. He points at his head and almost yells, "I'm listening to computer radio! Mike Schmidt! Comedy! *The 40-year-old Boy*! Podcast! Hilarious!"

When he catches your thousand-yard stare, he turns to his work and slams the old cab into drive. Daniel doesn't talk too much, either, still uncertain whether he's a paid informant or if you'll shoot him in the face.

Lt. Mathers had a knack for finding AWOL soldiers and getting them to come back to base without excess drama. With Willow in the hands of a couple of white supremacists, and more crazies on the way, a pant load of drama is guaranteed. However, you have the fat man's cell number and Lt. Mathers taught you an elegant solution for finding people who don't want to be found.

"Whatcha gonna do?" Daniel asks.

"Find the fat man. The best defense..."

"How are you going to do that?" Maybe Daniel is still worried about Lurch, crazed and tearing out a jugular with his dental nightmare of ruined fangs. To be fair to Daniel, Lurch does have zombie-worthy teeth.

"Are you going to track his phone?" Daniel asks. "Triangulate coordinates? I heard there was this guy in Colorado. Guy got lost in the woods and a mountain lion attacked. He managed to blind the cat with a pen and it ran off, but not before the animal ripped up his legs real bad. He thought he was going to die, but the cops tracked him down with the cell phone in his pocket!"

Closed Chicago storefronts flash past and each streetlight is a slow strobe that illuminates the anxiety in the creases and contours of Daniel's weatherbeaten face. He could be thirty or fifty. He's not meant for this. As soon as you don't need him anymore, you'll cut him loose and get him out of harm's way.

You sigh. "I figured I'd put a call out to my crack team of ninja monkey clone assassins. Then I'll just call for a helicopter with infrared cameras to zero in on the fat man. After that, I'll go all Klingon Christopher Plummer on his ass and 'Cry havoc! And let slip the dogs of war!'"

"I think that's Shakespeare," Daniel mumbles. "And I've heard the government can listen in if you just have a cell phone with you. You don't even have to be using it. As long as the battery is in, they've got you."

"Do I look like I'm the guy with the office under an active volcano, a monocle and a white Persian cat? I'm not exactly overloaded with resources, or cavalry for back up and a trunk full of cash, Daniel. I have an idea, that's all. The pizza trick works eight times out of ten." You try to sound confident, but you've had enough plans suddenly tip upside down that your voice comes out jittery. He gets your vibe and shuts up.

You pay the cabbie and urge Daniel to keep up with you. You're almost surprised when you turn a corner to find the white panel van — "a regular child molester wagon" Samuel had said just before he burned to death. It's parked exactly where Samuel said it would be: East Wesley and North Main.

You make the first phone call and Mathers' old hound dog trick doesn't work. You dial again and strike out again. Then you try a smaller pizza chain: Meanie Giodinni's. It's a go.

"I have a pizza order."

"Your telephone number, sir?" comes the bored voice from some wage ape praying for death.

You give the pizza place the fat man's cell number.

The order taker confirms the number is in their system. "So you want this order delivered to 19 Victor Young Street?"

"Sure, oh, uh...change of plan. Cancel that order and I'll call back. Thanks!" To Daniel, you grin. "Bingo. I know where the fat man is. "

"Slick. It's actually a little scary how easy that was."

"Now I need to make a car bomb to deal with Lurch." You've got a panel truck full of mines, but you're in a hurry so, to rig this device in a jiffy, you'll need to find an all-night convenience store.

The van's engine sputters to life. A few blocks away, Daniel points out a mom-and-pop with a dimly lit yellow sign that looks like a mallard in flight. The sign reads: 24-hour Convenience! Duck in! You do duck in, but you take the fat man's cell, the keys to the van and Daniel's request for a Slushie.

A few minutes later you return with a plastic bag that contains two long canisters of room freshener, a cheap little clock sporting a "Chicago Bears" logo, a ball of twine, a roll of duct tape and a tube of super glue. "No Slushie machine," you tell Daniel. "I got you a Coke and a Baby Ruth. "

It takes all your self-control not to break the speed limit on the way to the address where the fat man and Lurch are holding Willow. However, a traffic stop would make you more queasy than you already feel.

In this area, the streets are dotted with for sale signs. You miss the address and have to double back. Why doesn't anybody have their address displayed plainly? Very few houses seem to have numbers in this neighborhood, and many of those that do are either spelled out in an illegible script or the numbers are half-hidden behind bushes or posts. "I hope these people need an ambulance in a hurry some day. Serve 'em right!"

You had expected an abandoned warehouse or a broken down shack on the edge of the city. Instead, you spot the black Ford F150 with the foxtail tied to the roof antenna parked in front a two-story white house with fresh paint. The sign on the front lawn advertises that the house is for sale. Another piece of wood tacked to the bottom of the sign reads like a depressing capitulation: Reduced!

"Clever. So many underwater mortgages, there are plenty of empty houses to hole up in. I could have saved a lot of rent if I'd thought of that. I should have known the fat man would be squatting somewhere out of the way where he wouldn't have to use a name. He's so cagey he's almost invisible, except for visits from the pizza delivery guy."

"Think how I feel, looking at all these empty houses."

"Sorry, Daniel." For a minute there, you'd forgotten you sat next to a homeless guy.

You pull the van around the next corner. It's a decent observation post. You can see the front door clearly and the houses are spread out enough that you'd spot someone trying to sneak up on you through a side yard. You tell Daniel to stay frosty while you hurriedly construct the device that will help you kill Lurch.

You wind the duct tape around both air freshener canisters and yank the short red and black wires from the little clock's battery compartment. You attach the leads from the clock to the ends of the cylinders and apply even more tape. You wrap the twine around the whole contraption until you're satisfied it will hold together solidly.

"That's going to kill Lurch?" Daniel asks, frowning.

You pop the top on the tube of super glue and cut off the tip of the applicator with your knife. "You know, Daniel, for a guy with a Bible verse painted on his clothing with —what is that? White out? You don't seem to have much faith. Trust me. I'm Jesus."

HIT MAN

The trick will be to get the device in a spot Lurch will have to reach for it. Willow's on your mind and the thought of her at Lurch's mercy makes you want to run, but Lt. Mathers taught you well. "Run and people act like rabbits. Wander up casually and we won't get into a footrace with a guy fresh out of bootcamp," he said. "Those clowns are in the best shape of their lives."

You can't manage to go so slow it's a sidle, but you keep your speed to a solid amble as you approach the Ford F150. You stick to the sidewalk at first. No lights are visible in the house, so Lurch could be at the window, watching you come at him. If he runs at you out of the house, you'll lose both the element of surprise and the chance to outflank the enemy. Willow will be in even more danger. You don't know how long you have until dawn, but there's a better than even chance everyone left in this post-mortgage crisis/pre-apocalyptic neighborhood is still asleep. That just leaves meth head vampires on their way to bed and the bakers and morning shock jocks on their way to work to get in the way.

You pass the truck to get a glimpse in the back. Nothing there. Daniel's watching from the van. If Lurch popped out of the Ford's bed to slit your throat, you might die of embarrassment before all the blood loss took you away. A streetlight casts enough shine to see inside the cab. At a glance, you guess that antenna is for a CB radio. Very retro. Or for coordination of an attack.

You step into the street and look over your shoulder before you duck down behind the truck. This plan might work better in summer. You get your back and pants wet squirrelling under the truck to place the device. If Lurch spotted you already, you're in a vulnerable position. Your ears strain for the bang of a door or the crunch of a footstep in the snow.

You apply the super glue in several spots along the top of your device and press it into the truck's undercarriage with the clock face pointed at you. It's got to be attached solidly or you're screwed. The instructions told you to count to ten seconds for the adhesive to stick properly, but you've got to be *sure* it won't fall off. You force yourself to count slowly — one hippopotamus, two hippopotamus, three hippopotamus...— all the way to twenty. When that's done, you give the device a yank and it holds fast.

You scramble up and stalk away, trying to look purposeful, like you have urgent business elsewhere and can't seem to remember where you left your car. Cold and wet have soaked through your clothes and by the time you make it back to the van, the shivers have taken over your body and your teeth are chattering. If you live through this, you promise yourself you will start to dress more appropriately for these jobs. A black knit cap, a pea coat and a black turtleneck are a hit man's cliche, but they'd make more sense for Chicago in winter. On the job, you're always dressed like you're going to church or a funeral, which makes sense in its own way.

"What now, Jesus?" Daniel asks.

"Now you make a phone call for me. Here. Use the phone the fat man gave you."

Daniel takes the phone like it might be contaminated. "What should I say?"

"Warn him there's a bomb under his truck, of course."

"You want him to *know*?"

"Yep."

"What if he doesn't believe me?"

You point over your shoulder at the five wooden crates crammed into the back of the van. "He already knows I've got a van full of Russian mines. He'll believe it."

"But how would *I* know you put a bomb under his truck?" Daniel whines.

Your knuckles go white on the steering wheel and you count ten hippos before you answer. "*Relax*, Daniel. Do you remember the anthrax scare, not long after 9/11?"

"No."

"Doesn't matter. Listen. The FBI chased ghosts trying to figure out who was sending anthrax through the mail. Some people died. It was quite a panic. There was even worry that there would be copycats who'd send baby powder packages and shut down the mail service everywhere."

"Uh-huh. How does that help me?"

"The powers that be had to warn everybody that if you get an envelope with powder in it, *don't sniff it!* Think about that for a second. The World Trade Center had just come tumbling down and we thought terrorists were behind every rock and tree and people still had the survival instincts of deer in headlights. They'd get a letter full of powder and their first reaction is to take a deep snootful to see if it smelled like baby powder or anthrax, as if they'd know what anthrax smelled like."

"What if the fat man answers? He's not stupid."

"Everybody's stupid if you don't give them time to think. Tell them there's a bomb under their truck and it will go off at dawn."

"What do I say when he asks how I know that?"

"You don't wait for them to ask questions, Daniel. You hang up. I thought I'd made myself clear, but perhaps I didn't explain in enough detail." You whip out your SIG Sauer and let the cold muzzle graze Daniel's temple.

Daniel begins to hyperventilate. Hands shaking, he makes the call. "Th-there's a b-b-bomb!" He hangs up.

Since it's not helping, you pocket the SIG and sigh. "It would have been better if you'd been more specific, Daniel."

"I'm nervous! I get that way when anybody points a gun at me! Don't point a gun at me!"

"It's okay. It's okay. They'll call you back in a second. Just...just remember to tell them it's under their Ford F150 and it will go off soon. Say dawn."

The cell rings. Despite the fact that it's a cheap throwaway phone, you guess that it was the fat man who downloaded the ringtone. To your surprise, it's *I Get By* by Everlast, proving that even evil assholes can have taste.

"Should I answer it now?"

"Yeah. Presuming Willow is still alive, I'm in kind of a rush."

"It's Daniel."

You urge him to get to it, circling an index finger.

"There's a bomb under your car! Uh, under your truck! Under your Ford F1..."

You take the phone from Daniel and yell, "It'll blow at dawn!" and close the cell with a snap. It rings again, almost immediately. You roll down your window and toss it into a snowbank.

"What now?"

"Wait."

"It didn't work! Let's go! Call the cops and let them handle it! SWAT will clear this up and give your lady the best chance!"

"Wait."

"I screwed it up! I'm sorry! We've got to get out of here! When that bomb goes off and, you know, what with the gas tank — ! Oh, my god! If you hadn't pointed that g— "

"That's not a bomb, Daniel. The worst you can do with a couple of cans of air freshener is make somebody's asthma worse or maybe give them cancer over the long haul."

You pull the SIG out so fast this time, you accidentally bang him in the temple a bit with the butt.

At that moment, you spot Lurch burst out of the front of the house. The door bangs and echoes through the pre-dawn stillness. Daniel scrabbles for his passenger door, yanking at the handle but forgetting to unlock it. Before he starts clawing at the upholstery or trying to climb out of the window, you reach across Daniel, pull the lock and shove him out.

You twist the key in the ignition and the engine sputters to life as Lurch frantically circles his F150, searching. In a moment, standing in the street, he's spotted the device and doesn't hesitate to throw himself underneath to try to yank it clear. You pull out, but not so fast you risk attracting Lurch's attention. You need to act like normal traffic, not an avenging angel bearing down on your enemy, engine screaming.

You speed up as much as you dare and you see Lurch's long legs pointed out into the street. He got under the truck quick, but by the way his legs are jumping and wriggling, he's got two hands on the dummy bomb and he's struggling with all his might to overcome super glue. He may as well try to pry up a boulder with his dick.

At the last second, Lurch hears your van's engine and pulls his knees up, but you drive the van so close to the Ford that its rear fender takes out your driver's side mirror and it's not just a scratch you leave down the sides of both vehicles, but a layer of paint. The van lurches over each of Lurch's legs, bouncing over him in a sickening double bump.

His scream is...what's the word Liberty Montano used to describe the pain he inflicted? *Exquisite.*

You lock up the brakes and open your door and turn in your seat to peer back at him. Lurch is a real trooper. He's already flipped over on his stomach. He pulls himself out from under the truck by his elbows.

They made you do that in bootcamp, crawling for hours through deep mud that felt like it would suck you down to Hell and you'd be grateful for the rest despite the pitchforks and flames.

Sgt. Devin, AKA The Devil, would cackle, "You girls aren't dirty enough yet! Your legs and dicks are blown off! Pull yourself to cover by your elbows before Haji fires another RPG! Faster!" It was like Sgt. Devin was doing his best Samuel L. Jackson impression, if Samuel L. Jackson was having a bad day.

"Get your faces in that mud and *pull*, goddammit! Be my dirty girls! Nothing to it but to do it!" the Devil would say. In retrospect, by the way he enjoyed his job, The Devil was probably into some pretty sick German torture porn.

Lurch is in agony. You can't leave him like this. You did Samuel Clemont the favor of shooting him after he'd burned a while. You can do no less for Lurch on the off chance that it was he who likes Everlast's music and therefore may find forgiveness in the afterlife. He'll get no forgiveness from you, of course, but after he's dead, grace is somebody else's business.

"Hey! Speedbump! Justice is served, Nazi boy!"

Lurch raises his head to snarl at you, baring those ugly teeth one last time. Lurch is a big guy. The elevation of his forehead is just about even with the height of your back bumper when you slam the van into reverse and floor it. The sound surprises you. You thought it would be more of a crunch, but instead, when Lurch's head snaps back, it's a wet slap. He's under your left rear wheel and when you put the van in drive, the tires lose traction and spin red, white and brown gore. Lurch is a meat skid mark.

You shouldn't smile, but there's a little bit of a smirk on your face as you park. You jump out of the van and raise the SIG. *Nothing to it but to do it!* But Lurch is beyond need of earthly mercies.

A familiar feeling, like the ghost of a memory of a spider, crawls on the back of your neck. A pistol's hammer cocks behind you. You raise both hands slowly and turn, expecting that Daniel has turned on you.

Instead, it's the fat man pointing a nickel plated .38, so shiny it gleams in the streetlight's yellow glow.

"Shit." You drop the SIG in the snow gently.

"No swearing." He gestures with his weapon, once for you to put your hands down and twice for you to walk across the street.

You look right and left, confused. The Ford F150 was parked in front of the address the pizza place gave you. Lurch ran to his truck from that house. However, the fat man is so canny, he broke into the house for sale across the street, too. When the fat man gestures for you to climb into the trunk of a car in the garage, resistance is futile.

You've been had. Bad. Again.

THE USUAL SUSPECTS

"**W**hat, do you suppose, is the most painful way to die, Mr. Diaz?"

Burning to death is pretty fresh in your mind, but you don't mention that in case the fat man takes your whimsy as a suggestion. You're in a large cool room with a pillowcase over your head. At any moment you expect the fat man to do something terrible. He's taken your pistol and duct taped your hands in front of you and your legs are taped to the chair just below your knees. You still have the switchblade in your sock — the fat man was too uncomfortable in a crouch to reach that far — but you know from experience how useless it is to take a knife to a gunfight.

When you don't answer he continues. "Well, let's not talk about dying yet, Mr. Diaz. It happens I need your peculiar expertise, so let's talk about what's most painful that doesn't kill you."

"Old age is the worst. Let's try that."

"I recall the IRA's favorite trick with informants was to kneecap them. A shot in the patella is very persuasive."

"I'm allergic."

"One in each leg and you beg for death, I bet. What do you think?"

"I only bet on pool and when the Queen of England will die."

"Another thought occurs. When Reagan was shot, one of the Secret Service agents did what he was trained to do and took a bullet in the gut. I *loved* that assassination attempt. You're too

187

young to remember, but they showed it on television, over and over in slow motion. Very instructive. Did you know one of the people who helped foil that one was a hero construction worker who jumped on John Warnock Hinckley Jr.? They say it's easy to kill a head of state, but it's harder than it looks. Anyway, the Secret Service agent must have been wearing body armor under that suit, but the way he rolled around? It looked like agony. Don't worry. I could probably get all the information I need out of you before you die."

"Too risky for you. If you clip the inferior vena cava with that gut shot, I could bleed out before you could start regretting your terrible sin."

You listen carefully as the fat man moves around you, his breathing and footsteps heavy. "How is it that a guy like you knows words like 'inferior vena cava?'"

"A guy I knew died that way. I thought he was going to make it until his gut filled up like a balloon."

"I see."

"Well, let's just keep in mind that I have a lot of options. Whoever had this house before just walked away from it. The mortgage crisis in this country...terrible what criminals are allowed to get away with as long as they wear suits and work on Wall Street."

"I love wearing good suits," you say, "but I'm beginning to regret my vocational choices."

"My point, Mr. Diaz, was that upstairs in the kitchen, there's probably a carrot scraper. Keep that in mind when you don't feel like cooperating. I have lots of choices as to how I deal with you."

"Cool! I'm a big fan of free will. You might even decide to let me go."

"Oh, Lurch's widow would be very upset with me if I allowed that."

"His widow? Really? I thought you and Lurch made a lovely couple."

"This does not end well for you."

"I've heard that before. Let's not get ahead of ourselves. What do you want to know? I'm in a giving mood."

"I have a mine from your van. Soon I will go get all the mines. One at a time, I will soak them in hot water in the bathtub," the fat man says. "You're going to walk me through the bomb construction."

"Your informant got away," you say. "He was pretty freaked out and running for his life last time I saw him."

"Daniel," the fat man says. "I thought of him as Ezekiel. I like Ezekiel. Interesting fellow. He was a priest — the one in the Bible, I mean. I have no idea what Daniel's profession might have been before living on the streets, but Ezekiel? He had an amazing vision. He reported that he saw a wheel in the sky. Some crazies think he was talking about a UFO, but my favorite thing about the biblical Ezekiel was his prediction of the End Times. 'Wail...for the day of the Lord is near. A day of clouds' — nuclear, I suppose — '...a time of doom for nations.'"

"That's what I love about the Bible. All the emo Goth poetry."

The fat man moves closer. If you've offended his Christian values, he's probably about to make you bleed. You jump when he whispers in your ear, "How about Ezekiel's warning that no foreigner should be allowed in the temple? I wonder if that is God's little joke on us? A foreigner in the temple could mean a Kenyan in the Whitehouse, couldn't it?"

You sigh. Political talk makes you tired. However, one thing the military taught you was, if captured, keep the assholes talking, smoke their smokes and prolong the non-torture part of the adventure in the dim hope that you will get a chance to kill them. "Kenyan, secret Muslim...the dude was elected fair and square. By the way, even if he was Muslim, this is America. That's not supposed to matter. I get the feeling if he was a white guy — a secret Belgian, let's say — birthers wouldn't be so excited about his birth certificate."

"I believe in Manifest Destiny, Mr. Diaz. That doesn't simply imply we'll take over Canada one day, though we will. It means that, as a caucasian American, I'm one of the owners of this country. As an original master, I don't care to listen to lectures by a man who's not only Latino, but wasn't even born in my country."

"If you have to swim and fight for it, you appreciate citizenship more," you say.

"You imagine I'm the bad guy."

"I was thinking 'evil' with a capital E, but *po-tay-to, po-taw-to*."

"No. Not Evil." He sounds hurt. "When voters want to get something done and it doesn't get done, we're told to be patient. The politicians say we shouldn't make the Perfect the enemy of the Good. I'm not the enemy of the Good. I'm trying something new and different. New, unfamiliar things always look evil at first, but what all the sheeple don't understand is, what's coming? It's not simply about Good versus Evil. I serve the *greater* Good."

"Said every evil dude in history."

"And every patriot who wasn't too queasy about the relationship between ends and means."

"I wonder when Daniel will be back with the cops? I wish he'd hurry up. Shouldn't be long now."

He pulls the pillowcase off your head. You blink at the bright light. Daniel sits on the floor across the room. No, propped up in a corner and drenched in blood. His eyes are marbles, drained of life, accusatory.

"I caught up with him in your van not more than a couple of blocks from here. Sorry about the upholstery." The fat man points the SIG at your face. "I'm going to have a seat over there. You will help me do my job." He points at a long table eight feet away. "If you think you can tear out of that chair before I empty your pistol into you, feel free to try it."

"I won't." You mean it.

THE HURT LOCKER

A couple of beer bottles stand within easy reach of the fat man's seat behind the long table. Tools are strewn before him, including a roll of duct tape, brown butcher paper, three kettles, a row of screwdrivers, an adjustable wrench, and a large, flat plastic container usually used to store clothing under a bed. It is filled with water and through the plastic you glimpse a mine. You recognize it. It's a Russian TM40.

So far, your captor has demonstrated his confidence in what he knows. You have to drag him deeper into your world, where doubt can seep into his skin. "Did the clean up outside go okay? Are you sure nobody else called the police? SWAT's probably already circling the house."

"Actually, I didn't even drag Lurch's body into the garage," he replies breezily. "Before I drove over and picked up our homeless friend, I grabbed a snow shovel and covered Lurch up. All that blood, too. You sure made a mess, but the van is safely backed up in the driveway. No police. Thank you for your concern, but thanks to all those underwater mortgages, this street is the most deserted residential area in all of Chicago. I checked."

The fat man is going to kill you without a care in the world because some fat cat on Wall Street robbed people with bad deals and predatory mortgages years ago. It's all the little things that add up to the big picture, and that always seems to lead to blood and guts. Every misstep at the wrong moment, every turn left instead of right and a gift for bad timing: once again, loving the wrong woman has got you tied to a chair. If you believed God was interested in your tiny life, you'd be sure He has it in for you.

"You're going to help me, Mr. Diaz. Explosives aren't exactly my area of expertise. That was Lurch's thing. He loved to 'blow shit up' as he would say. I have four young men coming up here from Florida tomorrow at noon and I have to have the bombs ready. I need car bombs that will detonate on impact. I have to rig it so, in case the driver loses his nerve, I can be behind him, detonating it remotely."

"Just like they do with those suicide bombers in the Middle East," you say, hoping to provoke your captor and getting him off-balance. You won't be able to convince him you find the tenets of The Recipients' cause delightful — you're the wrong color for that — but nervous, angry people make mistakes. It'll take a huge mistake on his part to get you out of this chair.

"One for the Lincoln in the garage, one for the Ford F150, one for your van and I'll have to have one ready to install for the car the boys are bringing. We're on a tight schedule. You have no idea how hard it is to sucker four twits into becoming suicide bombers."

"Just like they do with suicide bombers in the Middle East," you offer again.

Instead of irritating him, the fat man smiles with pride. "Not at all like that. They've got bombs going off on the other side of the world every day. I really had to work hard to scare up four true believers. Between you and me, Osama Bin Laden had that part right. He tricked most of the terrorist teams on 9/11 into their suicide mission. That's what it takes. Discontent, malcontents and idiot true believers. Don't get me wrong. There are plenty who believe in the cause and the inner circle of The Recipients are some deep people. For the dabblers...let's just say it's difficult to convince a young fella to kill himself if he's got Internet access."

"Too much access to the 21st century?"

"Can't tear them away from the porn. In fairness, if we could get al-Qaeda more porn, we wouldn't have half the problems we do."

"I get it. You found some self-righteous, self-hating loser assholes."

"Oh, I wouldn't judge. From what I gather, a bunch of people might take you for a tool and an asshole, too. I looked into your background, so I know you have some history with technical problems like this. That car bomb you rigged back in New York? Did it take out the whole house?"

"Mostly just the front. But it was a *stone* house."

"I see. Well, you see the position I'm in. I wish Lurch were here. If he were, I'd put a bullet in your head and tell Lurch to get to work. I could be upstairs making bacon and eggs. Instead...well, here we are."

You hold up your bound hands, duct taped palm to palm in prayer position. "I don't miss Lurch. He didn't appreciate me as a person. I was thinking about that when the back tires were spinning and turning him into paste."

The fat man plops himself into his chair. He puts your SIG down delicately on the tabletop, picks up a beer bottle and takes a swig. It's infuriating. If he were a little closer and if your hands were free and if a freak asteroid strike obliterated him in a cloud of dust, you might have a chance at getting out of this basement alive.

"Where's Willow?"

"Upstairs. She's safe as long as you answer my questions and talk me through my technical problem."

You don't believe him but you let that go. Anything you could say about that now wouldn't help Willow and you're not going to go out a petulant whiner.

"I must say, munitions are fascinating," he says. "I was more interested in politics and history in school. Right now, I wish I'd studied more chemistry. When they talked about IEDs on the news, I never pictured mines. They used to call them boobytraps. Do you know why they changed that?"

The fat man is back in lecture mode. No wonder he doesn't know anything. He answers his own questions. "Fog of war. IED means Improvised Explosive Device, I know, but, to most people like me? Not so long ago, IEDs connoted explosives that the terrorists somehow cobbled together out of kitchen supplies and a visit to a desert hardware store. I never thought about Russian mines. Funny that. I mean, I was a member of Mensa in college. I possess a superior intellect. And yet, it never occurred to me, it's the Middle East. There are mines everywhere. We sold a lot of them and they all can be used against us...or for us, as the case may be."

He sets his beer on the table, all business. "This mine has been soaking in warm water for forty minutes. Is that enough time?"

You actually have no idea about that, but you nod earnestly.

"What do you know about these old mines?"

"The Hummers we had weren't armored, especially early in the war."

"Yes, I remember Rumsfeld telling the troops that you go to war with the army you have, not the one you wish you had."

"Yeah. The prick!"

"Proceed."

"We armored up vehicles as best we could and we packed sandbags on the floorboards of everything we drove. That saved some lives. Then a couple of my buddies got blown up about two-hundred yards from my checkpoint. The tangos got clever again and stacked the mines so the IED wasn't one explosive. It was three."

"Uh-huh. But do you know how to extract the explosive from this mine?"

"They taught us stuff. What I pick up, I remember."

"A good student, hm?" He looks dubious. Given where you sit, you can't blame him.

"You'll have to unscrew the top detonator. It's that cap in the center. Unscrew it."

"If I blow up, it won't just be you and me who will die. Your girlfriend is just upstairs."

194

"Then don't pull that pin as you unscrew the fuse housing."

"Good. Just so we understand each other." Nervous, his hands shake. "VBIEDs! Vehicle-borne IEDs! Military jargon. They do love the alphabet, don't they? I think it should stand for Very Best Idea Ever, Dummies! Samuel Clemont assured me there'd be enough explosive to destroy the target. It's very important we use it all. I have people to answer to, for one thing," he says fussily — almost to himself. "We have to use it all because the target will be in a vehicle and other vehicles will be around the target. They drive in defensive patterns."

Uh-oh. You have more than an inkling what this is about, and now this asshole just *has* to die.

He tries to unscrew the cap and fails.

"The stuff that makes this an explosive was injected at the factory," you say. "Try the wrench and don't be a wimp about it. It's not going to go off that easily."

His hands shake more and his face gets red as he tries to twist off the cap and fails again. You watch him strain and puff as more minutes tick by.

"I can't get the cap to turn!" he says and gives up.

"Hey. Mensa. Righty, tighty. Lefty loosey."

"Oh." A lot of guys would have shot you in the knee then, just because. The fat man is too embarrassed. "I couldn't figure out how to turn the hot water on in a hotel shower once. Same sort of thing," he says. These mines must have been sitting in a warehouse beside the crate of Scorpions for a long time. There's no rust and, when the fat man finally turns the cap the right way, it comes off.

"Lift off the top plate so you can access the inside." You lean back in your chair and wait while he pulls the metal casing up and away. He acts like it could blow up in his face any moment, but you're sure now that's not how he's going to die. It's all you can do not to smile.

"See that stuff inside? Does it look like it's in good shape?"

"How would I know that?"

"Does it look like green plasticine?"

He nods.

"Now smell it."

"What?"

"It's been in a warehouse for decades. Who knows if it's still good? Stick your face down in there and take a long drag. What does it smell like? Grandma's feet? Roses? What?"

The fat man picks up your SIG and points it at your crotch. "Respect, boy."

"Respect, man."

"Are you toying with me? Maybe I seem out of my element here, but I'm a fixer, Mr. Diaz. I problem-solve. Mess with me, and it won't just be you who suffers horribly."

"It should smell like almonds."

He puts his nose next to the casing and inhales deeply, coughs, and inhales again. "It does, in fact, smell like almonds, Mr. Diaz." He puts your pistol back on the table beside him and has another swallow of beer. "Now what?"

"If the water is warm enough, it should make the explosive material easier to scrape out."

He takes up a tablespoon and pulls out a few flakes of the green stuff.

"It'll be colder in the middle. Get in there and scrape it out from the sides."

"Ah. Yes." He's breathing heavier already and empties the bottle of beer before he continues.

You watch him work as the little pile of explosive clay becomes a bigger pile on a torn square of brown butcher paper. Toward the end, it's like he's trying to scrape very cold ice cream out of the bottom of a pail. He's red and sweating before he's done.

"What will we do after this, Mr. Diaz?"

"One step at a time. The longer it takes, the longer I live. It sucks a lot of the time, but I still enjoy breathing. Weird, huh?"

"You're thinking short-term. You should be more expansive. Help me here and you die quickly. I'm not a sadist. I'm not like Lurch. He was...like you. Animals. You two had a lot in common, I imagine."

"Maybe the same taste in music."

He coughs again and rubs an eye with the back of his hand. "I told you, I'm playing a much larger game than you can imagine. I see all the chess pieces. If it makes you feel any better, you're a small but critical part in something huge. I am not constructing bombs. I'm building history."

If this were an old Arnold Schwarzenegger movie, you could say, "You *are* history." However, you're still a long way from being able to stand without getting shot in the crotch. You lean back and try to breathe shallowly out of the corner of your mouth, unsure your distance will protect you.

"What now?"

"Pretend you're in elementary school. Remember making snakes out of Play-Doh? Roll the green plasticine between your palms."

"What does that do?" he asks, finally more suspicious, his breath coming shorter.

"The snakes make up the packing material for your bomb. Everybody thinks of car bombs as dynamite sitting under the hood. You can pack the stuff in the hub caps or the trunk, too. The wheel wells are a good place. You're fitting the bomb to the space so you can fit in more."

"I hadn't thought of that." He begins making snakes out of the explosive material. His cheeks are like stop signs. Sweat soaks his shirt.

"Is this on the test to get into Mensa? Maybe I qualify."

He laughs for the first time, though it turns into a ragged cough at the end. Then it hits him and he grabs his head and moans. The spoon clatters. He grabs for the SIG as he tips to the side, but he tips the wrong way and crashes to the floor.

You bend and get your knife. It takes a few minutes to cut through the tape and extricate yourself from the chair, but you have time. The fat man holds his head and writhes in helpless agony.

"Hey, Mensa. I've got some bad news." You remove your jacket and fashion a mask over your face with your shirt to avoid inhaling particles from the explosive. When you come around the table, the fat man's eyes roll your way and he goggles at your bare torso. Not many people have seen the grid of savage scars that criss cross your chest and abdomen.

You tuck the pistol in your waistband and bend to cut his sweaty shirt open. You knew it had to be there and it is: a large blue swastika tattooed over his heart. You use the arms of the sign of hatred as a guide for your cuts. When he tries to stop you, you cut his palms and fingers, too. He howls. The fat man's bloodshot eyes bulge wide.

He thinks his pain is bad. No. Not yet.

You lift the butcher paper — heavy with what looks like green plasticine — and, careful not to touch the explosive material, press it to the fat man's chest. His pain eclipses his ideas about how vast agony can be. His pain stretches out past Jupiter.

You step away and watch.

Nitroglycerine in a cut may be the worst pain on earth. Think wasps full of battery acid and then multiply that by fire and repeated kicks in the nuts followed by salt in the wound. Inhaling the mine's chemicals causes severe headaches and blurred vision. Handling explosives without gloves? He must have been lying about being a member of Mensa. When he clutches his chest with his cut hands, the nitro sears through his nerve endings and he flops around.

You watch the pain shudder up and down, like an earthquake has chosen only him to torment. You watch his torture the way straight men watch pornography together: transfixed, yet uncomfortable at having company. You won't have company long. His darkness closes around him. He's a traitor to his country, but the only kind of arrest he'll have is cardiac.

The fat man's rigid body starts to loosen. The would-be history maker stares up at you. Maybe, blurry vision and all, he finally sees the real you. You wonder which you he sees? The demon or the angel? You talk to yourself all the time, trying to separate your warring halves.

Or maybe you aren't at war with yourself. Everyone in group, in movies, in the world...they all talk about the war between good and evil. Maybe God needs you to be his avenging angel. With all you've done, you can never be the good guy, but perhaps God places you in these situations because he needs you to be the bad guy. Good guys finish last, but against evil? A bad guy has a chance.

As his heart pumps itself dead, your heart soars. You feel like you might be lifted off the floor and hover with sheer power and elation.

"I'm smiling," you tell him, "but it's not that I'm a sadist. I'm God's bad guy. I just realized — and I don't think it's just the aerosolized nitro talking — I get high on vengeance. Give me that, and I can feel good. I can even forgive you now."

His jaw finally drops, face muscles slack. The fat man dies surprised.

JESUS SAVES

Beyond the bedroom door, you hear a television or a radio playing. You pause. If it's locked, Willow is a captive and you're here to save her. If it's unlocked, Willow is probably dead. The permutations and combinations start piling up: raped and murdered, dead of an overdose, or perhaps just so high she's lying on the bed staring at...is that a *SpongeBob Squarepants* cartoon?

Another terrible possibility looms. What if Willow played you all along and she's a Neo-Nazi, too? Samuel Clemont was a racist asshole, but he was still her father. It's a gamble. Either the senseless hate took hold and she was just using you to get rid of the Lone Wolf and Skeet, or she's rebelled against her father like every other kid in America.

You bet on America and try the knob. It's locked, but the door is light and hollow. You break it down with one kick.

Willow is curled in the fetal position on an unmade bed. She looks up at you slowly, lids heavy, pupils spun wide, her mind in a half-world made of cozy dreams, thick quilts and heavy gravity. It is as if she sees through you. She turns back to watching television.

You recognize the *SpongeBob* episode. It's Pat Morita's last job before he died. The actor who played Mr. Miyagi in the original *The Karate Kid* does some voice-over work. In the movies, the damsel in distress rushes into the hero's arms, the music swells and all problems are erased. Instead, there's a couple of dead guys in the basement, a monster buried in a snowbank, four white supremacists on the way and you and Willow are watching a *SpongeBob Squarepants* cartoon.

But you aren't the movie hero, you remind yourself. You shot Chilli Gillie's friend and Willow's uncle, Thomas-not-Thomas. You let Willow's father burn a while before you shot him. That's a lot of secrets to keep before you even get to say, "I do."

"Willow?"

"Hm?"

"We can go."

"Go where?"

"I don't know."

"Okay."

She turns back to watch SpongeBob get rescued by a squirrel from Texas who is a superb martial artist.

A bottle of Vicodin sits on the night table. There are still lots of pills for both of you. You walk to the bathroom and flush them. When that's done, you're astonished you didn't even hesitate.

You guide Willow to the car in the garage. The Lincoln is more comfortable in the driver's seat than the trunk.

"Will. I want to be with you, You know that, right?"

"Mm-hm."

"But it won't work out."

"Um. Mm-hm."

"I'm sorry about your dad."

Now she looks at you, returning from the half-world. "My father's dead."

"Yes. I'm sorry."

"People always say they're sorry when someone dies. I don't know why. Sorry for what? It's not like they killed him."

"Uh...yeah."

Willow falls asleep against the passenger door. You drive in circles with no particular destination for a couple of hours. When you have a plan, you take her back to her apartment and tuck her into her own bed like a little girl. Maybe she'll wake up tomorrow and decide to change and live a life without drama and danger.

Willow's done it before. She could do it again, but not if you're around. Drama and trauma follow you around like hungry puppies. She can't have that in her life. The addiction counsellors were right. Relationships that start too fast, end too fast. You can't have girlfriends and instant future-wives, anymore...or at least not for a while. An evil guy might keep Willow by lying about who killed her father and uncle and never care that each happy day was a casual betrayal. You're just God's bad guy, so you have to go away and carry the weight of your sins with you.

But it's not as easy to walk away as you imagined. You watch the Queen of the Giants sleep, yearning to touch her blonde hair, fearing that she'll wake and you'll lose yourself to her eyes. Maybe you could lie every day. If you could make Willow happy, maybe redemption and forgiveness is possible for you.

Willow slowly opens her eyes. You don't know how long she pretended to sleep, but her tears reveal her deception. "Jesus," she says.

"Yes, my queen?"

"You think you love me, right?"

"I don't think. I know."

"Then what did you do with my Vicodin?"

"Flushed it."

She sits up. You were mistaken. Her eyes are not blue pools of gratitude. "If you love me so much, how come you didn't call the fucking cops, you moron? If you gave a shit about me, it would have been SWAT saving me, not you! Get out! Get away from me, you stupid asshole! And how could you throw away my Vikes? You fucking *dwarf*! "

You hesitate and look back but she just shakes her head and points you to her bedroom door.

"Little person. Dwarf is politically incorrect," you whisper and head out the door.

"Jesus!"

You turn around, hopeful.

"Of all the diners, in all the towns, in all the world, you walk into mine!" She rips the drawer from her night table and hurls it. The drawer cracks on the doorframe by your head and its contents spill across the floor. You lean in and close the door behind you to muffle her crying.

Since there is none for you, you now know the value of forgiveness. You should have fled to Nevada. What happens in Vegas, stays in Vegas. What happens in Chicago, stays with you.

JESUS DELIVERS

You glance at your watch. It will have happened by now. You don't mean to, but you speed up a little. The front wheels eat pavement. The back wheels push the miles behind you. In a couple of days, you'll be in LA. You need a lot of miles between you and Chicago.

Los Angeles is about as far as you can get without boarding a plane and you hate boats. With all the security cameras fitted with facial recognition technology and scanners that even detect your gait, airports aren't a safe place for you.

Chill rides stiff in the passenger seat, complaining about the potholes. He's out of the hospital, officially AMA, Against Medical Advice. "I'm stitched. I'll rest all the way to LA. Hospitals are full of sick people. The best place for me is in my own bed, healing in my own home." The big man sits slumped against the passenger-side door of his SUV as you play pilot on the Eisenhower Expressway past the Columbus Park Golf Course. You let your eyes linger there, wondering how many times Willow will pass this spot, seeing what you see, being where you are.

Willow will probably grow old in Chicago, but like Paulie said, she's a glamazon. She won't be alone for long. Liberty Montano is right. Willow's too smart not to kick the Vikes. Kids who should have been your kids are waiting, ahead in her time stream. Some summer day, she might even go golfing over there in some far off future with a husband who is...let's say an orthodontist.

In Group, Smug Tim said, "The two most powerful words in the English language, when slammed together, are 'Begin again'." You hope he's not wrong about everything. No matter how much you want to kick somebody in the teeth, the chances they're wrong about *everything* are pretty small, right?

Chill frowns at you. "Jesus. What are those two crates in the back of my truck?"

"Used to be more. It'll be fine as long as we don't get stopped by the cops."

"Oh, well, that's just peachy then. A brown man driving my car and me sitting in the passenger seat and he says, 'As long as we don't get stopped by the cops.' You better be avoiding Arizona altogether! You cross into Arizona even for a minute, they're going to be pulling over your brown ass and my black ass with it."

Sgt. Billy rises from the back seat. "Heart patient, here! Trying to sleep!"

"Sorry," you and Chill chorus.

"I can drive if you want. They'd leave an old white guy alone. I don't have a driver's license, but it's just a little dog's leg through Arizona if we cross into Nevada at Mesquite. And, hey! There's no White Castle in California! We need to stop at White Castle. In fact, we need to stop at White Castle every time we stop for as long as we can. I'm looking forward to seeing the Pacific Ocean before I die, but no White Castle is a heavy trade-off."

"Said the heart patient," Chill says.

"I won't be coming back this way."

"Fine. We'll go around Arizona. We'll hit a White Castle and you, old man, are not driving my SUV." Chill turns back to you. "And don't think I didn't notice you didn't answer my question, Jesus."

You glance at your watch again. 4 pm. You switch on the radio to catch the news update. In a moment, it's revealed why numerous alphabet agencies will want to talk to the Cuban assassin who's already linked to murder and a car bombing in New York.

"On the brink of President Obama's New Year's Day visit and speech tonight in the city where he began his political ascendance, and just weeks before his inauguration in Washington for his second term as president, the FBI reports that they have foiled a group of terrorists."

You can feel Chill's eyes on you.

The news announcer continues, "The investigation is ongoing and details are classified, but around noon today, a powerful explosive device, or several bombs, rocked a quiet Chicago neighborhood. An anonymous tipster called the FBI and several media outlets to say the terrorists were homegrown and members of the neo-Nazi affiliated Recip — "

You stab the button to shut it off and keep your eyes on the road, your teeth grinding. "Damn! It's New Year's Day! I totally missed out on making my resolutions last night and I was supposed to start work at a gym this week!"

Chill's laugh rumbles up to a high pitch. "You can make a new resolution any day, man. Like staying out of trouble from now on."

"I'm not in trouble. As long as they don't set up roadblocks or something, but...you know..."

"The FBI reports *they* foiled something, huh? How'd that happen, do you suppose?"

"Hypothetically? I'm guessing someone with excellent penmanship left a note on the front door telling Nazis to come on in and go down to the basement to see the fat man."

"What else would such a note say? Hypothetically."

"That's not the important bit. It's what the note didn't say, like maybe there were four charges rigged to the door in the basement. That might have made the house explode and slaughtered some assholes."

"That's a pretty specific guess," Chill says.

"I'm out of my mind with grief over a very recent failed relationship. Pay me no attention."

"So you avenged me and slopped extra vengeance on top, too?"

"Chill, in my defence, point one: You're a big, gay black guy. None of those assholes were going to make your Christmas card list. Second, it wasn't all about you. I was working out some rage issues at the time I rigged the detonators. Three, they were white supremacist suicide bombers. That shouldn't even count against me. They suicided earlier than they planned, that's all. And four, it would have been faster and easier to litter a bunch of mines all around the front yard, under the snow. I held back on that plan. I think I showed a lot of responsibility and restraint, don't you?"

"What held you back? You find God?"

You shake your head. "I remembered the Devil. But I knew I wouldn't be there to watch, so there didn't seem to be any point in going overboard."

"You blew up a neighborhood!"

"That's a gross exaggeration."

"Well, you blew up a house."

"It was foreclosed. Might have hurt the bank. Count that as a win for the little guy."

You spare Chill a glance, but he's not amused. He's wearing his serious face. "Jesus, what's in the crates?"

"It's an investment fund for a coffee shop. I'm going to sell it on the Silk Road and get Willow back on her feet. I think the woman who was going to be the future Mrs. Diaz should work in a nicer part of town. I'm going to set her up. One day, once I'm sure she's clean and sober and on track, she's going to get a beautiful anonymous surprise in her mailbox."

"Explosives?" Sgt. Billy asks.

"Money," Chill answers for you.

"Slow down," Sgt. Billy says. "You said Silk Road. What are you, trading with the Chinese?"

"The Silk Road is the Internet beneath the Internet. It's a place to buy and sell contraband. If that doesn't fly, there are always other ways. I'm thinking the best way to go is a bidding war among collectors for the Scorpions. That usually works out."

207

"Nah, man. Nah!" Chill says, waving his hands. "I owe you a favor. Here's what it's going to be. You come work for me."

"What's it pay?"

"It pays in not being in jail. It's a new year, man. Make a new resolution. It's pay enough that you don't have to sell a crate full of arms! You have to start planning for the long-term."

"I've never had much shot at a long-term, Chill."

"From now on, you're my Vice President in Charge of Special Projects."

"That sounds good. What's that like? Bodyguarding Beyonce?"

"Guarding Beyonce's chihuahuas, maybe. I just don't want you selling a bunch of weapons to assholes." He looks back at the crates again. It's wedged in, covered with a couple of bags of clothing Chill brought. Sgt. Billy has nothing but the clothes on his back and all you have is a backpack and the PS3 game station with *Lego Batman 2* you stole from Willow's uncle. Lurch hadn't even set it up for himself. He just took it from you for spite.

"Jesus, that *is* just the Scorpions, right? You didn't put any old Russian mines in my truck, did you?"

You smile and shake your head, your gaze riveted to the highway west. "That would be...bad. Right?"

"Oh, god. Watch for potholes."

"If you love her that much, how could you leave her?" Sgt. Billy asks.

You wait a long time for the answer to come. "I do love her, but," you admit, "too much to stay." You tell them how you found Willow on the bed watching *SpongeBob Squarepants*, high as angel pussy. "Someday, maybe soon, she'll climb down off that ride," you say. "When she does, she deserves better. We'd have made beautiful children together, and they'd have to love me. No matter what, you love your mother and father."

"But —?" Chill prompts.

"But there'd always be a but."

You drive automatically, switching lanes and keeping up with traffic, picturing what your children with Willow might have looked like. Chill talks about the bombing, but it's all a background buzz. You finally glance his way when, in some pain, Chill reaches out and gently covers your hand on the steering wheel. "Thank you, Jesus. He will never know of your secret service. But I know."

"Chill, I think this is the beginning of a beautiful friendship, but I do wonder when I'll ever get used to your *lithp*. Calling me *Hay-thuth, Hay-thuth, Hay-thuth*? Will I ever get used to that?"

"*Athhole*." Chill puts his head against the glass and closes his eyes to sleep.

You watch the road, eager to get out of the ice and into the sun that's always shining on California's picturesque mud slides, forest fires and earthquakes.

No, not evil, the fat man had said. He was so *sure*.

That's the hell of it, because you're pretty sure your story is classic bad versus evil, too. You could only forgive the fat man after you'd extracted the ultimate vengeance.

"You're named after someone who forgave, Jesus," Smug Tim once said. "Christ is for giving and forgiving. It's a good example, don't you think?"

"Asking me to forgive is like asking you not to run funny." Looking in Smug Tim's eyes, you wanted to rip off his prosthesis and beat him to death with his steel leg. Maybe then you could forgive him.

You're more the Old Testament kind of kick-ass. As long as you're confronting evil, you're sort of okay with that. Maybe more righteous kills will balance out the sins and close up some wounds.

Nothing to it but to do it! the Devil would say.

You can begin again, yes, but you're still the child watching your brother die in red water. You're always the kid in the Miami basement praying to God for help and hearing no divine reply. You're still the young teenager begging your captors to kill you. Tia Marta and the Bug Man were so beyond evil, they wouldn't allow such an easy escape.

In the rearview mirror, you catch Sgt. Billy shaking his head. He looks thinner than before. The lines on his face make a roadmap to a few laughs and many more tears. He lies down again in the backseat. His frail, papery voice reaches up to you like a ghost's whisper, "Remember? I ran away from the perfect girl once. I warned you. You find a woman like that, you stay and *change for her.*"

Does anyone really change, or are they actors, pretending they are the characters they play? Given time, you might have conned Willow, charmed her, helped her grieve and eventually won her back. You could even con yourself and kept the secrets of her father's and uncle's deaths forever. Killing off her family sure would make for an awkward wedding, though. Nobody on the bride's side of the church and all you've got on the groom's side are ghosts, the FBI and assassins.

The snow that had whispered down so gently now thickens, coming at you with purpose. You listen to the rhythm of the windshield wipers, smile and daydream of what might wait beyond Chicago's storm. With what you've got packed in those crates, any evil assholes on the West Coast better buckle up and brace themselves.

You don't need love and Vikes anymore. Justice is your addiction and there's no rehab for righteous violence. Vengeance is your drug now and nobody gets higher than Jesus.

AUTHOR'S NOTE

Books in the *Hit Man Series*

Bigger Than Jesus
Higher Than Jesus

Launching October 2014:
Hollywood Jesus, Rise of the Divine Assassin
*The Divine Assassin's Playbook, The Hit Man Omnibus
Edition*

If you'd like to get a glimpse of Jesus as a mature, more professional hit man, you can find him in *The Inevitable,* the story that started his character, in the short story collection, *Self-help for Stoners.* You'll find Jesus is more polished, but things still go awry.

The Divine Assassin returns in two new books in the Hit Man Series in Summer 2015.

Robert Chazz Chute is a former journalist and columnist turned suspense novelist living in Other London. Say hi on Twitter **@rchazzchute**. To discover more titles, blogs and podcasts by Robert Chazz Chute, please visit **AllThatChazz.com.** Don't forget to subscribe to the newsletter to be alerted to new books by the author. For media requests, please email **expartepress@gmail.com**.